PRIDE AND PORTERS

Visit us at www.boldstrokesbooks.com

By the Author

A Palette for Love

Love in Disaster

Canvas for Love

Pride and Porters

PRIDE AND PORTERS

by

Charlotte Greene

2018

PRIDE AND PORTERS

© 2018 By Charlotte Greene. All Rights Reserved.

ISBN 13: 978-1-63555-158-7

This Trade Paperback Original Is Published By
Bold Strokes Books, Inc.
P.O. Box 249
Valley Falls, NY 12185

First Edition: April 2018

CREDITS
Editor: Shelley Thrasher
Production Design: Susan Ramundo
Cover Design By Tammy Seidick

Acknowledgments

Shortly after seeing a big-screen movie adaptation of one of Jane Austen's novels, I used my allowance to buy a big compendium of her works, reading it over and over again throughout my teens. Austen was one of several authors that inspired me to become an English professor, and her works remain among my favorites to this day. I've had the privilege to teach her novels—including my favorite, *Pride and Prejudice*—to adoring undergraduates at various universities several times. Over two hundred years later, and her works are still among the best novels and romances ever written. This novel is a fan letter to her.

My hometown, The City of Loveland, Colorado, also deserves special recognition as the main setting and inspiration for this novel. Residents might note that I played around with the geography of the city slightly for my own purposes, but all of the locations except for BSB are, in fact, places you can and should visit. BSB was, however, inspired by my very favorite brewery, Loveland Aleworks. Their raspberry sour remains my very favorite beer.

My editor, Shelley Thrasher, as always, deserves my endless thanks for pulling this story from the morass that was the first submission.

And finally, to my lovely wife, who gave me the original idea and the title, as well as her usual endless support.

Dedication

For you, always.

CHAPTER ONE

Autumn along the Front Range is ever-changing, unfixed. Northern Colorado weather is notoriously fickle year-round, with extreme variance from one day to the next, but these extremes are never more obvious than the weeks before the first snowfall. This autumn, however, was what they once referred to as an Indian Summer. Unlike nearly every October that had passed before it, there had yet to be a hard frost by the first weekend, and the weeks before had been a uniformly pleasant mid-seventies. You can expect daily sunshine in most parts of the state, which meant that this Saturday afternoon, with the pleasant temperature and bright, almost cloudless sky, just about everyone in the state of Colorado was outside riding a bike.

The weather was particularly lucky for the Oktoberfest at Bennet Sisters Brewing (BSB), located less than a block from the Loveland bike path. The sounds of live accordion music and the smell of roasting bratwurst from the festival called cyclists riding by, siren-like. By mid-afternoon, every bike rack in a three-block radius of BSB was filled with the bikes of people stopping by "just a few minutes" for a beer and a brat. Most of them ended up staying all afternoon.

The Bennet sisters had opened BSB two years ago. In a brewery market of near-saturation in their small city, they had managed to keep their heads above water almost entirely because of their proximity to the path. Unlike several of the other breweries and tasting rooms nearby, they were located on the opposite side of the train tracks on Fourth Street, almost five blocks from the nearest restaurant. Their rent was less than in downtown proper, but there was far less foot traffic than the more popular downtown blocks. Without the bike path, they would have been forced to close down long ago. As it was, they were still struggling, and special events like Oktoberfest were critical to their ongoing success.

By four o'clock that afternoon, they had brought in more money than the whole of September. Earlier, Erin had called every single staff person they employed, and even then, she'd been forced to ask her friend Lottie to lend a hand.

Everyone working was wearing traditional German folk costumes, and Erin felt distinctly ridiculous. She wasn't what anyone would call "chesty," and the blouse she wore bunched uselessly where it should be filled with breasts. Her little sister Lydia also looked pretty silly. Lydia was beanpole thin, with their father's olive skin tone, and the getup made her seem sallow and odd.

Their older sister Jen, on the other hand, was like something out of a fairy tale. Unlike Erin and Lydia, her hair had remained a gorgeous, shining blond past childhood. This morning Jen had left her hair down, and her golden waves hung past her shoulders. Her cheeks, always naturally rosy, stood out against her bronzed, flawless skin. At five foot ten, she could have been a supermodel for German folk clothes. While the bike path had a lot to do with BSB's success, the other reason they were still open today was Jen. Once people saw her, they came from all over simply to stare at her— men, women, children alike. And beyond her appearance, Jen was a happy, genuinely warm and loving person, open and giving. It was hard not to fall in love with her immediately. Most people in town adored her. Eyes followed her everywhere she went.

Erin stood behind the counter, filling small tasting glasses of beer. She'd already had to switch out kegs several times today on most of their beers—a sure sign of success. Earlier she and Jen had changed roles every hour—behind the bar and out in the crowd—but even Jen had eventually agreed that they were best where they were now. Jen was better with people, and Erin was better with beer.

Their little sister Lydia wasn't good at much of anything, so they'd put her on bussing and dish duty, and from where Erin was standing, she could see several empty glasses on the tables around the room. Annoyed, Erin glanced around and saw Lydia chatting with a group of people sitting at one of the high tops. Ever since high school, Lydia had fashioned herself as something of a punk, and the four people at the table were all wearing black, tattooed and funky-haired. Erin could hear her sister's inane and fawning giggle. She couldn't yell at her across the crowded room, so Erin turned to her friend Lottie next to her.

"Hey, Lottie?"

"Hmmm?"

"Think you can handle this for a minute while I go strangle Lydia?"

"Oh, sure. It's quieting down anyway."

Erin was surprised to realize how late it had grown. She'd been so absorbed and busy, she hadn't had time to think of anything but beer for the last several hours. Outside, the light was growing softer, the sun marching closer to bed, which meant that more and more people were leaving to avoid riding their bikes home in the dark. It was still fairly crowded, and the extra tables outside were still full, but compared to three hours ago, it was much calmer. Erin wiped her hands on a towel and pointed out the orders that still needed to be filled before moving from behind the bar. She grabbed a few glasses off tables near Lydia, hoping Lydia would get the hint, but she didn't. She was so wrapped up in her new friends, she didn't seem to notice Erin doing her job.

Angry now instead of annoyed, Erin put several empty glasses on the bar for the dishwasher and turned around, intending to tear Lydia a new one. She stopped when she saw Jen approaching Lydia and her new friends. It was too loud to hear the two of them, but Jen touched Lydia's elbow to get her attention. The two of them talked briefly, and then Lydia immediately returned to work. Erin had to smile. If she'd gone over there and asked Lydia to start bussing again, even if she'd done it nicely, it would have been high drama, possibly with tears and screaming. Jen had a way with people—especially their little sister. Jen met Erin's eyes briefly and winked, and Erin gave her a wide, thankful smile.

Some hours later, about an hour before closing, things had distinctly slowed down, and everyone had moved inside to avoid the chill night air. The large gas grill was still set up outside to cook the last of the bratwurst, but the outside tables were empty and clean. Inside, most of the tables were still full, but they no longer needed wait staff. Jen and Erin stood behind the bar now, filling orders as people came up. Lottie sat at the bar, enjoying her payment for today: free beer. Lydia had left without telling anyone, but Erin was in a good mood regardless. Judging from the receipts in one of the two registers, they'd made a small fortune today.

"Lottie—you're a genius," Erin told her. Lottie had suggested that they hold an Oktoberfest.

She smiled. "I know."

Erin leaned across the bar and squeezed her hand. "Seriously—I owe you one."

"I just want you guys to stay open. You do that and keep making this gose, and you can consider me paid in full." Lottie took a long, deep drink of her beer, and her eyes closed in pleasure. She kept them closed a moment after she pulled the glass away from her mouth. "It's the best damn beer in the world."

Erin and Jen laughed, Erin more pleased than she could say. Most of the beers they brewed here at BSB were standard and never changing. They had a porter, a stout, an IPA, a red, an ESB, a saison, a lager, and a wheat on tap year-round. The two changing taps were either seasonal or experimental. This autumn, Erin had an Oktoberfest style on tap (to be replaced with their pumpkin ale at the end of the month) and a gose. Gose is salty and sour wheat beer and still somewhat rare in the US. The gose she'd brewed had been her first foray into something truly experimental, and it had been an enormous success. Though this was only its second month on rotation, rumor had spread. People from all over the area were coming in to try it. Already, Erin was thinking of making it a permanent fixture on their summer and autumn beer menu. She would have to work out the kinks to make sure she could produce something uniform every time, but it might turn into a BSB mainstay.

The door chimed, and all three of them turned that way. While they were open tonight until eleven, it was unusual for someone to come in this late. The people that entered were also not their usual type of customers. Colorado is a sporty state, with a kind of unspoken, nearly enforced uniform of casual sportswear, even in most offices. Tonight—a weekend night—all of the other customers in the room were wearing clothes that wouldn't be out of place on a hiking trail. The three people that walked through the door wore formal business clothes, the two men in suits and the woman in a skirt and heels. All three paused just inside the doorway, clearly unnerved by the attention they attracted. If a record player had been playing, it would have screeched and gone silent.

Erin glanced away to avoid being rude, and she and Lottie shared a shrug and raised eyebrows. A moment later, the three newcomers were sitting at the bar, and Erin glanced up from the sink she was standing at and into a pair of startlingly dark-gray eyes. The woman was about her age, maybe a year or two older—mid-thirties anyway—with platinum, almost white hair brushed off her face and expensively styled. She'd taken off her coat to reveal a dark silk blouse with white buttons, the color of which contrasted starkly with her pale, almost translucent skin. She had high cheekbones and full lips. She was striking, really, incredibly beautiful by any standards— an ice queen in the flesh. The woman's expression heightened this impression. Despite meeting Erin's eyes, she didn't smile or respond to Erin's grin. She simply stared at her. Erin wasn't sure if she saw dislike or disdain, but whatever it was, the woman seemed to think she was better than Erin, beneath the courtesy of a friendly, if phony, smile. Erin flushed to the roots of her hair, instantly embarrassed. Her grin died, and the woman still didn't respond. She did, however, glance away, as if uninterested in Erin's existence. Erin turned to the sink again, too flustered to do or say anything. She'd never been so completely put in her place with just a look.

Jen obviously missed this exchange, as she was soon talking to the three newcomers, taking and filling orders with her usual graceful efficiency. Erin kept her eyes rooted to the sink and the glasses she was cleaning until long after they'd starting chatting, and when she glanced up again, she saw Lottie watching her, her brows knit with concern. Lottie had something like a sixth sense, and she was clearly in tune to Erin's dampened mood. Erin shook her head, motioning with her chin at the three strangers to suggest they could talk about it later.

Jen and one of the men were chatting, and Erin suddenly heard someone call her name. She snapped to attention and saw Jen smiling at her, amused.

"Earth to Erin! Come in, Erin!"

She laughed. "Sorry, Jen. Woolgathering, I guess." Erin moved closer to them.

Jen indicated the man she'd been talking to. "This is Mister Charles Betters."

"Please—call me Charlie. Everyone does."

Erin froze. Charlie Betters Jr. was the new CEO of one of the largest craft brewers in the world. He'd inherited his position from his father, a legend in the beer world. Prior to the senior Charles's first foray into the market, craft beer had been so small and local and specialized that few people even knew it existed outside of local markets. When the Better Beer Company of Boston began mass-producing their famous beer, however, the popularity of craft beer spread across the country, and never more than in places like Colorado, Oregon, and California, where craft beer was as much part of the culture as breathing fresh air. Just as an example, Loveland, Colorado, a small city of 70,000 people, had more than ten micro and macro breweries, as did just about every town and city in the state. The population could support that many breweries because it was simply part of who Coloradoans were—beer drinkers. And most of this could be traced to Charles Senior—this man's father.

Just about everyone in the brewing industry had felt his death the past month. Already, rumors were spreading that his son—the man in front of Erin now—had no business running the company, and that Better Beer would be swept out from under him, and soon.

Charles Betters Jr., however, was clearly not letting these rumors get him down.

"I'm so very happy to meet you," Charlie said, his grin wide and friendly.

"The honor is mine," Erin said, grinning at him.

It was hard not to like the man immediately. His smile appeared genuine and honest, his face open and guileless. A fair man, with red hair and light eyes, he went nearly scarlet at her compliment. He shook his head and turned to Jen. "So, I know it's late for a visit, but we just flew in this morning, and we've been running around all day to local breweries. You're the last on our list. My lawyer Luis here is very particular about staying on track."

"Oh?" Jen asked. "What brings you to Colorado?"

Charlie colored again and stared down at his clasped hands. "You must know, Miss Bennet—"

"Please call me Jen."

"Jen, then. Well, you may or may not know, or you're good at hiding it, but my company is in trouble. Ever since my father died last month—"

"Oh, I'm so sorry to hear it," Jen broke in, genuinely concerned.

Charlie gave her a brave smile. "Thank you, Jen. I appreciate it. Anyway, ever since he died, the board of directors at Better Beer has been snapping at my heels. They're convinced I'm going to run my father's company—well, *my* company now, I suppose—into the ground. I've been given a six-month trial period, after which they might vote to cut me loose."

"From your own company?" Jen appeared upset, and Erin had to smile to herself. Jen had just met the man, and his problems were already personal to her.

Charlie smiled widely. "Exactly! Can you believe it! On the other hand, I don't exactly blame them. My father was very, let's say, *secretive* about his business. I know very little about brewing beer. And that's why I'm here."

Erin was interested now and couldn't help but interrupt. "Why here, of all places? It's thousands of miles from Boston."

"You can say that again." This was from the woman who had come in with Charlie, and everyone turned to her. Her expression gave nothing away, but once again, she stared at Erin evenly, coldly. Erin's face heated with angry embarrassment, and she glanced away to keep from snapping at her rudeness.

Charlie scowled at the woman, and when he looked at Erin, he shook his head. "Please don't mind my friend Darcy. She's a complete and utter snob. I don't know that she's ever been anywhere off the East Coast."

Erin decided to take him at his word and ignore her. She focused on Charlie again. "I still don't understand why you're here. I mean, I'm happy to meet you, but what's your plan?"

Charlie shook his head. "I'm sure you're aware, Erin, that Colorado beers are wildly popular. Even in Boston, it's difficult to find a bar that's not serving at least one beer from one of the larger microbrewers here. In some places in New England, you can even find beer from places here in Colorado that produce very little beer at all. In Boston, New York, Maine, Maryland—all over the Northeast and Mid-Atlantic—you'll find Colorado beers. And of course it's not just there. You can visit almost any state now and find them. Better Beer Company used to be the only craft brewer available in bars in my region, and now, gradually, we're being replaced, almost entirely by beer from here in your state."

Erin warmed with home-state pride. "Well, of course. It's because we're the best." She flushed, realizing she'd just insulted his beer, but he shook his head as if to dismiss her embarrassment.

"Exactly, Erin. I agree. Better Beer, while refreshing, has stagnated. It's been the same for thirty years. Of course I don't want to change our standard lager, but I do want to begin introducing some new beers to our lineup. So I'm meeting with all the brewers in Northern Colorado, the ones who agree to see me anyway, to learn their secrets."

Erin laughed. "So you can run us out of business?"

Charlie laughed. "Of course not. Do you think a Boston beer would ever compete with something brewed here in town?"

Erin grinned and shook her head. "No. Of course not."

"Exactly. I simply want to make better beer—that's all. And I imagine you have no objections to that."

She shook her head again. "No—I absolutely do not."

"Do you think you could set me up with your master brewer? I mean for a meeting about the craft?"

"You're talking to her, so yes. I think I can fit you into my schedule."

Charlie seemed surprised and then embarrassed again. "Oh, I see. I do apologize. I simply assumed—"

"That the brewer was a man?"

"My apologies."

"Nothing to be sorry about. Even I'll admit it's unusual to have a woman brew master."

"And she had to beg and cajole our business lenders to let her brew," Jen added, rolling her eyes. "After years of school *and* a five-year apprenticeship."

Charlie shook his head, scowling. "I can imagine they found it hard to believe that you would do it on your own. It's almost unheard of. Congratulations on proving everyone wrong. It appears you're running a great little spot here."

Erin felt herself color again, pleased, and grinned at him. She'd rarely liked someone as quickly as she liked this man. His tone and expression showed that he meant every word.

"In fact," he went on, "we tried to stop by earlier, and you were so swamped we decided to come back later. That was quite the crowd out there earlier today."

"It was the first day of Oktoberfest," Jen explained. "We're doing it again tomorrow."

"Fantastic. You serve food here, too?"

"Not normally. This is just a tasting room. We got a two-day permit to allow a food vendor outside. Just bratwurst and potatoes."

Erin listened to the two of them chat, watching her sister talk, primarily. Jen glowed tonight, happy about their success, and clearly happy to talk to such a nice man. However, something else was going on. Jen was attracted to Charlie. She was having trouble meeting his eyes and was actually curling her hair around one finger, her cheeks even rosier than they were naturally. It had been a long time since Jen had liked anyone, but Erin could always tell when she did. Luckily for her sister, Charlie also appeared to be smitten. Even when he'd been talking to Erin, she'd seen him flick his eyes toward Jen, almost as if to make sure that she was still there. And now, as the two of them conversed, he was obviously enraptured. This generally happened with straight men and her sister, but this was the first time in a long while Erin had approved of a man's adoration of her.

She decided to give them a little privacy and returned to the glasses she'd been rinsing in the sink. She took them out of the sanitizer and put them into the dishwasher before setting it to run. She emptied the sink and then grabbed several tasting glasses. When she held one up for Charlie, he nodded at her, quickly, before returning his attention to Jen. Erin turned to the taps, filling the first tasting glasses with their lightest beer. She deposited them in front of the three visitors and then did the same with the next darker beer, and the next, until each of the guests had a small, two-ounce glass of every beer they brewed in front of them.

"Jen, would you do the honors?" Erin swept her hand at the lineup in front of their three guests.

Jen eyebrows shot up. With another brewer, Erin always described and discussed their beers, so assigning this task to Jen was out of character. Erin simply wanted to give Jen the opportunity to keep talking to Charlie.

"Of course," Jen said, sounding less certain than her words.

"I have to go do some closing tasks in the back. Think you can handle it up here?"

"Sure, Erin. Go ahead."

"Charlie—it was very nice to meet you. And I'd be happy to talk about beer with you." She rooted around in her wallet and produced a business card. "Call me any time and we'll set something up. How long will you be in the area?"

"About two months."

Erin and Jen must have looked surprised, as he laughed at their expressions. "I know, I know. I should be back in Boston, kissing my board members' asses, right? But I really want to learn all I can, and I can't do that if I rush."

"Where are you staying?" Jen asked. Her face went red a second later with the implications of this question.

Luckily Charlie missed them. "Fort Collins, for the most part. We have a couple of trips to other parts of the state planned, but our base is around here. We're renting a house up there."

"Wonderful!" Jen said, and, when everyone turned to her, her face colored. "I mean…" She couldn't easily explain what she meant without giving herself away.

"She means it's always nice to meet new people," Erin suggested. Jen gave her a thankful smile.

"I agree, Erin, absolutely," Charlie said. "And if the two of you are an example, I imagine we'll meet wonderful people while we're here."

He had addressed both of them but was staring at Jen as he spoke. Erin turned to Lottie to share her amusement. Lottie had been sitting quietly to the side at the bar throughout all of this, simply listening, and when Erin met her eyes, Lottie put a hand over her mouth to avoid laughing. Good, Erin thought. It's not just wishful thinking. Jen and Charlie were clearly attracted to each other. She saw movement to her right and caught the tail end of the woman— Darcy—flicking her hair and then rolling her eyes at Charlie and Jen. She'd clearly recognized the flirtation between them, too. Erin wondered, and with no small amount of wicked pleasure, if Jen was stepping into this woman's territory.

You clearly don't deserve him anyway, Erin thought.

She spent the next hour doing tasks she'd normally have done with Jen and Lydia after the bar closed for the night. Still, starting early meant closing early, and she was glad that for once they might get home at a decent hour. Eventually Lottie joined her, complaining of boredom. Apparently, Jen and Charlie had eyes for only each other, and Lottie was tired of watching them flirt. The other strangers refused to talk to anyone else, so Lottie had been sitting there by herself with nothing to do.

Erin and Lottie dragged several rubber mats outside to hose them down in the alley—a dirty, wet, and cold task, even on a relatively mild autumn night. Finished with the hose, they stood there in the dark for a minute, breathing heavily.

"Thanks," Erin said between gasps.

"You owe me so big," Lottie replied, wiping some of the dirty water off her face.

Both of them froze when the door opened. From where they stood behind some pallets and trashcans, they were shielded from the view of whoever had just come outside. Very few customers used the alley door, but there was access to a small parking lot here, so it also wasn't unheard of. High heels tapped on the concrete, and Erin knew exactly who it was.

A whiff of sulfur followed a flare of light as someone struck a match. Cigarette smoke drifted toward them a moment later.

"Can you believe this shit?" the woman said.

"Oh jeez, Darcy. It's not that bad."

Erin didn't recognize the second voice and decided it was the other man with the newcomers.

"Are you kidding me? He's in there flirting with that—that—"

"Hot piece of ass?" the man offered and then laughed.

"Hot piece of ass or not, Luis, she's still a rube. I mean, did you see her? Once she heard he was *that* Charlie Betters, she was all over him."

"I'd hardly call that 'all over him,' Darcy. She was just being friendly."

Darcy scoffed. "If that was friendly, the word needs a new definition. If we're not careful, he'll be going home with her tonight—to whatever shithole she calls home, that is. Probably a doublewide down by the river."

"Damn, Darcy. You really are a snob."

There was a long pause, and the stink of cigarette continued as someone smoked.

"Maybe I am," Darcy finally said. "But I also don't want to see my friend getting taken for a ride again. Everyone just wants his money. That last bimbo, Kitty, just about killed him—you know it as well as I do. Then his father died. It was too much. He was barely himself for a while. He's just now starting to seem like Charlie again, and I want him to stay that way."

"I hardly think some beer server can do what Kitty or his father did to him, Darcy. Be reasonable. I'm sure he's just looking for some fun—bumping uglies with the locals and all that."

Darcy barked with laughter. "You're right, Luis. I'm sorry. I'm overly sensitive. I just don't want to see him hurt again."

"Well, I wouldn't worry about it. Jen what's-her-name isn't really, you know, something serious. Love 'em and leave 'em type, if you know what I mean. He could do worse for a short-term girlfriend."

Darcy laughed again. "You know—I think you're on to something there. Maybe she'll be just what he needs. Clean out the cobwebs and all that."

"You're nasty," Luis said.

They were quiet again. Eventually Erin heard someone stab out a cigarette butt in the little sandy tray by the door.

"What did you think of the sister?" Luis asked. "I got that dykey vibe from her."

"Hardly my type, Luis. I mean, really—a brewer?"

"I don't know. She's kind of cute in that androgynous way you seem to like."

"'Cute' is not the word I'd use to describe her. I think her sister got all the looks in the family."

The door opened and closed again as they went back inside, and Erin and Lottie were alone in the alley.

Lottie let out a long whistle. "Holy shit."

Erin shook her head. "No kidding. What a piece of work."

"She's a piece of something, that's for sure."

"Do you think she meant it?"

Lottie frowned. "What?"

"That Charlie just wants his—what did she say—his 'cobwebs cleaned'?"

Lottie shrugged. "I don't think so—at least that's not how I read him. He seems like a nice guy."

Erin raised her eyebrows. "A nice guy with terrible friends."

"Well, that guy Luis is his lawyer, and he's just fulfilling stereotype."

"Who's the woman?"

"I think she's a friend. They didn't go into detail while you were gone. It was mostly Jen and Charlie talking. He said something about knowing her from college, but I wasn't really listening by then."

They dragged the mats toward the door, using all their strength to get them up the little flight of stairs and inside. Charlie and the others had left by the time Erin checked on the front room. Soon after that, she and Jen locked up and spent the next hour completing the rest of their closing tasks, Jen chatting nonstop about Charlie. Erin let her talk without interrupting, quietly pleased her sister appeared so excited. Jen hadn't seemed this enthusiastic about a guy in years. Even if nothing came of it, it was nice to see her so happy. Jen was a lovely person, but she rarely did anything for herself. Being interested in a guy was exactly what she needed.

Just after one in the morning, Erin was finally alone in her own bedroom. She was happy to be home so soon. Normally on a weekend she and her sisters didn't get to leave for home until closer to two. Lydia hadn't come back to help close—but that wasn't a surprise. She was probably out getting drunk or stoned somewhere with those wastoids that had been in the bar earlier.

Alone in the dark, Erin thought about what Darcy had said about her. She didn't envy her sister's beauty—Jen couldn't help it, and she'd certainly never acted as if she thought she was prettier than anyone else, even if she was. No, what bothered Erin right now was the clear dismissal in that woman Darcy's voice when she'd talked about her. According to Darcy, Erin wasn't even *cute*. So if she wasn't cute, what was she? Ugly?

Erin didn't know why this possibility bothered her so much, but she hoped that if Charlie actually arranged to come see them again, he would be on his own. She never wanted to see Darcy again.

CHAPTER TWO

Jen and Erin always took Tuesday off, and by Tuesday that week, they both needed a break. Their Oktoberfest beer had been such a success they'd already had to switch out that line for their pumpkin ale—two weeks earlier than Erin had planned. While this was, of course, a sign of success, now they had a little pressure to get the holiday beer that would follow the pumpkin ale ready earlier than she'd scheduled—mid-November instead of Thanksgiving week. The beer would be ready and brewed by then—that wasn't the problem. Bottling and casking it were, and both would have to be fit into the work schedule much earlier than planned. Erin spent most of Monday morning and afternoon working it out on a calendar and Excel spreadsheet, and while she could schedule it in early November, time would be tight, and it might entail a lot of overtime hours, which BSB could ill-afford.

When Erin woke up that Tuesday, exhausted, she almost decided to stay in bed. She could, however, hear Jen talking somewhere in their house, and, sighing, she dragged herself up. She took a quick shower and slipped on some shorts and a long-sleeved Henley before running her fingers through the short mop of dark curls on top of her head. She glanced in the mirror to check her hair. The sides of her head were shaved, and as she never wore makeup and was slim and narrow-hipped, her gender presentation was distinctly androgynous. She sighed at her reflection. Despite her best efforts, Darcy's remarks still stung. She looked tired—that was true, but she'd always thought of herself as cute, if nothing else. She would be thirty-four in February, so maybe her cute years were behind her. She shook her head, angry with herself for caring. Normally a stranger's offhand comments wouldn't bother her—she'd heard just about every insult imaginable growing up with her face and figure—but she couldn't forget Darcy's words.

Jen was cooking breakfast and smiled at Erin when she appeared. She was still on the phone, so Erin waved at her and sat down at their little kitchen table.

"Of course, Dad," Jen said. "It's not even a question. We'll be there at seven."

Erin made a frantic cutting motion with her hands and mouthed the word "no" as clearly as she could.

Jen rolled her eyes and ignored her. "Yes, Dad. Erin will be there, too." She was quiet for a while, and a tiny line appeared between her eyes. Finally, she sighed. "Dad, I have to go. And I wish you wouldn't say things like that. I said we'd be there and we will. Tomorrow at seven." She paused again, listening. "Okay, bye."

"What the hell, Jen?" Erin said, the moment she hung up. "I don't want to see Dad."

Jen stared at her evenly. "Oh, really? I never would have guessed."

"Why did you do that? If you wanted to see him, you could have gone by yourself. Anyway, Lydia will be there. You don't need me, too."

Recently Lydia had needed to move in again with their father. She'd done this on and off since her late teens, unable to keep up with her bills when she lived on her own. Their father didn't mind, but Erin had always thought that if he put his foot down for once, it might be better for Lydia. She might get her act together if she didn't have a safety net to fall back on every six months. When Lydia had lost her last job, their father had basically bullied Jen into giving her one at the brewery, and the situation had, as predicted, turned into a fiasco. Lydia was constantly late or calling in sick, and she was completely unreliable even when she did show up. She did the bare minimum—often less. Even more galling to Erin was the fact that Lydia was paid a little more than their much-better tap-room attendants, all because of their father. If it was up to Erin, Lydia would have been fired weeks ago.

Jen sighed again. "I know Lydia will be there, but that's not the point. Look, Erin, you know as well as I do that we need that money. We can keep this up what—another six months? Eight, tops? We need that extra space if we're ever going to get our heads above water and keep them there. Oktoberfests don't happen every weekend, after all."

"But he *likes* you, Jen. You're the one who should ask him for the money. You know he'll never give it to me."

Jen's expression fell a little. "I know. But it's *our* business, Erin, not just mine. I'm going to ask him, but you should be there too, even if you don't say anything."

Their father ran several successful restaurants in the area, but none were more successful than the centerpiece—The Steak Lodge—in downtown Loveland. After almost fifty years in the business—ten in training and nearly forty running his own places—their father was finally retiring. He'd also decided to sell off all his restaurants, including The Steak Lodge. He told Jen last month that he wanted to take the money from the sales—what would likely be a moderate fortune—and invest it for future grandchildren she might give him. Both she and Jen, however, had immediately thought this might be the answer to their prayers.

Their business had been struggling so much partly because of a space problem. Their current venue consisted of a small tasting room attached to a much-larger brewery—but both were still small by most local standards. They needed to expand so they could increase their beer output and seating area. If they could brew more beer, they could start selling more of it outside of the tasting room, at more local bars and stores, for example. And if they had more space, more people could sit in the tasting room more comfortably, buying the bigger quantities they were producing.

Luckily, they were already in a good position to expand. There were currently rental vacancies on either side of their brewery, so they could simply take over those spaces. They wouldn't need to move completely—just expand where they were, which would save them a ton of money and time. Still, the minimum price for expansion was around one hundred and fifty thousand dollars. That cost didn't include the specialty brewing equipment they would need to increase production. Erin and Jen both knew they would never get another bank loan for the amount of money they needed, no matter what kind of plan they proposed. They needed an angel investor—someone with money willing to take a chance on them, and Jen hoped that angel would be their father.

However, while their father adored Jen and Lydia, he and Erin did not see eye-to-eye, primarily because they were too much alike—stubborn grudge holders with quick tempers. Growing up, Erin and her father had argued about everything from her major in college to her profession to, as her father called it, her "choice" to be a lesbian. Their father was much older than their mother when they married, making him closer to the age of most of their friends' grandparents. She and Jen were in their thirties now, but their dad was just a few months away from his seventy-fifth birthday.

Jen always excused his homophobia in part because of his age, but Erin had never allowed it to be that easy for him. She refused to stay in the closet in front of his friends, refused to hide her girlfriends from him, and could never resist talking about gay rights when he was around. Needless to say, some time ago they'd basically become estranged. Despite living in the same small city, Erin and her father almost never saw each other. Her mother had died four years ago, and since then she'd barely visited. Erin couldn't even remember when they'd last talked. For the last three Christmases, she'd gone skiing rather than face another holiday with the man.

All of this was in Erin's mind, but, seeing Jen's expression of defeat, Erin felt terrible. She touched Jen's hand. "Hey—don't do that."

"What?"

"Look like we've lost before we've even tried. Dad might not like me, but he loves you. He'll do almost anything to make you happy."

Jen grinned, but her eyes shifted away, a little guilty. "You think so?"

"I know so." She squeezed her hand again. "Okay. I'll come with you. And I'll even keep my mouth closed for once. I'll try anyway. And hey—what's the worst that could happen? If he says no, we won't be any worse off than we are now."

Jen was about to reply, but her cell phone rang again. Erin made a "go ahead" motion with her hands, and Jen answered. Her cheeks colored when she heard the voice on the other line, and Erin knew who it was before her sister mouthed the word "Charlie" at her. Charlie had been calling Jen since Saturday a couple of times a day, and Jen was excited every time. Erin had decided not to tell her about what she'd overheard his friend Darcy say in the alley. She wanted to take Charlie on faith. He'd seemed like a nice guy no matter what his friends had insinuated.

Excusing herself to her sister, who barely noticed her leaving, Erin grabbed her wallet, phone, and keys and went outside into the late-morning sunshine. She paused on their front porch, stretching and peering up and down their street with distinct pleasure. She and Jen had moved downtown together soon after opening their brewery. This particular neighborhood was one of the cutest in Loveland. Many of these small homes had been built in the twenties and thirties. They were only a few blocks from the city recreation center, and just a few more blocks from their brewery. Their place was a small, cottage-style house with two bedrooms and a tiny front and backyard. Most of the houses on the block were just as modest, but everyone around them took great care with their yards, making their street a kind of centerpiece for the town. Most of their neighbors were young couples with professional jobs, most of whom had chosen to live in a smaller house for environmental purposes.

Erin went around the side of their house, passing Jen's yellow VW Beetle—a car she and Jen had managed to keep running since high school. Erin didn't own her own car, preferring bicycles. Passing the Beetle, she walked into their little garage and rolled out one of her bikes. It was so beautiful and quiet out today, it was perfect for a long ride. She kept a little fanny pack attached to the bike for her belongings, and she clipped it on after putting her keys, wallet, and phone inside. She went into the house and filled her water bottle in the kitchen, then held up her bike helmet to Jen. She waved a hand in acknowledgment, still obviously distracted by her phone call. Grinning, Erin went outside, buckled on her helmet, and took off down her street toward the city bike path.

Her ride passed in a daze of happy exertion. While no expert, Erin could bike for hours, and she liked to use her days off to explore as often as she could. She frequently rode to other breweries in Loveland or Fort Collins—almost all the local brewers were her friends—but today she needed the outdoors. The weekend had been a success, but it had been noisy and crowded. She needed quiet and sunshine to restore her sense of self. She rode west for a while before hitting Wilson Avenue, where she left the trail and headed north along the road. At about the hour mark of her ride, she was passing Coyote Ridge Natural Area, a series of trails between Loveland and Fort Collins, and she turned into the parking lot. There were mountain-bike trails here, but, as she was on her road bike, she locked it and set off on foot on one of her favorite hiking trails.

It had been weeks since the last rain, and she kicked up a lot of dust. The first part of the trail had no trees, and the sun beat down on her. She finally made it to the bottom of the foothills, which were somewhat shaded, and turned around to take in the prairie she'd just passed, marveling at the warm weather this late in the season. Though Colorado's open plains were brown and dried out this time of year, she'd always found a bleak beauty in them. From here, she could see far away on the horizon, and the sky was a bright, crystalline blue. She took a deep breath, the relaxation she'd craved settling into her bones. She turned and started hiking up, the trail a steep scramble from here on.

Halfway up the ridge, she was glad she'd brought her water bottle, and once she'd passed the halfway point on the sloping hill, she realized she needed to turn around or she'd run dry. It was now very hot, and she hadn't brought a hat. Still, this could very easily be the last week of nice weather. Any day it could grow chilly, and she was glad she could take advantage of the trail one last time until next summer.

By the time she reached her bike, worn out and sweaty, she felt relaxed and loose-limbed. She stopped at a public water fountain to fill her bottle and then washed her face and hands. She was covered in dust and splattered with mud from her earlier bike ride, but she couldn't have been happier. She greeted a fellow biker on his way toward the mountain-bike trails and then unlocked and climbed on hers after putting on her helmet. She was about to push off toward home when her phone rang.

"Hello?"

"Hey, Erin. It's Jen. Listen. I've been having some beer with Charlie and wondered if you could pick me up. I mean, if you're nearby. I didn't eat before I came, and the beer went right to my head. I was going to call for a ride but thought I'd check in with you first in case you're around."

"Where are you?"

"At Zwei Brewing. Charlie and the brewer here had a meeting this morning, and he invited me to join them."

Erin glanced down at herself and wrinkled her nose. Aside from being filthy, she was pretty sure she stank, too. "I don't know, Jen. I'm kind of a mess right now."

"Oh, Charlie won't mind. Please come? I could Uber, but I hate leaving my car."

Erin sighed and did a quick mental calculation. "Okay. I'll be there in half an hour or so. You better have a big glass of ice water for me when I get there. I'm hot as hell."

"Done. Thanks a million, lady."

The ride to the brewery was less pleasant than the ride she'd taken to the trails because the roads were much busier. Fort Collins is larger than Loveland and, despite being very bike-friendly, still has some work to do to make some roads safe for bicycles. Twice she had to slam on her brakes to avoid being hit by a car, and by the time she rolled into Zwei Brewing's parking lot, she was hot, thirsty, and rattled. She made herself pause outside of the tasting room for a moment to collect herself, not wanting to embarrass her sister.

Inside it was blissfully cool and dark, and it took Erin a moment to spot Jen and Charlie. Just as she realized they weren't alone, and almost as if she'd called out to her, Darcy turned and met her eyes. Erin saw her look her up and down and then, suddenly, recognition dawned on the woman's face, followed by something like horror.

"Great," Erin muttered to herself.

Breaking eye contact with Darcy, she walked toward their table, and a moment later Jen spotted her. She leapt up when Erin came closer, giving her a solid hug.

"You came!"

Erin laughed, recognizing the signs of Jen's drunkenness. Her usual quiet friendliness and warmth had turned effusive and loud.

"Of course I came, you ninny. I told you I was on my way."

Jen was grinning like a maniac, and she held Erin out at arm's length, scrutinizing her. "My god, Erin. You're filthy."

Erin had to agree. She'd been dirty before, after her hike, but now she was a mess. While it hadn't rained for a long time, there were always puddles, and Erin had managed to hit or be hit by every one. Mud and dirt had splattered her clothes, and a strange black slime coated one leg.

Charlie laughed from the table behind her. "Hey, we don't mind. This isn't the Ritz. Please join us, Erin."

Erin smiled at him gratefully and then sat in the empty chair, ignoring Darcy. A large glass of ice water sat at her place, and she gulped it down without stopping. After she finished, she glanced at Darcy, who was staring at her with a strange expression. It took Erin a moment to realize that it resembled actual interest, and Erin averted her eyes, blushing.

Jen and Charlie had moved their chairs close together and were chatting and animated. For a moment, Erin felt a little pity for Darcy. She'd likely been the third wheel since Jen showed up.

Charlie turned and grinned at her, his boyish face pink with embarrassment. "I'm sorry, Erin. Your sister and I were just finishing a conversation about hops. She knows a lot about them, and I find it fascinating."

Erin had to smile. Only her sister could be wooed with such a topic. "Yes, we both do, actually. We've recently had to switch to using hops out of Oregon for almost everything we brew. I wish we could use exclusively Colorado hops. I use local for everything else. But this just isn't the climate for them."

"You can say that again," a voice said behind them. Erin turned and was pleased to see one of the Zwei brewers she was friends with. She stood up and gave him a quick hug before remembering how filthy she was.

"Your friend here has been schooling me all morning," Charlie explained. "He was just showing us some of the new equipment in the back before you got here."

Erin turned to the brewer, excited. "You got it?"

"You're damn right. Last night, as a matter of fact. Me and the other guys have been basically standing around admiring it since it got here."

Erin was almost breathless. "Can I see it?"

He laughed. "Of course! Follow me. You guys can come see it again too, if you want."

Everyone jumped to their feet and followed him into the brewing room. Erin's breath caught in her throat. Zwei had recently been able to buy a much larger, four-vessel, steam-powered brew-house precisely the size Erin wanted to install at BSB. At BSB, she'd been using a smaller electric version since they'd opened, and the maintenance, cleaning, and size were becoming a problem. The brewer showed her around the equipment, pointing out all the features she'd been reading and dreaming about for months.

When she climbed down the ladder, Charlie and Jen were smiling broadly, clearly pleased. Darcy still had that strange, hard-to-read expression, and once again, Erin's face heated up under her gaze. She turned to the brewer.

"It's really incredible. I'm so happy for you guys. Congratulations."

"Thanks, Erin. That means a lot. I think it's really going to change things around here."

"I'm sure it will."

As they walked into the tap room, Erin couldn't help but feel a stab of true envy at Zwei's success. She'd long slavered over a new brewhouse, but even if BSB could afford to buy one—which they couldn't—they simply didn't have enough space to put it in their brewing room. Until they could expand, she'd never be able to buy one. Even if she somehow got the cash and managed to get the new brewhouse, they would have to upgrade all their other equipment, in capacity at least, to meet the new quantities they could create. The amount of money involved was staggering.

All five of them sat down at the table again, and she and the brewer caught up on local brewing news for the next half hour as she rehydrated with glass after glass of water. She had one small sample of Zwei's Oktoberfest Ale, pleased to find that she objectively thought her own brew much better. He must have read this conclusion on her face, as they had a lively debate about it for a few minutes before he excused himself to return to work. When she turned to the other people at the table, she once again found Darcy staring at her. This time she made herself maintain eye contact, and after a moment, to her surprise, Darcy smiled at her.

"You certainly know a lot about beer, Miss Bennet," Darcy said.

"I should hope so. It is my profession, after all."

"I like to see someone committed to something, wholly and totally. It's obvious you have a true passion for your work. And, having tried your product, that passion is well placed. Yours has been the best beer we've tried so far in Colorado."

Erin couldn't help but flush in pleased surprise, and Darcy's smile widened further. Erin tried to align Darcy's words with the Darcy she thought she knew, but it simply didn't compute. Darcy must be trying to trick her for some reason.

Instead of responding, Erin turned and saw that Jen and Charlie had both overheard this exchange. Charlie was giving Darcy a lopsided grin, and Jen was beaming at her. They clearly believed what Darcy had said, and again, Erin had a moment of doubt. Could Darcy actually mean it? Too confused to figure things out right now, she launched herself to her feet.

"I'm so sorry, Charlie, Darcy, but my sister and I need to be going."

"But Erin—" Jen said.

"No, Jen. Really. We need to go. Now."

She and Jen had a silent conversation with their eyes, and Jen finally sighed, seeming defeated by Erin's determination.

"Fine." She turned to Charlie. "Thank you so much for inviting me. I'm sorry we have to leave so soon."

"The pleasure is mine, Jen. I know you're both very busy at the brewery, but I do hope we can do it again sometime soon."

Jen's smile nearly doubled in size, and for a moment, it appeared that the two of them—Jen and Charlie—were deciding how to say good-bye. Erin was fairly certain that, had it been just them, they would have kissed, and it seemed like he might at least hug her, but Jen, awkward as usual, simply held out her hand. Charlie seemed surprised, then shook it before shaking Erin's as well.

"Until next week," Charlie said to Erin. He'd arranged to get a tour and hear about their brewery on Monday.

"Until then," Erin said.

They went outside together, and Erin unlocked her bike and rolled it over to the Beetle. It had a bike rack on top, and they managed to hoist her bike up there and lock it in place. They climbed inside, and Erin was about to start the car, but she paused and turned to Jen. It took a moment, but Jen finally noticed and looked over at her.

"What is it? Is something wrong? Why did we rush out of there like that?"

Erin shook her head, unable to explain the panic that had washed over her when Darcy smiled at her. "It's nothing. I'm sorry. I just want to get home and take a shower." She paused, staring out the front window and then at her sister. She wasn't sure how to broach the topic of Charlie, but avoiding it was starting to feel a little like lying.

"Jen—are you and Charlie seeing each other now?"

Her sister's face went dark red, and her eyebrows shot up. "Seeing each other? What do you mean?"

"It's obvious you like him, and he likes you."

"So what? That doesn't mean we're dating. He lives in Boston, for crying out loud."

Erin continued to stare at her, long enough that Jen blushed again. She glanced away, clearly embarrassed.

"Anyway, even if we did start dating, what difference does it make?" She was almost pouting.

"It makes a lot of difference, Jen. You know that."

They sat there quietly, both watching the traffic on the busy road beyond the parking lot, neither of them saying a word. Erin felt a little better for bringing up the subject—she'd wanted to say something earlier, but she also didn't want to make Jen feel guilty about anything. She was an adult, after all, and could make her own choices.

Erin touched Jen's hand. "Hey, Jen, I'm sorry. You can do whatever you want. I just don't want you to get hurt."

Jen met her eyes, frowning, but then she sighed. "It's okay, Erin. I'll be careful."

While she knew that Jen believed what she was saying, Erin didn't buy it. Jen was clearly falling for Charlie. Still, at least she'd said something. She'd feel worse if she pretended, like Jen, that nothing bad could happen.

CHAPTER THREE

After two busy days of prepping the holiday beer for casking and bottling, Erin was tempted, despite her promise, to back out of going to her father's for dinner. While they needed the money he could loan them—needed it desperately—as the hour drew closer for the visit, and despite what she'd told Jen, she started to doubt if it would be worth even trying. Jen could forgive anyone basically anything, but Erin had always thought that if you love someone, you should love them unconditionally. Their father did anything but. In fact, he had spent the better part of Erin's teenage years and young adulthood doing everything he could to change just about everything about her. When he'd failed, their relationship had turned from annoyance to sour antagonism to deep dislike. Every moment Erin spent with the man was torture. Still, she'd promised Jen she would go, and she knew she should. Erin hated breaking a promise, especially to Jen.

Erin was lying on her bed, dressed in a nice, long-sleeved button-up and khakis, taking deep breaths to calm down. Lottie had come over to help her get ready, and she was sitting in Erin's reading chair idly flipping through an illustrated Jane Austen novel.

Erin sat up and shook her head. "Christ, Lottie. I don't know if I can do it."

Lottie laughed. "Of course you can. How long will it be—a couple of hours? Three, tops? You can get through anything for that long." She laughed. "I once went on a three-hour date with a man that couldn't stop talking about *Mortal Combat*—the movie, not the video game. I survived."

Erin laughed, but her smile soon died. "You weren't there the last time I talked to Dad, Lottie, and neither was Jen. He said some things that were…" She paused at the memory and shook her head. "Unforgivable."

Lottie seemed sympathetic. "I don't doubt it. I've heard him speak to you before, Erin, and I saw you after the last time the two of you met. But let's keep the broader picture in mind. Your father can help you, and you need help. I think you can hold your tongue for three hours if it means staying in business."

Erin wavered. Part of her still wasn't sure if staying open was worth talking to him again, but of course that was ridiculous. Their brewery meant everything to her and Jen. Erin had grown up wanting exactly what they had now—had gone to college and gotten apprenticeships to train in exactly what she was doing now. She wasn't about to give up now, especially when a possible solution like her father was right in front of her.

She grinned. "You're right again."

Lottie sniffed. "Of course I am. Am I ever wrong?"

Erin threw one of her pillows at her, and the two of them laughed.

A moment later, Jen came through the door, grinning. "I heard laughter. Does that mean your crisis is over, Erin?"

Erin sighed and launched herself to her feet. "Yes, it's over. I'm ready." She straightened her clothes. "How do I look?"

Jen peered at her critically for a long moment and then shrugged. "I mean, at least your clothes are clean."

Erin glanced down at herself, confused. "What's wrong with what I'm wearing?"

Jen sighed and shook her head. "Nothing. But you know Dad."

Erin flushed with anger. "You know I won't wear a dress for that man, Jen. Ever."

"I know. I just thought…well, it doesn't matter. Let's go." Jen walked over and gave Lottie a long hug. "And thanks for helping today. I couldn't have gotten her ready on my own."

Lottie smiled. "That's what I'm here for."

Erin slapped her forehead. "Wait—I just thought of something. Do you think we could take Lottie with us? Dad likes you, Lottie, and with you there, he might be less likely to say something nasty."

Jen seemed surprised, then turned to Lottie. "Well, yes, I guess so. Do you have plans tonight?"

Lottie shook her head. "No—I've got some time. And if you think it'll help, I'd be happy to." She waved at her casual outfit. "But I'm not really dressed for a dinner party."

"I can lend you something. Come on, though. We need to hurry if we're going to be on time."

A while later they were in Jen's little car, driving across town to their father's house. They had grown up in a more modest home in a different part of town, but when their mother died, her father had sold their childhood home and upgraded to a large, McMansion-style house in a brand-new subdivision. Jen and Erin hated the new house, and Erin couldn't help but feel like he'd betrayed their mother's memory by selling their old place. It was just another piece of the tension between her and her father—one of dozens. Still, she'd promised Jen she'd be on her best behavior and attempt to ignore such things. Nevertheless, as they pulled into the driveway to a house identical to all of its ugly neighbors, Erin felt a sharp pang of disgust and anger at her father's choices.

Lydia sat outside on the front stoop of the house, smoking. In her black clothes and heavy makeup, she looked distinctly out of place in this sterile, generic neighborhood. She didn't bother to get up and greet them and did little more than move over an inch or two when they got closer.

"Where were you this morning?" Erin asked. "You were supposed to help with the dry-hopping."

Lydia blew out a stream of smoke and shrugged. "I didn't feel like it."

Erin felt a bright-hot flare of anger, and Jen, as if sensing this reaction, touched her arm to stop her from yelling. Erin took a deep breath and let it out, making sure her voice was still calm before continuing.

"Well, I had to call Kyle in to help. You could have at least let me know you wouldn't be there so I didn't have to call him at four in the morning."

Lydia didn't respond, seemingly unimpressed, and Erin again had to fight the urge to yell at her. She might have done it anyway, but the front door opened, and suddenly she was staring at her father. She'd seen him in passing a few times over the last year, but they'd barely spoken more than a couple of words. He'd aged a lot since she'd last seen him up close. His shoulders were a little stooped, his hair wispy and thin compared to the full head he'd managed to keep most of his life. He was staring at her, too, and his eyes seemed to bore into her for a moment. Then they were sliding away, dismissing her, to land on Jen. His entire face transformed, his smile wide and happy, and he and Jen embraced. He spotted Lottie next and gave her a similar hug.

"What a pleasant surprise!" he told her. "I haven't seen you in ages, Lottie. I'm so glad you came."

"Nice to see you too, Mr. Bennet," Lottie said. She threw Erin a guilty glance, as if she were betraying her, but Erin shook her head. It was hard not to be charmed by her father. He was incredibly warm with the people he liked.

He paused in front of Erin, and the two of them seemed to debate for a long moment, waiting for the other to make a move. Erin didn't, and neither did he, and the moment stretched into awkward silence.

"Oh, for goodness' sake," Jen said, her face red. "Can we go inside already? The two of you are ridiculous."

Erin flushed with shame. She should have given him a hug, even if it was a false one. She'd already failed her sister.

Her father didn't seem embarrassed at all, however, and stepped to the side to make room for them. "Yes, please. I have a special surprise for you all. Come in!"

Erin followed Jen, Lydia, and Lottie inside, closing the door behind her. She paused by the door, closing her eyes and taking another calming breath. You can get through this, dammit! she told herself. Get it together.

When she opened them, she was startled, once again, to see some of her mother's antique furniture here in this modern monstrosity of a house. Her mother's ancestors had been some of the first pioneers in what became Colorado, and her mother had inherited a lot of the original furniture and decorations that had traveled first across the ocean from the Netherlands and then via wagon from the East Coast. Erin had long thought that she and her sisters should have inherited all her mother's things, which was yet another reminder of an argument she and her father had many, many times.

She heard laughter in the dining room, and after squaring her shoulders, she walked toward it. The table had been set with a serious spread of food. While it had been years since he worked in a kitchen, their father had initially trained as a chef before buying out the first restaurant he worked in. He was always an amazing cook, making just about every holiday and Sunday meal for the family when they were growing up.

For a second, Erin felt a sharp stab of nostalgia at the sight of her sisters and father laughing at the dining-room table. It almost felt like old times. While she and her father had never had an easy relationship, they had, at least before she was a teenager, been close—close in the way only two very similar people can be. They'd argued, yes, but many of her childhood arguments with him had been more like friendly debates. Her father would push her buttons in order to motivate her to do something or think more clearly about a topic. She'd enjoyed his ribbing then. Was it possible for them to return to the way it had been when she was little? It was the first time in a long while that she'd even entertained the idea.

A moment later, however, a strange, middle-aged man came into the room from the kitchen, and everyone went silent. Her father was beaming at this man, and he moved closer and put an arm around his shoulders.

"Girls—I want you to meet Will Collins."

"Hi," Will said, smiling. Tall, with a heavy build, he appeared as if he might have, at one time, been simply solid, and while he wouldn't exactly be called overweight now, by almost any standards, his face and stomach were rounded—almost swollen. His eyes were a little sunken and squinty, and his skin was sallow, pale, and blotchy. With his upturned nose and balding head, he resembled a pig.

Erin couldn't think of any reason for her father to invite this man tonight. Here she was, at his house for the first time in over a year, and he'd brought in some outsider. Lottie didn't count—she'd more or less been a part of the family since they'd met as children. This man was different. She'd partly agreed to come tonight—despite being incredibly busy at the brewery—for a chance to mend some fences and possibly set up the conversation she and Jen wanted to have with him about the money. They hadn't planned to literally ask for money tonight, but they had planned to lay the groundwork for that conversation sometime in the next couple of weeks. Now, with this man Will here, even that first step couldn't happen. Erin was furious. It was typical of her dad to ruin every event.

"Actually," their dad said, "I'm being a little facetious. All of you have met before, but it was such a long, long time ago, I can't imagine that you'd remember each other very well. Even you met him, Lottie."

"I did?"

"Yes. It was over twenty years ago. He stayed with us for a week in the early nineties."

Erin suddenly flashed to the time her father was talking about. She was about ten or eleven, Jen twelve or thirteen. Her dad's friend from high school had come to stay with them for a week that summer with his little boy. She remembered Billy, as he'd then been called, as a bitter, nasty little kid that pulled her hair and teased her for being, as he put it, "a weirdo" for being into sports and other "boy things." Something else had happened between her and Billy that week too, and Erin had never told anyone. She had been terrified. Jen had felt sorry for him then, Erin remembered, because his parents were getting divorced, but that hadn't been enough for Erin to forgive his nastiness or what he'd done to her, or how he'd made her feel. She'd been incredibly relieved to see the last of him when he and his father moved on.

"Oh!" Jen said, clearly remembering that week as well. "I do remember you now. How nice to see you again, Will. Was that really twenty years ago?" They shook hands.

"A little over, I think." Smiling did nothing to improve his looks. If anything, it accentuated his piggish features.

"You were with your dad, right?" Lottie said, squinting at him.

He turned his smile to her. "Exactly right. My parents were getting divorced, and my dad and I spent the summer with friends and family before we settled in Denver."

"Oh, I'm sorry," Lottie said, her face falling. "I didn't mean to bring up bad memories."

He shook his head. "It's so long ago now—please don't worry about it."

"So why are you in town, Will?"

Lydia broke in. "He's here to take over Daddy's businesses."

Erin and Jen stared at her. Erin was shocked to her very core.

"W-what?" she sputtered. She turned to her father, so incredulous she could hardly breathe. He was grinning at Jen. Erin glanced at her sister and saw that her face had drained of color.

"What?" Jen echoed, her voice barely above a whisper.

Their father's grin grew, if anything, broader. "Lydia's right, pumpkin. Will is here to take over my restaurants. I've decided to avoid selling almost all of them for as long as I can."

"But why?" Jen asked, her voice still weak.

"Why not?" He shrugged. "Every restaurant I own is bringing in more and more money every year. Still, I'm man enough to recognize that I'm getting worn out. I can hardly keep up anymore, and I need to stop before I make a fool out of myself. I wanted to sell, but after I mentioned my plan to Will's dad, he suggested I talk to his son first. So when I contacted Will for advice, he offered to manage them for me for a few years before he buys me out."

Erin couldn't help but jump in. "But why him?"

He glanced over at her, clearly annoyed that she'd spoken. "I would have explained that to you if you had even an ounce of patience, Erin, but, as usual, you don't."

Hot rage flashed through her. "You didn't answer my question."

He sighed, rolling his eyes. "I wanted to bring in Will because he has years and years of investment experience, most of it in restaurants."

"But you've never actually worked in a restaurant?" Erin asked him. She couldn't help but sound disgusted.

Will shifted uncomfortably, but he shook his head. "No, not exactly. But I have a lot of experience revamping and revitalizing restaurants, making them better, and finding the best staff possible. No matter how great a place is being run, it can always do better. If I start working with your father now, by the time he's ready to sell, every place he runs will be worth much more than it is today."

"It's win-win," her father said, holding his palms upright. "More money for me, more money for him."

Erin and Jen shared a look, and Erin saw her own dashed hopes reflected in her sister's eyes. If her father wasn't interested in selling anytime soon, their own business would probably be sunk within the year. Jen was better at holding herself together and hiding things, though, as a moment later, she was congratulating Will and chatting with him, seemingly friendly. Erin felt as if the world had just dropped out underneath her. She felt disoriented—dizzy, almost. She hadn't admitted it to herself, but some small part of her had genuinely believed they would somehow convince their father to loan them the money.

She should have known better. Her father was obsessed with his restaurants. When Jen told her a few months ago that he was thinking of retiring, Erin had been stunned. She couldn't imagine her father relaxing. He'd been in motion every moment of her life. It made perfect sense that he wanted to keep them running into his retirement. Having someone else manage the restaurants meant he could still keep his toe in the water, as it were. This new development was, of course, something she and Jen should have expected, but they hadn't. Hope had blinded them to one constant they'd known their whole lives: her father's work defined him. Without it, he was nothing.

Erin decided that if she didn't leave now, she would explode and say something she couldn't take back. She pretended to take a phone call and, after excusing herself, talked to no one for a moment in the kitchen, and then walked into the dining room.

"I'm so sorry," she told everyone. "Kyle—our coworker—just called and said there's an emergency at the brewery."

She could tell from their expressions that no one, except perhaps Will, believed her, but at this moment she didn't care.

"Anyway, I have to run," she said. "Lydia, can you give Jen and Lottie a ride home later?"

"I'll be happy to," Will offered. "I'm staying downtown for now, so it's no bother at all."

"Thanks, Will. I appreciate it. Good-bye, everyone."

She nearly dashed from the house. A moment before she'd left, she'd seen Jen's hurt expression, but she didn't care. She needed to get as far away from her father as she could.

She drove the little Beetle hard and fast, much faster than the old engine could take anymore, at least for long. At first she simply drove, not paying attention to where she was going, but eventually she turned west, heading into the mountains. The winding road to Estes Park took a lot of concentration, and for a while all she thought about was the dark road in front of her, basically empty at this time of night. She was being reckless driving so fast. Even without the dangerous, hairpin curves she was flying around, she could hit animals out here. One wrong move could mean plunging into the Big Thompson River or into the canyon wall.

She'd initially planned to head to Estes and hit a little bar she knew there, but, as she drove, she thought of the very first trail she'd ever finished hiking as a child. She and her father had climbed it together for the first time when she was about six years old. Her sisters had never been outdoorsy, by any stretch, and while he'd made the others go occasionally, she and her father had often camped and hiked together alone when she was a kid.

After a moment's debate, she pulled into the parking lot for the trail—deserted now that the sun had set. She climbed out of the Beetle and opened the trunk, searching around beneath boxes of promotional materials for the brewery. At the very bottom of one pile of junk, she found the black duffel bag she kept handy for hiking and camping and, after rooting around in it, found her headlamp. She strapped it on, lighted it, and headed up the trail, nearly jogging.

By the time she made it to the top of the first long hill, she felt better. She paused at the branch that signaled the beginning of two trails, breathing heavily from exertion, and as she caught her breath, she peered into the dark woods around her. She'd come up here a few times for full-moon hikes over the years, but never when it was like this—almost pitch-black. The headlamp's light barely penetrated the dark beyond the ten- or fifteen-foot circle of light she was standing in. Reaching up, she turned off the headlamp and was immediately plunged into the kind of darkness that exists only in places far from the city lights. She peered up into the sky, marveling at the Milky Way and the bright stars above her. She stood there for a long time, letting the sight calm her, her insignificance always so poignant in the face of eternity.

Her headlamp had a low-light setting, and after turning it on, she continued on the shorter trail. She stepped lightly, hoping to see animals, and a moment later, as she rounded a bend, she managed to see an owl taking flight into the woods. She smiled. The joy of nature was so fulfilling, so startling every time she came face-to-face with it. She glimpsed several more animals in the woods—a fox, a raccoon, a porcupine, all of whom fled from the light, but the owl remained her best sighting of the night.

The last stretch of the trail was very short but very steep, and she paused at the bottom, considering her options. She wasn't exactly dressed for a rock scramble. Aside from her nice clothes, she was wearing her newest Converse sneakers—not exactly hiking boots.

Still, she was this close, and it felt silly to turn around now. She took a deep breath and starting climbing, slipping a little here and there, but happy to find that the trail wasn't as bad as she'd anticipated.

When the little stone lookout cabin finally appeared, she felt a familiar sense of triumph. The trail she'd just hiked was designed for families with small kids—it was short and had a Nature Trail pamphlet you could follow along with, but it was still somewhat difficult, especially in the dark. She suddenly remembered the first time she'd seen this little cabin with her father. She'd been incredibly proud of herself, hooting and hollering as she raced toward the small building. Her father had laughed along with her.

In their living room growing up, a large photograph of the two of them from that first hike had hung on the wall for several years. Then, one day in her mid-teens, Erin had realized that it was gone. She'd never asked her parents what happened to it, but she'd always suspected it disappeared around the time she came out of the closet.

The lookout cabin had a sloping wooden roof and stone walls, with open doorways and windows holes instead of actual doors or windows. The CCC had built it during the Depression for the contemplation of nature, and it had the rough, clunky, and functional architecture of that era. She'd been here many, many times, yet it was still a magical spot.

She went inside the cabin and sat down on the bench by one of the open windows. The bench was made from a hewn pine trunk and covered in a thick, clear gloss. She leaned back into the darkness, turned off her headlamp, and closed her eyes. The air was colder up here than in town, and she had to suppress a shudder. She breathed a deep lungful of cold, piney air and felt almost happy again.

While she'd been here so often she couldn't remember every visit, she did recall a very significant trip here in high school. She'd been wooing a girl in her biology class—unbeknownst to the other girl, or so she thought. At school, she'd done everything she could to get closer to the girl—Kim. They'd been in different social groups, and it had been an uphill battle at first. Erin had a crush on her for years before she finally had the opportunity to talk to her, and even then it wasn't easy to move beyond casual greetings.

Biology class had finally brought them together. They'd been assigned as study partners, and a kind of fawning, one-sided friendship had sprung up. Kim had been the dictator, and Erin had done whatever Kim wanted. At the time, Erin thought this was fair. Having Kim to simper over was enough—she didn't care how poorly she was treated. Kim took this as her due. She was beautiful as only that kind of blond, blue-eyed girl can be, and Erin had thought of herself as anything but beautiful then.

At some point, Erin had somehow convinced Kim to agree to this hike with her. Erin couldn't remember the exact circumstances, but it must have been for class. She'd bought, packed, and lugged a huge lunch up here, and the two of them had shared the meal sitting on this very bench. Despite the fact that she'd bought all of Kim's favorite foods and carried them up here on her own, Kim hadn't thanked her; instead, she criticized Erin's choices, clearly trying to make her feel bad. It had worked, and Erin had been on the verge of tears for most of the meal.

Erin shook her head, dismissing the memory with a sad smile. She'd gone on to have lots of crushes and one-sided relationships like that before she'd learned to respect herself more, but she was still attracted to that kind of woman, even now.

That thought brought Darcy to mind, and she frowned in the dark. Darcy was exactly like a grown-up version of Kim, yet Erin hadn't been able to stop thinking about her. She was convinced now that Darcy had indeed been flirting with her the last time she'd seen her, but why? She was probably bored and had simply toyed with Erin to pass the time.

Dismissing her again, Erin got to her feet and went outside to the actual lookout. Highway 34 was just visible below, a very occasional car passing, but otherwise she could barely see a thing. Mountains loomed in the dark, visible only because they blocked out the stars. She took one more deep breath of cool mountain air and turned around to head back to the VW. She was starting to feel a little sheepish now. She'd left her father's in a teenage-like sulk, she'd driven around like a madwoman, and now she was in the mountains, on her own, in the dark. Talk about reckless. She'd long grown out of going out and getting reckless in town—sleeping with strangers and drinking too much—but what she'd done tonight was dangerous.

Still, by the time she made it to her car, she felt much better. The hike had done her a lot of good, and she could think clearly again about her father and their situation without the fury that had clouded her judgment earlier. After all, nothing was settled yet. Perhaps, even now, she and Jen could convince her father to sell some of his holdings and help them out. And even if they couldn't, maybe things would turn out all right in the end.

CHAPTER FOUR

E rin let out a long breath and then bent down to stretch her back and upper legs. The gym was busy this time of morning, and even the space set aside for stretching was filled with people. In the past, Erin didn't like going to the gym, in part because of the crowds. All of her life, she'd been very active, but she preferred her exercise to come from an activity rather than an artificial routine inside. Then, last Christmas, Lottie had given her a year's membership to the Chilson Recreation Center, close to Erin and Jen's house. When she'd opened the little envelope Lottie had handed her and seen what it held, she'd stared at Lottie like she'd lost her mind. Lottie, red-faced and stammering, had explained that she'd bought herself the same thing. She bought Erin a membership so they could go together.

"For motivation," Lottie had explained.

"Yours or mine?"

Lottie face took on a darker shade of embarrassment. "Mine."

Erin had left it at that, understanding in an instant what Lottie wanted. She and Lottie had met in elementary school and been close ever since—despite the fact that they had very little in common. Erin was a natural athlete. She'd been team captain in several sports throughout school and eventually president of their senior class. Lottie, on the other hand, was a nerd. She'd been somewhat active behind the scenes in their middle and high schools' theater departments, but mostly she read books and played Dungeons and Dragons with the other weirdos. She was, with most people, extremely quiet, staying in the background to avoid talking to just about anyone. In middle and high school, she'd started to put on a little weight, and by the time she and Erin were graduating college together, she was quite heavy.

Erin knew that Lottie's weight bothered her—she'd seen her avoid a lot of situations where food was involved, for example, just so she wouldn't be seen eating in front of other people. Additionally, she'd always seemed a little wistful when either Erin or Jen talked about the active things they'd done, as if she didn't think it was possible to do them herself. Buying herself and Erin a gym membership was a big deal, and getting one for Erin was her way of asking for help.

They'd started by going once or twice a week before work. Both of them had relatively flexible schedules at their respective jobs, so they'd begun going mid-morning, when the gym was almost empty. Erin had helped Lottie get to know the weightlifting equipment and had given her a light cardio routine. Erin really didn't do much more except show up to work out with her, but it had been enough. After a month or so, Lottie had started to seem more confident, and she'd lost a few pounds. Then, as the months passed and winter turned into spring, Lottie's weight loss had continued, and her confidence both in and outside of the gym had started to grow.

At the beginning of the summer, she'd asked Erin if they could start going earlier in the morning so she could attend the classes the rec center ran then. Erin had reluctantly agreed, knowing it would probably be best for Lottie to have professional help, and now they came to the gym almost every weekday morning. Erin had gone to a couple of the classes with Lottie, but, once Lottie was used to the experience, she could do it on her own, and Erin continued her former workout upstairs in the gym.

Most mornings, Erin ran around the little indoor track for a few miles, listening to music or audiobooks on her phone. Afterward, she'd do weights with one part of her body, and she swam three days a week. She wouldn't say she was a gym convert yet—she still preferred exercising outside, but now that she'd been working out here for ten months, she could appreciate the fact that, no matter the weather, she got some exercise almost every day. It had certainly helped her stress levels, and she'd also seen some gains in her stamina hiking and biking on her days off. Whether she bought another year's membership on her own was still up in the air, but she probably would. Even beyond her own workouts, Lottie still liked having her here, and Erin was happy to oblige. More recently, they rarely saw each other at the gym beyond showing up and leaving together, but Lottie still seemed to need her here.

Erin got down on the ground to stretch her legs some more, debating whether to swim. It was Monday, a usual swimming day for her, but she didn't think she had enough time. Normally it wouldn't matter, but she had to get to work earlier than usual to meet Charlie for the tour. Earlier, she had run two extra miles beyond her usual three. Between putting on her swimsuit and the extra time she'd need in the showers to get the chlorine out of her hair, it didn't make sense to try. She'd just swim some extra laps Wednesday instead.

She stood up to head over to the weights just as Lottie appeared on the stairs. Erin had to smile. Lottie had lost a lot of weight this year—twenty or thirty pounds. Erin, however, didn't care as much about Lottie's weight loss as the fact that she had started to come out of her shell. She was holding herself higher, more confidently, and she met people's eyes more often now. Lottie had told her that her parents, who had, as long at Erin had known them, basically ignored her, had recently complimented her new appearance, but it was this personality benefit that made Erin the happiest. Lottie seemed more like herself now, even with strangers.

She spotted Erin and smiled before joining her.

"Hey, you," she said.

"Hey, yourself. What are you doing up here? Shouldn't you be in class now?"

Lottie shrugged. "I left a little early. We had a substitute instructor today, and he kind of sucks. Thought I'd come up and work out with you for once."

"Well, I'm almost done." Erin paused and grinned. "I just need to do my chest, arms, and shoulders."

Lottie groaned. When they first started working out together, she'd always dreaded these exercises since they were her weakest muscles.

Erin laughed. "Oh, come on. It's been weeks since I tortured you. Anyway, I bet you'll be surprised how much stronger you are now after all those aerobics classes."

"Okay." Lottie sounded anything but happy.

They approached the dipping and chin-up bars. Erin decided to give Lottie a break and go first, and positioned herself for dips. She started dipping, and Lottie watched her with something like dread.

They were quiet for a while as Erin counted, and then Lottie asked, "What's been happening with Jen and that Charlie guy?"

Erin paused mid-dip and then continued through to her final rep. She got down on the ground and sighed. She waited to reply until Lottie climbed up onto the bar and started her own workout.

"I don't know the details—she doesn't really talk about him. But I'm really starting to worry. I haven't exactly been on board since they met, but Jen's already getting a little moony. I mean, at first I didn't mind so much. He's really a nice guy, and I'm glad she's found someone to be interested in after all this time, but where could it possibly go? I mean, the guy lives in Boston."

They switched places again. "Yeah, but you never know, right?" Lottie said. "Maybe they could do long distance or something. I mean, stranger things have happened. He'll be here for a while yet. Maybe they'll both fall in love."

Erin had to laugh. Despite being almost chronically single, Lottie had always been a romantic. She always egged Erin and Jen on in their relationships, being something like a cheerleader any time either one of them was dating someone. She wanted everyone in the world to be paired up. Her own love life was somewhat lackluster, so she seemed to be living vicariously, though God knew why. Erin had always thought Lottie sold herself short. She was, in fact, charming, sweet, and adorable, and once others got past her initial shyness, they learned what a fantastic, caring person she was, too. Erin had seen men looking at her with interest over the years and pointed it out many, many times, but Lottie had always laughed the possibility off as ridiculous.

Erin moved to the side, and Lottie got on the bar for her second set.

Erin shook her head. "I don't know. I guess they could end up together, but it's more likely she'll have her heart broken. Again."

Throughout high school and into their late twenties, Jen had been a serial monogamist, dating one loser after the next. She seemed to be genuinely attracted to assholes, as every guy she dated either cheated on her, or dumped her unexpectedly, or both. After Jen's fiancé Jacob left her three years ago, she had refused to talk about why they'd broken up. She'd been something like a ghost for six months, hardly talking to anyone, so Erin hadn't pushed her, hoping that with space and time she'd decide to discuss it. She never had. Since then, Jen had simply stopped dating. As far as she knew, Charlie was the first guy she'd been interested in since Jacob.

After Lottie finished, the two of them moved over to the chin-up bar, and Erin climbed the little steps up to it.

"It could happen, Erin. I mean it. Has she told him how she feels about him?"

Erin laughed and placed her feet on the steps and stared down at Lottie in disbelief. "They just met!"

Lottie shrugged. "Yeah, but when it's love, it's love. It's always better to be honest with someone. If she doesn't tell him, how could he know?"

Erin laughed again and continued her chin-ups, struggling through to the end. She'd clearly overdone it running earlier, as she was nearly spent. Both of them decided one set was enough, and after seeing the long lines for the free weights and the other weight machines, they decided to call it a day.

After showering and getting into their work clothes, they stopped by the little coffee shop in the bookstore down the street—their Monday, Wednesday, Friday ritual. They came often enough that the barista started making their coffees the moment they walked in the door. Erin and Lottie took their favorite seat by the window.

They chatted about work until their coffees were served and paid for, and then Lottie suddenly resumed their earlier conversation. "Look—about earlier—I don't mean to sound like an ass about Jen.

I just want her to be happy. I'm probably being unrealistic, but I've seen the way she's been since she met him. She's on cloud nine."

Erin frowned. "I know. I've seen it, too. And that's what worries me. She's getting in too deep, too fast. She basically spent all weekend with him, and I'm pretty sure they slept together."

Lottie's eyes widened. "Really?"

"Unless they had separate hotel rooms. She went with him to Denver overnight Saturday."

Lottie appeared uncertain. "But it could have been innocent. Right?"

Erin gave her an even glare. "Come on, Lottie—what are the odds?" She paused. "I'm not saying the sex is a bad thing. I'm pretty sure it's been years since she slept with anyone. But I know my sister. She's never been the kind to have sex with someone just because she's attracted to him."

Lottie raised her eyebrows and nodded. Jen didn't sleep around.

Erin sighed. "I just don't want to be picking up the pieces later, you know? But maybe it's already too late."

Lottie touched her hand. "Jen's a grown-ass woman. She gets to make mistakes, too. We all do. We don't know how she'll take it, and we don't know if what they have is going anywhere or not." She held up her hands before Erin could interrupt. "Look, it's unlikely that it will be anything more than an autumn romance—I'm not a complete idiot—but it could work out. Like I said, stranger things have happened. Why don't we just let the cards fall where they may and hope for the best?"

Erin laughed and moved around to give Lottie a quick hug. "That's what I love about you, Lottie. You're an actual dyed-in-the-wool optimist. You sound like a motivational poster." She paused again, thinking about her sister. "And you're right. I mean, maybe not about it working out for them—I genuinely doubt that—but maybe Jen just needs someone to get her back in the game." She glanced down at her watch. "Shit. We're both going to be late now."

Usually their schedules allowed them to go in more or less when it suited them, but both had needed to be at work by a specific time today.

Lottie's eyes widened. "Oh crap. My boss is going to go ballistic. We have a huge project this week, and no one can start until I'm there." Lottie worked in a web-design company in town.

"Let's get the hizzle, then."

They hugged outside by Lottie's car, and Erin set off toward the brewery at a fast pace. She'd thought of bringing her bike this morning but had decided to walk to the gym, and it was too late to go home for it now. It was only ten minutes from the coffee shop to work, but she should have been there twenty minutes ago.

Out of breath and a little sweaty, she spotted Charlie's luxury rental car a block away from the brewery and jogged the last few yards. The front of their tasting room was almost entirely glass, and she was surprised to see Charlie already sitting inside. The mystery was solved a moment later when she saw Jen appear from the back, and when she tried the front door, it was already unlocked. Both of them turned her way, clearly startled.

"I'm so sorry, Charlie," Erin said, still a little breathless. "I meant to be here when you showed up."

He smiled. "No problem, Erin. Your sister was kind enough to let me in."

Erin shared a look with Jen, and Jen widened her eyes a little, silencing her. Jen hadn't told her she would be here this morning. As far as Erin knew, the plan had been for Erin to do the tour alone today. She was the master brewer, after all, and Charlie wanted to talk about brewing. Jen did the business end of things, and while she knew more than a layman about flavor and palate, she knew very little about the craft. She'd clearly shown up just so she could see Charlie.

"Oh?" Erin said, stalling. "That's great—I'm so relieved. I had an image of you sitting here waiting all by yourself."

"Nope," Charlie said, eyes glued on Jen. "Not a problem."

Erin couldn't help but roll her eyes. The two of them were still staring at each other, oblivious, so they didn't notice.

"Okay then. Let's get started."

It took an extra moment for the two of them to realize that Erin had said something, and they both seemed to snap out of it, almost physically. When they looked at her, almost dazed, Erin had to stifle a laugh. Maybe Lottie was right. Charlie was starting to seem just as besotted as her sister.

By the time they finished the tour, it was only a few minutes before the brewery opened to the public. Jen excused herself to go see to the staff that had shown up. She was the staff manager as well as doing all the financial stuff. Jen also worked two or three hours behind the bar most days, and Erin usually a bit less than that. Their jobs were primarily behind the scenes now. To Erin, this was both a good thing and a bad thing.

During her last apprenticeship at a brewery in Fort Collins, she'd been behind the counter a lot, and she'd often enjoyed explaining beer to new and old drinkers alike. She loved the moment when someone found a beer they loved, especially someone who came in claiming they didn't really like beer. Now, she spent most of her working life in the brewing room, rarely talking to anyone except her fellow brewers. She kind of missed talking to regular people.

They employed two full-time counter service specialists, several part-time specialists like their sister Lydia, and three assistant brewers. That was all the staff they could afford until they got bigger—if it ever happened—which usually meant that if someone took a day off or called in sick, either she or Jen had to cover their hours in the taproom. But Erin generally didn't mind. Sometimes it was nice to go back to where she started.

While Jen talked to the four staff members behind the bar, Erin poured Charlie and herself a small glass of her favorite beer—the porter. They walked around the side of the bar and out into the taproom, sitting at one of the tall, long tables in the center of the room. Charlie took a long pull on his beer, his eyes closed in pleasure, and Erin couldn't help but smile. She loved seeing people enjoy her work. When he opened his eyes, he blushed a little, obviously embarrassed to see her watching him.

"You'll have to excuse me, Erin. People always tell me I wear my heart on my sleeve, and I'm having a hard time hiding how much I love your beer."

"Why would you?"

He laughed and wiped off some of the foam on his lip. "I guess I want to seem impartial. I've tried a lot of beer here in the state and still have a lot to try. I don't want to pick a favorite just yet." He indicated his glass. "But I can tell you it's going to be hard to beat this porter."

Erin flushed in pleasure and was about to say something when she noticed he was no longer looking at her. His eyes were rooted on something behind her, and she turned to follow his gaze, not surprised to see that he was watching Jen. She was setting up the register at the bar for the staff, oblivious to them. Erin looked at him and almost laughed out loud. His eyes were so wistful, so full of happy longing, she could tell exactly what he was feeling. He finally wrenched his gaze from Jen, and when he met Erin's, he flushed scarlet and stared down at his hands. They were quiet for a moment as he regained his composure, and then he finally met her eyes again.

"Listen, Erin, about your sister. I mean, about the two of us..."

Erin's heart started hammering. "Yes?"

He opened his mouth as if to speak, and then the front door opened a few feet away. They looked over, and Erin was startled to see Darcy standing in the doorway, taking off her sunglasses and glancing around. Their eyes met for a moment, and then Darcy saw Charlie.

He got to his feet and gave her a hug. "Hey, you! I haven't seen you in few days. How was Aspen?"

She shrugged. "It was Aspen."

Charlie laughed. "Whatever that means."

"Oh, you've been there before—you know what I mean. Bunch of rich assholes with nothing better to do than to sit around being rich. They don't have enough snow there yet, so I couldn't even go skiing to get away from them."

"Was your aunt there?"

She nodded and rolled her eyes. "Yes. Unfortunately."

Charlie barked a laugh. "That bad?"

She nodded again.

"Is she still trying to set you up with that hotel woman?"

Darcy's eyes grew wide, and she glanced over at Erin, alarmed. She leaned closer to Charlie. "Can we talk about this later?"

Erin held up her hands and got to her feet. "Hey, don't mind me. I was just leaving."

Charlie looked as if he wanted to stop her, but Erin walked away as quickly as she could to give them privacy. The last thing she wanted to hear was gossip about Darcy's love life.

She greeted the two counter employees and then went in the back to find her sister. Jen was in the miniscule office they'd made for her, which was also a storage room for hops and barley. So many sacks of things were in here, you couldn't see the walls, but it smelled absolutely heavenly. Along one wall, they'd placed Jen's desk, computer, and other office equipment, and she'd complained repeatedly again about not having enough space. If they managed to expand, this entire room could be converted into her office once the new storage room was built, and Erin could hardly wait so she wouldn't have to hear her gripe.

"Hey, Jen. Darcy just got here. Didn't you say you guys were going to go to lunch together?"

"Yes," Jen said, her brow furrowed. "And I assumed you'd come with. Don't you want to? Charlie's paying."

Erin sighed. "And if it was just you and Charlie, I would. But once you mentioned Darcy, I thought better of it, and after seeing her out there, I don't think I can go through with it."

"What is it between you two? You've barely spoken a word to her. She's actually quite lovely once you get over her reserve. You should know that, being friends with Lottie."

Erin felt a stab of guilt. She hadn't told Jen about the conversation she'd overheard in the alley, not wanting to cause some kind of rift between her and Charlie, but now she regretted not being more forthright. It was too late to fill her in now.

Instead, she said, "She's a bitch, Jen, pure and simple. I don't want to get to know her better, and I don't need to. I'd be happy to get to know Charlie, but not while she's around. What's she doing here with him, anyway? Is she one of his lawyers, too?"

Except for the first night, they hadn't seen the lawyer Charlie had come in with. He was apparently flying back and forth from Boston to take care of things while Charlie was here.

Jen shook her head. "No—she's just his friend. They've known each other a long time, I guess. College friends."

"It's hard to imagine two less-similar people. I seriously don't understand how they could be friends. Does she work with him or something? Is that why she's here?"

"No. She's some kind of reporter, I think. At least that's the impression I got from some of the things I've heard them saying. I haven't thought to ask. She might just be independently wealthy or something. I do know she's rich as hell, just like he is."

"Well, anyway—you go on ahead and have lunch with them. I have a lot to do here today. I'll get one of the others to go get me a sandwich or something."

Jen raised her eyebrows but didn't argue, clearly seeing it would be fruitless. Erin would go a long way to please her sister, but she would rarely fake being nice to a complete stranger. She could barely make nice with her father, let alone Darcy. If she and Darcy were put together for any great length of time, she'd end up telling the woman off, and no one needed that. Best just to avoid her.

After finishing a backbreaking task with two of the other brewers, Erin went into the little office to sit down for a bit before heading home. Jen had returned from lunch and left already, and it was dark outside. The walk home would be chilly, and she was worn out.

Realizing the office computer was still on, Erin reached over to shut it down and then thought of something Jen had said earlier today. She clicked on the web browser and typed Darcy's full name into the search bar. The first response listed her as a writer for *Food and Beverage* magazine.

Erin's stomach seized with dread. She clicked on the link to Darcy's articles, and the first one that popped up was a review of a local brewery. Feeling sick now, Erin opened the article and read a scathing, horrific diatribe against the brewery and its beers. While most people might not read this article before visiting the brewery, it could significantly hurt their business. Erin opened another tab and ran a search on the brewery reviewed in Darcy's article, and sure enough, after the brewery's website, the review was the second link in the search.

Erin once again read the article through to the end, and this time, when she hit the bottom of the page, she scrolled down and saw something that made her go cold with horror. Under Darcy's byline was a little paragraph:

> *Darcy Fitzwilliam will be reporting from Colorado breweries for the next few weeks. Her articles will appear on Mondays and Fridays throughout the autumn, bringing you the latest reports on brewers in the Rocky Mountain state.*

Erin could hardly breathe. She was so angry and so upset, it took her a long moment before she realized that Darcy had been in their brewery twice now and had tried all of their beers at this point more than once. She was clearly going to do an article on BSB, too.

"Oh, shit."

Chapter Five

Erin waited a week to tell Jen about Darcy's review. At first she thought she might be able to hide it from her—Jen didn't react well to stress. But as the days passed, and Charlie and Jen saw more and more of each other, Erin started to feel like she was being disingenuous. Her sister had a right to know what was coming, whatever the review might say. It would be worse to spring it on her after it had already been written.

Although she usually took Tuesdays off entirely, Erin had decided to go to the gym to see if she could catch Lottie, but she hadn't seen her there. She'd wanted to ask Lottie's opinion about the news all week, but now it was too late. It was unusual for Lottie to miss a weekday at the gym, and Erin wondered if she should call her later to check in. She did a quick run and some weights before heading home. When she walked into the house, Jen had clearly just woken up. She was in the kitchen reading the newspaper, eating her oatmeal standing up. She looked startled when the door opened.

"Where were you?" Jen asked. "I thought you were still sleeping."

"I woke up early." Erin put her keys on the island and sat on one of the stools.

"I wanted to talk to you about something, Jen. Can we sit for a minute?"

Jen raised an eyebrow, but she moved over to the other stool and sat down next to her. "Sounds serious."

Erin sighed. "It could be." She grabbed her phone and opened the article Darcy had written on her browser before handing it to Jen. "Read that."

Jen frowned, took the phone from her, and spent the next couple of minutes reading. Her face became grave the longer she read, and when she finished, she was a little pale.

"Shit," Jen said.

"That's exactly what I said."

"Do you think that means—"

"That she's writing a review of us? Of course she is."

"Shit."

They were both quiet. Finally, Jen shrugged. "Oh, well!" She got up and started cleaning her breakfast things.

"What do you mean 'oh well'? It doesn't bother you?"

Jen shrugged again. "Not really. I mean, what can we do? She's probably already written the review, right?"

"But doesn't it bother you? Shouldn't they have said something to us?"

Jen stared at her. "Of course not. That's not how reviews work, Erin. They're supposed to be anonymous."

"But at least Charlie should have warned you. Don't you think?"

Jen rolled her eyes. "Why? And again I ask you—what could we have done? Refused to let them review us? That's stupid."

"What do you mean?"

Jen set down her soapy bowl and sighed. "Think about it, Erin. If Darcy gives us a good rating, we'll benefit from it, won't we? I mean, I don't know if many people who read *Food and Beverage* will go out of their way to visit some random brewery in a small town in Colorado, but we could publish the article on our website, and that could only help us with people around here."

"But what if it's bad?"

Jen laughed. "Then we don't put it on our website! Anyway, didn't you say she likes our beer? Don't you have faith in it yourself? I think we're making some of the best in the state right now, Erin. I really do."

Erin had no response and sat in stunned silence as Jen bustled around the kitchen. Jen always amazed her. She was completely and totally right. Of course the beer would speak for itself, and of course the review had a high chance of being positive. All week, Erin had been dreading the idea of a write-up in a national magazine, when really, it might end up being one of the best things to happen to them right now.

When Jen finished cleaning the kitchen, Erin got up and gave her a hug.

Jen laughed. "What was that for?"

"For being you. You're so much smarter than me in some ways."

Jen looked puzzled. "Thanks? But really, you need to go shower and get dressed. They'll be here in twenty minutes."

Erin groaned. "Do I have to go?"

"Yes—you do. No buts."

After Charlie's tour at BSB, when they were having lunch, Jen had agreed to go with Charlie and Darcy up to Estes Park to show them the breweries there. She'd volunteered Erin to come along without asking her about it—something about having an expert with them. Erin had been trying to get out of it all week but couldn't. They both had the day off, and Erin had talked to Jen recently about wanting to go to Estes before the snow fell in earnest.

After she showered and dressed, Erin came into the living room to find Charlie and Jen sitting on the little love seat together, chatting happily. Darcy was perched on the edge of their recliner, clearly out of place and ill at ease. Erin couldn't tell if she was uncomfortable because she'd been put in the position of the third wheel again or if it was from being here in their house. But Erin couldn't help feel a little smug—anything that brought the ice queen down a peg or two was a good thing.

The car ride was exceptionally awkward in part because it was longer than usual. Big Thompson Canyon between Loveland and Estes Park had recently closed to repair a road damaged during a flood three years ago. A temporary fix had been put in place soon after the flood, but the county and the state had decided they needed a permanent, better-constructed repair. The road would be closed all winter, the low season, and possibly again next year. All of this meant the four of them had to take the long way to Estes through Lyons.

Besides the trip being unusually long, Erin was forced to sit in the backseat with Darcy the entire time, listening as Jen and Charlie chatted almost nonstop. She felt incredibly uncomfortable sitting there not saying anything either to the couple in front or to Darcy, and about halfway up, she'd finally had enough. She turned to Darcy, wanting to ask her about her reviews, and was surprised to see that she'd fallen asleep. Erin couldn't help but stare at her. Her face, normally composed and rigid, seemed softer, kinder. Her pale hair had fallen across part of her face, making her appear less put-together, almost ruffled somehow. In a word, she was incredibly sexy.

Erin finally wrenched her eyes away, startled to realize that her heart rate had picked up. She wouldn't deny that Darcy was beautiful—she'd thought it from the beginning—but this sleeping Darcy was attractive in a way Erin found disturbing. She didn't want to like her. These thoughts distracted her the rest of the way to Estes, and when they finally pulled into the parking lot of Estes Park Brewery, she was surprised to suddenly be there.

The elevation was higher here and the air much cooler than down in the foothills in Loveland. Patches of snow lay here and there, but Estes still hadn't had a big snowfall. Erin and Jen had dressed for the colder weather, but Charlie and Darcy were surprised by how much cooler it was. The day was remarkably clear, the sunlight and blue of the sky so vivid and bright it hurt their eyes. All four of them spent a few minutes admiring the majestic views of the snow-capped Rocky Mountains around them before heading inside the brewery. A fire burned in the fireplace, and despite the high ceilings, the restaurant was warm and cozy when they entered.

Erin caught Darcy taking the measure of the space itself, reminded once again of what she did for a living. She hoped for the sake of the owners today that the staff was nice and the beer was fresh. If her previous article was any indication, Darcy was a ruthless reviewer.

It was a weekday afternoon, so they had the run of the place. The hostess seemed surprised to see them. She led them to the best table, and they sat next to a bank of windows with views of Longs Peak. Darcy and Charlie were so enraptured by the view that they seemed to forget where they were. Jen and Erin shared a grin. Despite growing up in Colorado, Erin had never become immune to the natural beauty around her. The views of the mountains in Loveland certainly weren't as spectacular as those in Estes, however, so even for Erin and Jen it was a treat to be here. Erin was up here nearly every week in the summer to hike or camp in Rocky Mountain National Park, minutes away from Estes, and she often stopped at this brewery before heading home. She hadn't been here since August, and it felt a little like coming home.

They ordered lunch and two flights of beer to share, and when their beer arrived, Charlie and Jen immediately started drinking from the flight closest to them. They were soon chatting away again as they sipped each taster, and Erin and Darcy shared an amused glance. Darcy raised one eyebrow at her and indicated the beers in front of them. Sighing inwardly, Erin moved her chair a little closer to hers so they could drink together.

"So you come up here often?" Darcy asked.

"In the summer, yes. Almost every week. Usually to hike up in Rocky."

Darcy smiled. "I knew you were one of those."

"One of what?"

"One of those granola lesbians."

Erin flushed. "What's that supposed to mean?"

Darcy held up her hands. "Nothing bad—really. I admire someone who enjoys the outdoors, getting dirty and all that. It's refreshing. Not what I'm used to at all. Most of the women I know in Boston and New York haven't even seen a hiking trail, let alone walked on one."

"Does that include you?"

Darcy paused and then shrugged. "Not exactly. I'm not a mountain person, per se, not in the summer anyway, but I do like to ski." She took a sip of the lightest beer and considered it for a moment. She swirled it around in her mouth before swallowing. Then she gave a little satisfied smile, and Erin couldn't help but feel relieved.

Realizing she'd been simply staring at her, Erin backpedaled in her mind. "Downhill or cross-country?"

"A little of both, actually." She smiled at Erin's expression. "Does that surprise you?"

"Yes. I wouldn't take you for a cross-country skier."

"Oh? Why not?"

Erin thought about it for a moment and then shook her head. "It just seems a little, I don't know, hardcore or something. At least, that's the reputation it has here. I don't know what it's like in the Northeast. Most cross-country skiers in Colorado do it in the backcountry."

Darcy raised her eyebrows. "So I've heard. I've done a little of that, in the backcountry, I mean, but it's definitely harder in the mountains nearest to me. Snowmobilers have overrun most of the backcountry trails. When I was a little girl, my father would take me and my sister almost every weekend up to the White Mountains, but it's been getting harder to find trails reserved for skiers. If I do cross-country now, I usually have to go to a resort."

"You have a sister?"

Darcy smiled, her eyes warm and far away. "Yes. She's a lot younger than me. My father remarried when I was a teenager, and she was born a year after that. She just started at Julliard a couple of months ago."

Erin was going to ask her more, but their food arrived. As Erin ate, she couldn't help but picture Darcy skiing. It was a pleasant thought. Darcy had a long, svelte body, and with her pale hair and eyes, she would be every bit the Nordic princess in her snow pants and sweater. Erin flushed at the image and had to wrench her eyes away from Darcy's face to stop herself from staring again. The confused tumult of her thoughts soured her stomach a little, and she pushed her food away, nearly uneaten. Jen threw her a concerned glance, and Erin shook her head at her to dismiss it. She spent the next few minutes staring out the window as everyone else finished their lunch, trying very hard not to look at Darcy again.

She was still annoyed that the woman was hiding the fact that she was writing reviews of every brewery they visited, but Erin was starting to become accustomed to the idea. After all, it was her job, and being anonymous meant that the reviews would be authentic. Still, part of the reason she'd started to forgive Darcy was the growing attraction she felt. It wasn't the kind of attraction she would ever act on, but she was easy on the eyes—no one would deny that. Yet the dishonesty was still there, and Erin knew she'd need to bring it up soon or risk being in the same position as Darcy—lying by omission.

"So," Charlie said, pushing away an empty plate, "where to next?"

"There's a newer brewery in town I haven't had a chance to try yet," Erin said. "I didn't even know it was open until recently. It was one of the reasons I've been meaning to come up here before winter."

Charlie grinned. "You don't know how lucky you are to have so many breweries to choose from. It's incredible that the populations here can support so many."

Erin smiled, proud again of her home state. There really was no place like Colorado for a beer drinker.

"Shall we, ladies?" Charlie asked, standing up.

They followed him outside, all of them surprised to see that the weather had turned in the hour they'd been indoors. They hadn't been able to see the storm coming from the mountains in the west, and now the sky was exceptionally ominous. Up here at elevation, the clouds seemed very close, almost within reach, and they were roiling with energy and darkness, like a thunderstorm, headed right for them.

"Oh, crap," Jen said. "That doesn't look good at all."

"I thought the weatherman said it would be nice up here today," Darcy said, frowning.

Erin and Jen laughed, and Jen said, "You can't rely on the weather up here or down in Loveland, for that matter. At all. It can change on a dime and often does."

"I've been caught in storms so many times, I can't even tell you," Erin added.

"What do we do now?" Charlie asked. "Should we drive down to Loveland, or do we have time for a quick stop at the other brewery? We could get a growler to go."

Jen and Erin considered for a moment, and then Jen shook her head. "No. I'm sorry. It probably won't be a big storm—not if it wasn't on the weather this morning—but it could make driving dangerous later today if we wait even a short time."

All four of them made their way over to the car, deflated. Charlie seemed the most put out by it, but then, after he unlocked the doors, he stopped and slapped a hand to his forehead. "Hold on—I just had an idea."

"What?" Jen asked.

"When do you two have to be in to work tomorrow?"

Jen and Erin glanced at each other and shrugged. "Ten or eleven, I guess," Jen replied.

"Do you think the roads will be okay by tomorrow morning? I mean, if it snows?"

Jen nodded. "With a fast-moving storm like this one, they should be. They're good about keeping up with the roads around here when it snows. They have to be."

"Let's stay over then!" Charlie said happily. "I'll pay, of course. We could find some little cabins or something. Rough it a bit. What do you say?"

All three of the others turned to look at Erin, knowing she would be the deciding factor, and Erin had to laugh at their identical, pleading eyes. "Fine, fine. We can stay. Especially if you're paying, Charlie."

Jen let out of whoop of triumph, and they all laughed. Charlie put Darcy on cabin duty as they got in the car, and by the time they'd parked at the second brewery, Darcy had reserved two cabins nearby.

"What a treat!" Jen said as they got out of the car again. "We almost never get to stay up here in Estes. I mean, we've camped overnight in Rocky a million times, but not often in an actual hotel or anything. I've only done it once or twice. What about you, Erin?"

"Same here—once or twice. It's so close to Loveland, it just seems silly to stay over."

"Well, I'm glad to oblige," Charlie said. "And now I can have a little more to drink, too, since I don't need to worry about driving."

"We still have to get to the cabins," Jen said, laughing.

"We can call a cab!"

When they entered the new brewery, Erin was surprised to find how small it was. It even made their brewery in Loveland seem large by comparison. Rock Cut Brewery had clearly traded space for location, however, as, like Estes Park Brewery, it was directly on the route in or out of Rocky Mountain National Park. Unlike the other brewery here in town, Rock Cut was, like Bennet Sisters, only a taproom with no food, and after Charlie expressed confusion about this situation, Erin explained the different laws about breweries in Colorado and why they'd decided to open a taproom only. This was, however, only part of the truth. In reality, by the time Erin and Jen were in a position to open BSB, Erin had been in and out of restaurant work at one or another of her father's restaurants for so long she couldn't stomach the thought of working in another, even if it was her own. Getting the cheaper license to open a taproom had been a win-win for her since it meant not working with food ever again.

Erin spoke to the server and was able to arrange a quick tour with one of the brewers. After showing her around the small operation, the brewer joined them at their table for a while to talk shop with Erin, and it wasn't until they'd been conversing for several minutes that Erin realized Darcy was listening. She threw her a quick glance and couldn't help but blush under her intense scrutiny. Darcy grinned but kept staring, and for the rest of the conversation, Erin's face felt hot under her gaze. When the brewer finally excused himself to go back to work, Erin turned toward her, and Darcy smiled more widely.

"You're really passionate about your work," Darcy said. "I like that."

Erin blushed harder and couldn't help but look away. It was hard to meet Darcy's eyes. She wasn't used to this kind of forwardness. She turned her eyes to Charlie and Jen, who had moved their chairs so close together they might as well be sitting in each other's lap. Without any other options, she turned her gaze to Darcy, who was also eyeing Jen and Charlie. Her expression was cold, unhappy. This impression disappeared a moment later when she looked at Erin, but Erin knew what she'd seen. Darcy clearly wasn't entirely happy with what was going on between Charlie and Jen, and while Erin still had her own reservations about them, Darcy's concerns made her want to leap to their defense.

She shook her head to dismiss her annoyance. "Yes—I am passionate. It's my whole life, really."

Darcy leaned forward onto her forearms. "Tell me about it. How did you get into the business?"

Not able to stop herself, Erin asked, "Is this on the record?"

Darcy's eyebrows shot up and she laughed. "So you figured me out? I'm the big, bad reporter from the big, bad city. Did you Google my name or something?"

Erin felt her color rise again, as that was exactly what she'd done. She nodded.

Darcy considered her for a moment as if weighing something in her mind, and then she shrugged. "Well, if the cat's out of the bag, I don't mind talking about it. As long as you don't spread it around. But no, my question is not on the record. I just talk about the wine and beer I review, and sometimes the wineries or breweries themselves, not the winemakers or brewers."

"And ruining the reputation of actual people while you do it. That review I read was brutal. If word got around, they'd be destroyed."

Darcy shrugged again. "That's their problem. I can't help it if they're serving swill."

Erin went deadly cold. "You don't mind if a business closes because of your review? Most people depend on their jobs for their livelihoods. Those people—the ones who produce the product you so casually put down—they're friends of mine. Who knows what will happen if they have to shut down. You're talking twenty, thirty people out of a job. Not all of us have a trust fund to fall back on." Erin immediately regretted saying that bit about the trust fund, but she was still angry.

Darcy narrowed her eyes for a moment. "Let me ask you this then, Erin. Do you like their beer? Do you honestly think they're making good product, or is it just that you like them personally?"

Erin flushed again. "That's not the point—"

"Ah, but it is. That's exactly the point. My job is to review the *product* of a winery or a brewery, not to talk up the people who work there. And I'm always honest."

They were quiet for a while, both of them focusing on the beer samples in front of them to avoid more awkwardness. Part of Erin understood what Darcy was saying, but she couldn't get over the idea that another brewer—a brewer like her—might soon lose their business because of this woman. It was difficult not to take it personally. Despite being in a market that supported and sustained a great many microbreweries, like any small business, most breweries were only four or five months from disaster at all times, sometimes less. One bad review could end any of them.

Again, unable to let it go, Erin asked, "Are you reviewing every brewery you visit?"

Darcy didn't respond to the hostility in Erin's voice. Instead, she shook her head. "No—only the exceptional ones, good or bad. I'm trying to do a couple from every town we visit. I might do a kind of concluding article that mentions some of the others I don't go into in depth. Maybe with some kind of starred review chart. I'm still weighing my options."

Erin continued to stew and drink in silence. She glanced once or twice at Jen and Charlie, both of whom were so wrapped up in each other they seemed to have no idea what was happening on the other side of the table. She was happy that her sister was enjoying herself, but it was difficult not to feel like a third wheel around them, even with someone to talk to. While it was true Jen hadn't dated anyone in a long time, the same could be said for Erin, too. She'd had a few one-nighters in the last couple of years and had even seen one woman more than once, but she hadn't seriously dated anyone in years. This thought, coupled with the beer that was starting to muddle her head, made her feel morose and self-pitying, and she lashed out at the nearest, easiest target.

"Hey," she said to Darcy. "I haven't seen you go out for a cigarette all day."

Darcy looked confused. "I don't smoke."

"That's funny, because I could have sworn you did. The first night I met you, you were outside. Someone was smoking—I thought it was you."

Darcy's confusion lasted another moment, and then her eyebrows rose and her face paled. "Oh. That was Luis. You were there?"

"I was there. You didn't see me and Lottie."

Darcy leaned forward, her face sympathetic and worried. "Listen, Erin, I'm sorry about what I said and how I behaved. We'd been drinking all day on very little sleep—"

"You don't have to apologize."

Darcy grabbed her hand. "I do. My remark was insensitive and rude."

Erin's resentment faded as she stared into Darcy's eyes. Her hand was warm on hers, and she was very tempted to simply hold it for a moment. Her heart rate picked up, and her mind went into overload. What was she doing? This woman was toxic. She needed to get away from her and soon.

Erin jumped to her feet, her chair squealing loudly. The others stared up at her, clearly surprised. "I'm going outside for a minute and get some air. Be right back." Darcy leaned forward as if to say something, but Erin turned and hurried through the door before she could object.

The temperature had taken a significant dip in the last hour, and the sky above was a dark, leaden gray. Nothing was falling yet, but it looked like it might start snowing or sleeting at any time. Still, the cool air felt marvelous on her overheated skin, and she closed her eyes and took several deep breaths.

Finally calm, she was just about to go inside when she saw something that stopped her dead. Lottie was walking across the parking lot, hand in hand with someone Erin recognized: Will Collins. Her heart squeezed with dread. How on earth had this happened?

Lottie, as if sensing her gaze, turned and spotted her, and even from this distance, Erin saw her react, almost flinching. Will paused with her and, turning too, saw Erin. He smiled and waved, and the two of them strolled over to her.

"What are you doing here?" Lottie asked. Her eyes were flicking around nervously, unable to meet Erin's. She was still holding Will's hand.

"I might ask you the same thing." Erin's voice was quiet.

Will, oblivious to the awkwardness, jumped in. "I came up here as a kid when we were staying with you guys, but I wanted to see it again. Lottie was kind enough to offer herself as my escort."

Erin kept her eyes on Lottie. "Your escort?"

Lottie flushed bright red and looked away again.

Again, Will didn't seem to notice what was happening. "Yep! She told me she comes up here all the time with you, so I knew I'd get the locals' point of view. She took the day off, and here we are."

"Imagine that," Erin said, still staring at Lottie.

Will finally seemed to sense something between them and frowned slightly. "Anyway, we have to get moving if we're going to stay ahead of the weather. You'd be smart to get on the road soon, too. That sky looks deadly."

Erin finally wrenched her eyes away from Lottie's face to his. "We're staying over."

"Oh?" he said. "How nice. Well, have a good time then."

"Thanks. Have a safe trip home."

Lottie didn't say anything, and Erin watched them walk over to Will's car, both of them only releasing hands when they climbed inside. Erin's surprise and disgust was so acute that she completely forgot her earlier awkwardness with Darcy. It had been a couple of weeks since they'd all been at her father's place, and somehow in between now and then, Lottie had started dating that odious man. They seemed fairly comfortable with each other, so it likely wasn't a brand-new thing. They'd probably been together ever since the dinner party, and Lottie hadn't said a thing about him. Erin saw Lottie almost every day. In addition to her disgust, Erin felt betrayed and hurt. While Lottie wasn't aware of the details about Will's behavior to her when they were children—no one was but her and Will—Lottie knew that Erin didn't like him. So, in addition to Lottie's omission, she clearly didn't care how Erin felt at all.

She rejoined the others, and some of her feelings must have shown on her face, as Jen immediately asked, "What's wrong? You look like the dog died."

Erin shook her head. "I just saw something terrible. Outside in the parking lot. Lottie and her new boyfriend."

"Is it Will Collins?" Jen asked.

"Yes, it was. How did you know?"

Jen colored slightly, her face falling. "You didn't know?"

"No. I didn't."

Jen opened her mouth to explain, but just then the server brought another round of tasters. As the four of them tried their extra-large samples, Erin decided to let the subject drop for now. It didn't make sense to discuss it with Charlie and Darcy here. They knew Lottie only in passing. She would bring it up later when she and Jen were alone.

Another hour passed. Erin, still upset by both by her conversation with Darcy and with the revelation about Lottie and Will, drank in earnest. While the others sipped all their tasters, Erin drank all of hers and finished theirs. By the time Charlie and Darcy got up to settle their tab, she was past tipsy and well on her way toward being drunk.

"We should get a growler or two to drink in the cabins," she suggested.

Jen leaned close enough to whisper, "I think you've had enough."

"Pshaw!" Erin said, laughing. "There's never enough."

Jen's face crinkled in concern. "Come on, Erin. Don't get plastered today, okay?"

Erin put her hand on her sister's arm. "I know my limits, Jen. I am an adult."

"Well, you're not acting like one right now. I'm asking you nicely to stop drinking. Don't embarrass yourself or me."

Erin was about to snipe a response, but Charlie and Darcy returned. Darcy was carrying two growlers of beer and held them up. "Thought we'd take some back to the cabins with us."

"A woman after my own heart," Erin said.

Darcy smiled, apparently confused, and Jen's face darkened perceptibly. "Let's get going then," Jen said. "It's really starting to come down out there, and we need to pick up something for dinner."

CHAPTER SIX

They stopped at a small grocery for sandwiches, snacks, and some toiletries before heading up to the little resort where they were staying. The flakes were falling from the sky in lazy, wet drops, but so far the roads were clear. By the time they drove across the little bridge to the resort, it was getting a little hard to see, and with the mountains all around them, the sun had already begun to set. Charlie insisted on checking in by himself so they could stay dry, and when he climbed into the car, his shoulders were covered in wet snow.

"We're just up the road," he explained, holding out a set of keys for Erin. "They said they'd bring some wood in a few minutes for fires. I guess we're the only guests tonight."

Erin took the keys, confused, wondering why he hadn't given them to Jen. A terrible idea occurred to her, but she dismissed it. No way would Charlie and Jen make her stay with Darcy. That would be too much even for them.

The two little cabins were next to each other, and Erin was relieved when all four of them went into the larger one together to have an early dinner. At least they would discuss the sleeping arrangements later. In the meantime, she'd try to get Jen alone and convince her to stay with her. It would be way too awkward otherwise.

Darcy popped a bottle of sparkling wine for them, and while Charlie and Erin were game for a cup, Jen frowned a little when she saw the wine. Erin decided to ignore her. She could be a real spoil-sport sometimes. They each took a little Dixie Cup of the bubbly, and Darcy made a quick toast.

"To new friends," she said.

"Hear, hear!" Erin said and then drank hers down in one long gulp. She held out her empty cup for a refill, and Darcy obliged before sitting down. Jen was giving her a dirty look, and Erin turned in her chair to give her sister her back.

"You like wine, too?" Darcy said, grinning slightly.

"I do. The only thing I don't drink much is hard liquor—though I will imbibe a margarita now and again. But yes, I love wine. In fact, I did six months of my job training in a winery in Oregon."

"Oh? Is that usual?"

"Not exactly. I did it mostly so I could have some training on the supply and business end of things. Jen's the expert in that for us, but I needed to know a bit about it so I wouldn't be completely useless in that department. I originally signed up to do a kind of internship with a brewery up there, but when it fell through, I decided that since I'd already rented a place in Oregon, I might as well go, and I found the winery pretty quickly after that. I'm sure if I'd grown up there or in California or somewhere on the coast, I'd be a winemaker instead."

"Did you have other training beyond that? You've mentioned internships, but did you go to school for it, too?"

"Are you asking me if I went to college?" Erin asked. Seeing Darcy's embarrassment, she laughed. "It's okay. I know most people just assume that brewers are just the grown-up version of the slackers from high school."

Darcy's pale cheeks lit up, and Erin laughed again. She reached out and touched her arm. "It's okay—I make assumptions about people, too. But yes, I did go to college. Colorado State, in Fort Collins."

"Close to home, then."

"Yes. I studied food chemistry and nutrition, and when they started offering the Fermentation Science and Technology BS, I got one. After that, I did some internships, got my MS in food chemistry, and then I won a grant for some advanced certificate programs at the Siebel in Chicago and a six-month training in Europe."

Darcy's eyes were wide. "Impressive."

Erin shrugged, pretending nonchalance. "I've done a little more training than most of the brewers I know, but almost all of us have some kind of formal education. My dad wanted me to work for one of the big breweries in the area, but I was set on opening my own place. Then, finally, Jen and I got our loan, and here we are."

"Well, it definitely paid off," Darcy said quietly. "You make incredible beer. You're very talented, you know."

Erin's stomach dropped perceptibly, and she was unable to tear her eyes away from Darcy's. Darcy's eyelids were lowered a little, her lips twisted into a slight grin. She was, Erin realized, flirting with her again. Erin suddenly saw that she was still touching Darcy's arm. She yanked her hand away and turned toward her sister to break eye contact with Darcy, only to look away from Jen almost as quickly. Jen and Charlie were making out on the other side of the table. Erin and Darcy shared an amused glance, and Darcy got to her feet. Charlie and Jen broke apart, Jen's cheeks flushed and red.

Darcy motioned toward the door. "Come on, Erin. We should give these two some privacy. I want to get our cabin warmed up a little, too."

Charlie colored slightly and stood up, pulling Jen with him. He cleared his throat, obviously uncomfortable. "Actually, Darcy, Jen and I should be the ones to leave." He gave them both a sheepish smile. "The other cabin has only one bed."

Everyone was embarrassed now. Dumbstruck, Erin watched as her sister and Charlie left. Darcy followed them out and then came in a moment later, carrying an armload of wood.

"Is this enough? I don't know how much we'll need. I've never made a fire before."

Erin found this incredibly funny, and, her drunkenness now verging on what her sister would called "plastered," she struggled awkwardly to her feet to help. She suddenly realized that she didn't care at all about Jen and Charlie. No, that wasn't quite true—she cared, but she didn't mind being left alone with Darcy. Darcy had been cordial and friendly with her all day. She hadn't let the awkwardness of their conversation about the reviews and the overheard insults ruffle her feathers at all—in fact, she'd been honest about both. It also didn't hurt that she was so attractive, and now, after so much wine and beer, Erin wanted to stare at her some more.

As Erin put the kindling and logs in the fireplace, she could feel Darcy's gaze traveling across her, warming her wherever it landed. She couldn't suppress a small shudder, and when the fire started to blaze, she stood up and turned to find Darcy, as expected, watching her closely.

"Listen," Darcy said, stepping a little closer, "about earlier. About what you overheard—"

"Really, Darcy, let's forget about it. I'm not even upset anymore."

"Anymore?"

Erin sighed, her embarrassment making her angry and hot. "Fine. What you said about Jen and about me bothered me. Are you happy now?"

Darcy shook her head. "No. I'm not happy at all. I feel like an ass."

"Well, you were an ass—that night anyway."

Darcy laughed and raised an eyebrow. "But not tonight?"

Erin shrugged. "I don't know. Something's changed, I guess. And I'm sorry I keep making things awkward. You've been nice to me all day, and I don't even know why. I've been a pest."

Darcy took another step closer, and now they were close enough that Erin could see the fire dancing in Darcy's gray eyes. A slight odor hung in the air—citrus—which Erin realized was her perfume.

"I was wrong, you know," Darcy said. Her voice was low, almost purring.

Erin had to lick her lips a couple of times and swallow before she could talk again. "Wrong about what?"

"What I said about you."

Erin flushed with heat. The sensation was so immediate, so sweeping, she started trembling all over. She reached out to surreptitiously grab a chair nearby, her legs actually weak.

"Oh?" she managed.

Darcy nodded and thankfully turned away, moving closer to the fire. With her back turned, Erin had an opportunity to take in the whole of Darcy's figure at length. She was tall—three or four inches taller than Erin, and lithe. It made sense now to know that she was a skier, and Erin predicted that if she asked, she'd find that Darcy was also a runner—she had that lean build. It took almost every ounce of Erin's willpower not to walk up and grab her from behind, and she put her hands in her pockets to steady herself.

The silence dragged on—both of them standing in the same spot, doing nothing, saying nothing—and finally Erin couldn't take it anymore. She spotted the beer they'd bought earlier and blurted, "Want a beer? We've got two growlers just for us. Jen and Charlie forget to take one."

Darcy turned toward her and laughed, clearly understanding that Erin had asked simply to say something. "We could save some for later."

Erin wrinkled her nose. "Beer doesn't last long in these things. It'll be stale in a couple of days."

Darcy smiled and shrugged. "Sure—I'll take a beer. Do we have anything besides Dixie Cups to drink it in?"

"Let me look around. Might be some glasses somewhere."

Erin started poking around, surprised by how dark the cabin already was. Not wanting to ruin the mood created by the fire in the living room, she stumbled around in the semi-darkness and eventually found two tumblers in one of the bedrooms. The tumblers weren't much bigger than the Dixie Cups, but at least they were glass. She gave each a quick rinse in the little sink in the bathroom, and then, just as she was about to turn to leave, she caught her own reflection in the mirror. Her hair was a little mussy, and even in the dim light, she could see that her eyes were a little watery and drunk.

"What are you doing, Erin?" she asked herself. "Are you really going out there with that woman? What's the end game here?" Her reflection didn't answer, and no longer caring, she left the bathroom, grabbed the growler off the table, and rejoined Darcy in the living room.

She was sitting on a pile of pillows on the floor. Her platinum hair shone and flashed in the firelight. Her skin, normally so pale and cold-looking, seemed warmer in this light, and her eyes sparkled with amusement as she watched Erin fumble her way toward her. Erin's breath caught in her throat and she swallowed, hard, stopping abruptly at the sight of her. She had to force herself to take the last few steps before sitting down a few feet away.

The cabin had been designed with a fairly large space in front of the fire for lounging like this, and Erin couldn't help but notice the intimacy of the dim, warm light. She handed Darcy a tumbler and poured them both a small glass full of vanilla porter. They both sat, quietly drinking, staring into the fire. After a few minutes, Erin started to relax. Despite the awkward position the others had put them in, it really wasn't that bad being here alone with Darcy. Nothing was going to happen. Erin glanced at Darcy surreptitiously and then quickly away. In this light, she'd changed from beautiful to stunning.

"This is nice," Darcy finally said, holding up the beer. "I'm glad we brought some with us."

"Yeah, I like it, too. And I usually don't like flavored beers."

Darcy poured them some more a moment later, and they watched the fire again. Erin's hands were starting to sweat, and it wasn't from the heat. Suddenly, without necessarily meaning to, she looked over at Darcy again only to find her staring, her lips curved in a slight smile.

"What? What is it?"

Darcy's smile widened. "Nothing. I just like the view."

Erin flushed, but she managed to keep her eyes on Darcy's. They sat there, staring at each other, and the tension in the room grew denser as they stared at each other. Erin's heart was racing, and she felt hot and jumpy. She licked her lips nervously. Darcy's eyes grew dark, and then they rushed at each other, glasses of beer flying aside. Erin met Darcy's lips in an anguished crush, their arms wrapping around each other in something like desperation. Both Erin and Darcy were on their knees now, kissing as they kneeled. Darcy's lips were flavored with the vanilla from the beer, and Erin sucked on her lower lip urgently. Darcy let out a little moan of pleasure, and the heat racing through Erin's veins caught fire. She moved her lips to Darcy's throat, sucking at her pulse point, and Darcy groaned and gripped her shoulders, pulling Erin closer. Their breasts collided, painfully, but Erin continued to kiss and lick Darcy's neck. She pulled one earlobe into her mouth, and Darcy gave a brief shout, seeming surprised.

Suddenly Erin was on her back, Darcy topping her easily. Darcy was surprisingly strong despite her slimness, and Erin didn't fight her. Several pillows were underneath her, and she squirmed beneath Darcy to move them. Darcy fought back a little, grinding into her between her legs to still her, and Erin let out a gasp of pleasure, becoming almost completely still at the cascading sensation of pure lust that raced through her. Darcy moved her hands up under her sweater a moment later, brushing her long fingers along the bottom of Erin's breasts. Again, Erin froze in anticipation, and Darcy pinned her to the ground with her mouth. Erin responded, snaking her tongue out to touch Darcy's lips, and when they finally parted to let her in, Erin couldn't suppress a whimper of triumph. Darcy smiled against her lips and moved her hands more firmly onto Erin's breasts, squeezing them and rolling her nipples. Erin sighed and threw her head back, arching into Darcy's hands.

Footsteps sounded outside on the little porch, and they froze in place, listening. After a light knock sounded, Darcy sprang up, hurrying to her old spot a few feet away. Erin sat up equally fast, smoothing her sweater into place just before Charlie opened the door. Luckily, he was looking down as he came in, kicking the snow from his feet, which gave them a couple of crucial seconds to get themselves farther apart and settled.

He finally looked up, and his smile faltered for a second. A knowing grin followed, and he winked at them.

"My apologies for intruding. Jen and I forgot our growler. I hope you don't mind."

"Not a problem at all!" Erin sprang to her feet with nervous energy, hurried to the little table, and then carried the beer over to him. "We were going to drink it if you didn't come back."

"Got here just in time, then," he said. He met Erin's eyes, and, from the merry twinkle in them, Erin could see that he knew exactly what he'd just walked in on. "Anyway—thanks. You two have a good night, now. See you in the morning."

He turned and went outside, and Erin closed and locked the door behind him. She stood there for a moment, breathing heavily, trying to calm down. She finally turned around, and Darcy had a hand over her mouth to stifle her laughter.

"Jesus," Erin said, chuckling. "Two minutes later and he would have had a real show."

Darcy continued to giggle, and then she wiped her eyes. "I guess I should have locked up when they left."

Erin put a hand on her hip, pretending to be put out. "So you were planning this all along?"

Darcy laughed. "Of course. I've been trying to get you alone for a while now."

Erin grinned at her, amused. She'd thought Darcy was flirting on a couple of occasions today, but she hadn't been sure. "Oh, you were, were you?"

"Yes." Darcy's face was serious now, her voice quiet. "I find you very attractive, Erin. That should be obvious by now."

Erin experienced a momentary thrill of triumph, but the feeling faded almost as quickly as it came. Darcy was beautiful—stunning—but she was also dangerous. Just judging from their own minimal interactions, she was changeable, unreliable. Erin had already seen her coldness and indifference to others' pain, including her own. Was this really someone to get involved with? At the very least, it would be awkward for the rest of the time she and Charlie were here. It wasn't as if they would suddenly become lovey-dovey with each other like Jen and Charlie. How would they act around each other? As if nothing had happened? Erin didn't think she could. If they had sex, Erin's world would become a thousand times more complicated and confusing, and she didn't need that.

Darcy got to her feet and came closer, her face wrinkled with what seemed to be concern. She took Erin's hands. "What is it? You look…I don't know, scared?"

Erin shook her head. "Not quite. I don't know what I'm feeling. But I'm starting to regret something we haven't even done, and I don't think that's a good sign."

Darcy frowned slightly and released her hands. They stood that way for a long time, gazing into each other's eyes.

Finally, Darcy nodded. "You're right. It might be a dumb thing to do."

Relief flooded through her. "Not that I don't want to! But yes…"

"It would be a bad idea. I'll be gone soon, and I'm sure we don't need any," Darcy paused, "complications."

Neither of them moved, both seeming to wait for the other to make the final decision. For a moment, Erin almost pulled her into another kiss. Her desire, which had died down significantly in the last few minutes, was still there, roiling underneath the damper she'd thrown over it. It would be back instantly if Darcy gave any indication she was ready to act on it.

Finally, Darcy broke eye contact and turned away, going to the small kitchen sink and grabbing a rag. "I think we spilled some beer. I'll clean up while you get ready for bed."

Still, Erin hesitated. She watched Darcy move around the room, bending down and standing up again as she cleaned. Erin's temptation was so strong she had to fight an urge to rush over to embrace her. She closed her eyes, took one deep breath, and then grabbed her little bag of toiletries before heading into the bathroom. She closed the door behind her, resting her forehead on it for a moment, breathing heavily. Finally, she turned toward the sink to brush her teeth.

Once in bed, she tossed and turned, both overheated and worked up, her mind whirling with regret. Finally, when the light outside started to turn the fuzzy purple of dawn, she fell into a deep, exhausted sleep.

❖

Erin could barely move her head the next morning without feeling sick. When everyone met outside by the car, Charlie and Jen seemed a little shamefaced, too, so the entire ride down to Loveland was awkward, tense, and painful. Erin kept her sunglasses on the whole time, barely speaking to anyone, and by the time they arrived at the brewery, she was ready to burst from suppressed anxiety. She popped out of the car almost the moment Charlie parked and rushed toward the brewery before Jen called out to her.

"Jeez, Erin, you could at least say good-bye."

Erin had to stop and take a deep breath to keep from shouting at her, but she managed to plaster a smile on her face and turn around. She walked the few steps and shook Charlie's hand. "Sorry, Charlie, just anxious to get to work. I need to do about a million things today. Thanks so much for the trip. It was…fun."

Erin was so embarrassed she hadn't met Darcy's eyes all morning. Still, she couldn't help but glance her way once in parting. Darcy, however, wasn't paying attention to her. Instead, she was looking at something behind her, in the direction of the brewery, and when Erin turned her head to follow the direction of her gaze, she was surprised to see Darcy staring at her sister Lydia. Lydia was standing next to some guy Erin didn't recognize. Lydia was working the opening shift today and was clearly waiting for them. Darcy seemed unhappy, angry even, at the sight of her, and Erin wondered what the hell that meant. She was about to ask, but Jen was suddenly there, giving Darcy a light hug.

"It was so nice to hang out with you yesterday, Darcy. Thanks for keeping my sister occupied."

Erin was amused to see both Jen and Darcy blush. Erin didn't think Charlie had told Jen what he'd seen last night, so both of them were thinking about different things, but for the first time that day, Erin almost laughed.

"We need to get going, Jen."

Jen sighed. "Okay, Erin. Jeez. Go let Lydia in, and I'll be there in a minute."

Knowing Jen wanted a good-bye moment with Charlie, Erin excused herself and went over to the front door. Lydia and the man she was with were leaning against the glass windows, and Erin had to suppress the urge to yell at both of them—they were leaving a smudge. Lydia seemed washed out and pale, as if, like Erin, she'd been up all night. The man she was with had shoulder-length, dirty hair and threadbare clothes. Erin had the impression she'd seen him before, but she couldn't place him.

"Took you guys long enough," Lydia said.

Erin glanced at her watch. "We don't open for ten minutes."

Lydia rolled her eyes. "You're the one that always yells at me if I'm not thirty minutes early, Erin."

Erin sighed. "I'm sorry. You're right. We should have been here half an hour ago." She looked over at the man. "Who's this?"

Lydia smiled. "This is my boyfriend, Geo. We met at Oktoberfest."

"What's up?" the man said. He didn't hold out a hand to shake, so Erin didn't offer hers. She remembered him now. He and his punk-rock friends had come in to drink during Oktoberfest, and Lydia had been mooning over them all night. She'd disappeared with them, but as far as Erin knew, that had been the last of it. Apparently not.

"Hi," Erin said. "Nice to meet you."

As she turned to unlock the door, Lydia and Geo embraced, and Erin kept her eyes firmly in front of her to give them privacy. Once inside, she glanced back a single time to see both of her sisters in their respective lovers' arms. Darcy was leaning against the side of Charlie's car, arms crossed over her chest, bored or impatient. Erin continued to watch her for a moment, and a momentary sting of longing pierced her. She dismissed it immediately. The last thing she needed was to get involved with someone who lived so far away. She'd made the right decision last night. The same could obviously not be said of her sisters. Both of them were headed for heartache and pain. The only question now was when.

CHAPTER SEVEN

The Northern Colorado Brewing Festival is held in Fort Collins at the end of October. Most of the breweries in attendance submitted two types of beers for a competition between themselves. The competition and festival were open to the public, which was queried on preferences and tastes, but the public's opinion accounted for only 40 percent of the total score submitted for each beer. A panel of judges blind-tested the beers at a special event before the public festival, and they determined the bulk of the score.

Last year, BSB had been a fifth runner-up in the porter category, but their second beer had been completely ignored. This year, Erin had decided to submit their porter again, in part because she thought it much improved over last year's recipe. After a lot of debate, they'd also submitted their gose in the fruit-and-sour category. Jen had a lot of reservations about using the gose, since it was so unusual, but Erin had argued that its strangeness would make it stand out. It remained to be seen whether the gamble would work. The winners would be announced that afternoon.

Jen and Erin had worked overtime in the week preceding the competition, trying to manage both their regular work at the brewery and the setup for the competition. Erin had wanted to man the booth at the festival herself, with one or two helpers, but Jen had wisely—and perhaps cunningly—suggested that they use two of their employees with an All-American attractiveness that served them well in the taproom. It had been a good strategy, as the brewery had been so busy that Erin and Jen hadn't had time to go to the festival until the last afternoon. Also, by all measures, the two employees managing the booth had been a success, as Erin had needed to take keg after keg of their beers up there for tasting. She'd taken the last of them this morning, deciding that if they ran out today, the public votes they'd already received would simply have to do. She'd returned to Loveland for a couple of hours to work, and then she and Jen finally managed to head up to the festival together for the last afternoon and the announcement of the winners.

They got out of Jen's little Beetle several blocks from the festival warehouse, and Erin was struck not only by how many cars were here, but also by the large number of people she could see heading inside. Given that it was Sunday afternoon, she'd expected the crowds to have thinned out by now, but, if anything, there were more people here than yesterday. She felt a little tremor of anticipation, suddenly terrified that she'd made poor choices with her beer selections for this weekend. While beer connoisseurs might like the nutty malts of their porter or the biting tang of their gose, neither one was really what one might call a people's beer. Though public opinion was only 40 percent of the vote, if they completely bombed out with the public, they wouldn't even make the top ten in either category.

As if sensing her anxiety, Jen pushed her arm. "Hey, Erin, lighten up. You look like someone died."

Erin laughed. "Not someone—some*thing*. My career."

Jen stopped and waited until Erin turned to her. "What are you talking about? This kind of thing can only help us—you know that. Lots of people that come here learn about our beer for the first time. Even last year, when we didn't really stand a chance of winning, we managed to generate a lot of new customers because we competed."

Erin nodded, and they continued toward the warehouse together. Near the door, they saw Lydia and her boyfriend Geo waiting for them, and for a moment, Erin's annoyance replaced her nervousness. She and Jen had dressed up a little today, just in case they won and were called to the stage and, in general, because they wanted to look professional as they walked around the festival. Lydia and Geo wore ratty, faded, black clothes, and both of them were pale and sickly. Lydia had lost some weight recently, and Erin wondered if she was sick or simply not sleeping well. She'd been calling into work a lot lately—not that that was anything new—but now Erin wondered if she might actually have a reason for her absences.

"Hey, girls," Geo said, lifting a hand in a halfhearted wave.

Erin had to stop herself from snapping out a response. She hated it when anyone, especially men, called grown women "girls." Jen saved her by warmly greeting both of them and giving Lydia a quick hug.

"Are you feeling okay?" Jen asked as she pulled away. "You're burning up." She held a hand on her forehead, and Lydia pushed it away, obviously annoyed.

"Stop it, *Mom*. I'm fine. Just getting over a cold."

Jen continued to peer at her closely, clearly concerned, and Erin felt moderately better about her earlier judgement. She wasn't the only one who saw the changes in Lydia's appearance and demeanor. While she was never the most reliable employee, she liked getting a paycheck, and she used to keep her absenteeism under control— once or twice a week, tops. Now that Erin thought about it, she couldn't actually remember the last time Lydia had come to work, and when she had come sometime last week, she'd been late. All of this had happened since she started dating Geo, and Erin suspected it all stemmed from him.

Lydia sighed, clearly becoming annoyed. "Can we just get going already? I don't know about you, but I actually wanted to drink some beer today."

Geo rubbed his hands together. "Yeah, man, me, too."

Jen and Erin shared a quick glance, and Erin shrugged. It wasn't the time or place to get into it, but they would need to talk about whatever was going on. Jen raised her shoulders, and the four of them turned toward the festival entrance.

Each brewery received only two special brewers' passes into the festival, so Erin had to pay for both Lydia and Geo to attend. The entrance fee for drinkers was quite expensive. Neither one agreed to be a designated driver, who could get in for free—so Erin had to cough up fifty dollars for each of them.

The noise inside was nearly deafening, and Erin estimated at least a couple of thousand people were here. The event used to be held outside, but with Colorado weather so fickle, after it had been postponed a couple of years in a row because of storms, the organizers had decided to move it inside. With the autumn as warm as this one, it was a shame to be inside today, and Erin sighed, remembering how much nicer the festival had been when held outside in the park and streets near Old Town.

Lydia and Geo almost immediately disappeared into the crowd, neither one of them thanking or acknowledging Erin for paying their entrance fee. She and Jen shared another look, but, like outside, this wasn't the time or place to talk. Fighting the crowds, they made their way back to their booth, and by the time they got there, they were stunned and amazed to realize that the longest line they'd seen was for BSB.

"Holy shit!" Jen said. "Look at all the people!"

"No kidding," Erin said. "What the hell?"

"Why don't we ask someone in line? Why they're waiting, I mean."

Erin nodded, and they walked over to a young couple, both of whom smiled as they approached.

"Hi," Erin said. "How are you?"

"Good," the man said, still smiling.

Erin cleared her throat, suddenly nervous. This guy didn't know who they were, and she didn't want to give herself away as the brewer. She indicated the long line in front of him. "What are you waiting for?"

"Only the best beer in the whole place," the woman said, grinning widely.

Erin flushed with pleasure. "Have you had it before?"

"Yeah," the man said, "a couple of hours ago. Then we walked around and tried some others, but both of us wanted some more BSB."

"Really?" Jen asked.

"It's really good," he said. "I like the gose, and she likes the porter."

"Wow," Erin said, still stunned. "It must be really good if you're willing to stand in this line."

"Totally worth it," the man in front of them said.

"Absolutely," a woman from behind piped up.

"Maybe I'll get in line, then," Erin said.

"You should," the woman from the couple said. "Rumor has it they're almost out of the porter."

"Already?" Erin said, glancing at her watch. She'd dropped off the kegs a little over two hours ago.

The woman grinned. "Exactly. If I don't get some more today, I'm going to drive down to the brewery and get it—it's really that good."

"I'll keep that in mind," Erin said.

She and Jen moved away from the line, both of them grinning like fools. Erin had long thought that she and Jen made some of the best beer in the region, but this was one of the first times she'd seen that other people thought the same thing.

"So what do you want to do until the announcement?" Jen asked.

Erin turned toward her to answer and saw that Jen was peering around them, almost wildly, as if searching for something. Or some*one*, Erin thought.

"Do you want to go find Charlie?" Erin asked.

Jen stared at her, and her skin turned a rosy shade of pink. Erin laughed. "You're not exactly subtle, Jen. You can go look for him if you want to. I'll talk to some of the other brewers."

Jen smiled, and then her expression faded a little. "I don't want to leave you on your own. Why don't you come with me?"

"I don't want to be a third wheel."

"You won't be—I promise. Anyway, you know more about the beers than I do. I'm sure Charlie will be interested to hear what you have to say about them." She paused. "And Darcy's here with him anyway. If anything, you'll save *her* from being a third wheel."

Erin went hot with embarrassment. She'd been trying not to think about what had happened with Darcy last week and had done a fairly decent job avoiding her. They'd seen each other a few times in passing, but Erin hadn't said more than necessary—just quick greetings or good-byes. Every time she thought about that night in the cabin, she felt foolish and ridiculous. She should never have let herself get into that situation, no matter how long it had been since she had sex or how physically attractive she found Darcy. She could blame it on the alcohol, and had tried, but something like loneliness had made her stupid that night. She'd been a little fragile, yes, feeling like she'd been left behind by Jen and Lottie, but that didn't excuse her actions. Darcy was a ticket to heartache, and she had to avoid her.

Some of these thoughts must have shown in her face, as Jen suddenly looked confused. "What is it? I thought you and Darcy were getting along now. We all had such fun when we hung out together in Estes. Did something happen?"

Erin hadn't told anyone about what went on that night, and she didn't want to. But she couldn't possibly avoid Darcy today without drawing attention to herself and giving something away. At the very least, she could, as Jen had suggested, talk to Charlie about beer for an hour or two until the end of the competition.

She gave Jen a reassuring smile. "It's fine. We can go find them together if you want."

Jen's happy response calmed some of Erin's nerves, and they set off through the crowds. Jen tried calling them a couple of times, but the nearly deafening sound of the merrymakers made it impossible to hear a phone ringing. Erin finally decided to climb up to a small balcony that ran the length of one wall and spotted Charlie and Darcy almost immediately. She pointed them out to her sister below. Jen ran toward him when she spotted him, and they embraced and kissed.

Erin climbed down from the balcony and met the three of them, and immediately, Jen and Charlie moved to walk in front of them, their two heads close as they whispered and giggled. Erin was left with Darcy—exactly what she had wanted to avoid. She decided to maintain silence as long as she could and ignore her. She felt Darcy's eyes on her occasionally as they strolled along, and it was all she could do not to turn and meet them. Just when she thought she couldn't take it anymore, she heard Jen shriek a greeting over the noise and saw Lottie and Will coming toward them. Jen gave Will and Lottie a tight hug, and soon all six of them were standing together in a little circle.

Lottie and Will were holding hands, and once again Erin was struck by something like horror. When she'd seen them in Estes, she'd been both shocked and dismayed, but she was beginning to feel angry now, too. Why would Lottie want to date this repulsive man? After running into her in Estes, Lottie had completely avoided Erin, even at the gym. She hadn't stopped by the brewery at all and hadn't returned a single phone call. Considering that they'd seen each other just about every day since childhood, it was obvious what, or rather who, had caused the change. Erin should have apologized for her coldness to Lottie up in Estes, but she couldn't make herself do it. She still felt about Will as she had then, so an apology would be a complete lie. Erin had never been the kind of person who could lie easily, even when it meant saving someone's feelings, and she wouldn't try now. She still thought Lottie deserved better, and she hoped Lottie would see that herself, soon.

Jen seemed oblivious to Will's repulsiveness and was chatting with him freely. Erin suddenly realized that Darcy was still staring at her, and when their eyes met briefly, she saw a hint of concern. It was almost as if Darcy was reading her mind. Erin felt a flash of embarrassed anger. She hated the fact that this woman could see through her so easily. It made her feel cheap.

Jen elbowed Lottie in the ribs. "I was just telling Erin on the way here that we haven't seen the two of you around since Erin ran into you in Estes. Have you guys been honeymooning?"

Both Lottie and Will went a scarlet shade of red, and Erin's dread deepened into a real alarm. She'd been hoping that the two of them would be having, at most, a kind of dalliance, but judging from their reaction, this was something more.

Will gripped Lottie's hand a little tighter and laughed uncomfortably. "Something like that."

"I'm sorry I haven't been around lately, Jen," Lottie said. "But yeah—we've been busy."

She and Will shared a loving glance, and Jen laughed out loud. "I just bet you have. I'm so happy for you both."

Erin could hardly believe her ears. Jen liked Will about as much as she did. How could she lie like that? Again, some of this reaction must have shown in her expression as, when Lottie finally looked over at her, her face fell a little with regret.

"Anyway," Lottie said, glancing away, "we should get going. We don't want to intrude."

Jen waved a hand dismissively. "Don't be ridiculous. Come with us. We're heading over to the booth of one of our favorite breweries. Charlie and Darcy haven't tried it yet."

"You don't mind?" Lottie asked. Her eyes strayed back to Erin, and for a moment Erin felt genuine remorse. She was about to say something to reassure her, but Will jumped in.

"Hey, babe, she said it was fine. We've been wandering around long enough. Let's let the experts show us the good stuff."

"Okay," Lottie said. She threw Erin another hurt glance and took Jen's arm.

Once again, Erin and Darcy brought up the rear as they traveled across the rest of the warehouse. Jen and Lottie were in front, chatting away, and Charlie and Will were talking, seemingly with ease. The universe appeared to be conspiring against her today. No matter what she did, she knew she'd end up next to Darcy all afternoon. Further, Erin was angry with herself now. It simply wouldn't do to hate Will—it would drive Lottie away. She needed to figure out how to hide her repugnance a little more convincingly.

"You seem upset," Darcy said, breaking her reverie.

Erin looked at her, surprised. She frowned and shook her head before shrugging. "Sort of. I mean, I know I shouldn't be—I should be happy for Lottie, but…"

"But you can't stand him?"

Erin's stomach dropped. "Is it that obvious?"

Darcy laughed. "That's one of the things I like about you. You're easy to read."

Erin blushed. She'd said *one* of things she liked—implying there were more. She cleared her throat, a little nervous. They weren't drunk, yet Darcy was flirting again. "I don't mean to be. Easy to read, I mean."

"It's not a bad thing—really. I like that there's no bullshit with you. It's nice."

They walked in silence for a while longer, the crowds making it difficult to get anywhere quickly. Erin reflected on what Darcy had said and had to admit that it was true. Being easy to read was one of her primary character traits. It had made growing up with her father so difficult—he could read her anger and dislike in just about every interaction with him since puberty.

"So why don't you like Will?" Darcy asked. "I mean, other than the obvious fact that he's a bore and kind of pig-like, somehow."

Erin couldn't help but laugh, and she clapped a hand over her mouth to silence herself. The two of them paused there, letting the others move ahead a little, and Erin removed her hand and giggled a couple of times until she calmed down. Darcy looked pleased with her reaction, and Erin couldn't help but give her a wide grin.

"He's right in front of us!" she whispered.

Darcy shrugged. "Don't worry—he didn't hear us. He's too busy talking to Charlie, who's too nice to tell him to shut up."

Erin grinned again. "Charlie is nice, isn't he?"

Darcy nodded, almost gravely. "He's the best."

Erin had a wild compulsion to grill her about him, but she quickly suppressed it. This was neither the time nor the place. She'd do it soon, once she found out what was going to happen between him and her sister. Right now, everything was still up in the air. They were clearly falling for each other—anyone could see that—but would it go anywhere? Jen and Charlie still lived thousands of miles apart.

"We should catch up to the others," Erin said, waving at them as they disappeared into the crowd. Darcy nodded and they started walking again.

"You didn't answer my question," Darcy said.

"About what?"

"Why you don't like him. Will, I mean. Other than the obvious."

Erin sighed. "He was awful to me when we were kids. I know it's not fair to hold that against him—a lot of kids are little shits, and he was going through a rough time. But it's hard to let go. Jen remembers part of it, but she doesn't know all the details. She just thinks he was your everyday, average bully."

"He was more than that?"

Erin stared at the ground in front of them. Even now, over twenty years later, she felt a desperate flash of terror and anxiety at the memory. She'd rarely been as scared. For a moment, Erin was tempted to tell Darcy about it. After all, she would go away soon, and the secret would still be safely between her and Will.

Darcy paused again, and when Erin met her eyes, she seemed genuinely concerned. She touched her shoulder. "Hey—are you okay? I didn't mean to make you uncomfortable." Her face suddenly hardened, and her voice went darkly quiet. "Did he hurt you somehow?"

Erin suddenly felt like she might cry. Darcy looked around quickly and then put her arm around her shoulders. She steered them toward an empty table by a large potted plant. There was only one small bench-style chair, so they had to sit almost on top of each other, their legs and the side of their bodies touching. Darcy kept her arm around her as Erin desperately worked to stop herself from crying.

A tear or two slid out anyway, and she laughed, wryly. "Christ, I'm sorry," she said, wiping at her face furiously. "I can't believe I'm crying about it after all this time."

"Don't apologize," Darcy said, her voice quiet and soothing. "You can feel however you need to feel about it—whatever it is."

Erin gave her a pained grin. Their faces were very close, and Erin caught a whiff of her perfume again, faint and almost citrusy. She'd never denied that the woman was beautiful. And now, gazing into the depths of her gray eyes, Erin saw something there. She couldn't quite tell what it was, but Darcy was clearly and genuinely concerned.

Erin began to feel humiliated. She shook her head. "You're going to laugh when I tell you what happened. It's stupid, really. Kids' stuff."

Darcy remained quiet, gazing at her evenly and patiently, and Erin had to glance away. She felt teary again.

"I've never told anyone about it."

Darcy stayed quiet to let her speak. Erin felt a little ray of hope. She'd repressed the memory of that day for so long, she almost couldn't believe she was going to tell someone, let alone Darcy. But Darcy's eyes were not judging her and wouldn't, no matter what she said—Erin knew that without asking.

She took a deep breath and let it out. "I was eleven or twelve. Billy—that was Will's childhood name—was staying with us that week with his dad." She swallowed the lump in her throat.

"One day, my friend Lisa was over. She was my first, sort-of girlfriend. I mean, we didn't really know what we were, but we liked to kiss each other and hold hands, that kind of thing. Neither of us knew what it meant, but we knew enough not to do it in front of anyone."

Darcy nodded.

Erin cleared her throat again, surprised by how nervous she was to say this out loud. "Anyway, one day Lisa was over, and we were in my room when Billy waltzed in on us. He'd been doing it all week—hoping to catch me or my sisters naked, I think. Me, Jen, and Lydia had told on him to our parents several times, and he'd gotten in trouble for it, but he was still doing it. That day, he didn't knock or anything, so when he came in, he saw everything. I mean, it was fairly innocent, but we were kissing on my bed."

"Shit," Darcy said.

Erin shook her head at the memory. "Lisa was so scared, she starting crying and carrying on. Eventually, I talked Billy into letting her leave to go home." She paused, flushing at the memory. "He was so smug. He told me he would tell my parents, her parents, my sisters, everyone. And I believed him."

"How old was he then?"

"A couple of years older—maybe thirteen or fourteen. His voice was changing. I remember that."

"So he knew what it meant—at least more than you did."

"I mean, I knew Lisa and I could get into trouble, but I didn't really know why yet, either. Does that make sense?"

Darcy nodded.

Erin closed her eyes, remembering that biting terror. She opened them and looked up at Darcy again. "Anyway, he lorded it over me the next few days. He loved having me in his power. First he wanted all my desserts, and then he took my allowance, and then I was doing all his chores, including the ones he made up."

She was quiet long enough after this that Darcy finally said, "Was that all?"

Erin hesitated and finally shook her head. Her voice, when she said it, was almost a whisper. "He made me undress in front of him. I had to stand there for thirty seconds while he looked at me." She shuddered. "That was the last straw, and he knew it. I think he realized he'd gone too far, that I had just as much dirt on him as he had on me. After that, he ignored me." She shook her head. "I was still scared for a while after that—even after he and his dad left. Scared that he would tell, I mean. But he never did."

They were quiet for a long time, both of them staring out at the crowd. Darcy still had her arm around her shoulders, and Erin didn't feel the least bit uncomfortable about it. Telling her had made them closer—at least for the moment. It didn't need to mean anything more than that right now.

Darcy finally released her and took one of her hands. She waited until Erin met her eyes before saying, "I'm so very sorry, Erin. You didn't do anything to deserve that, you know."

Tears filled Erin's eyes again, and she nodded before wiping them hard, with her palms. She took Darcy's hand again. "I know. At the time, though, I felt really terrible. Dirty, even. What kind of asshole makes another kid feel that way?"

Darcy shook her head in sympathy. "I don't know. And now he's dating your best friend."

"Exactly."

"Have you thought about telling her?"

Erin shook her head. "Not really. It's ancient history. I don't even think he remembers—at least not the details. It was only traumatic for me."

"Well, maybe you should tell her. Maybe it would help her understand why you don't like him. Maybe she would see what she's getting into."

Erin shrugged. "Maybe."

But that wasn't true. No way could she tell Lottie now, or Jen, for that matter. She'd only told Darcy because Darcy was safe, removed from her real life. Jen and Lottie would be really upset, and what would it help? Nothing at all.

"There you are!"

Darcy and Erin jumped at the voice and turned to see Charlie and Jen grinning at them. They let go of each other's hand almost instantly, and Erin couldn't help but blush in embarrassment.

Jen was still grinning. "We've been looking everywhere for you two. The winners of the competition are about to be announced. Come on! Let's go wait by the stage."

Darcy slid out first, and Erin followed her, immediately missing the warmth of her body. Darcy and Charlie walked ahead this time, chatting, and Erin watched as he gave her his glass of beer to try. Darcy smelled and then tasted it, and Erin's mouth almost watered in some strange kind of sympathy with the glass. She had a momentary impulse to take the glass from her and try the beer herself so she could taste what Darcy was tasting.

"Holy shit, Erin," Jen said next to her. "You've got it bad."

Erin's cheeks flushed with heat. "What are you talking about?"

Jen lifted one eyebrow. "You can't lie to me. I know when you like someone. When did this happen?"

Erin looked away before starting to follow the others again. "I don't know what you're talking about, Jen. I mean, I might have misjudged her a little, but I don't like her like that."

"Suuuure, you don't. You just hold hands with every girl that gets near you."

Erin couldn't help but laugh. "Shut up."

Jen shoved her playfully, and Erin laughed louder. Charlie and Darcy turned around, an identical expression of confusion on their faces, and Erin and Jen laughed harder, too amused to explain themselves. Charlie started to laugh along with them, and even Darcy was eventually smiling.

They finally made it up to the front of the warehouse where the winners were being announced, and Jen spotted the others. Lydia and Geo had found Lottie and Will, and as they joined the others, Erin couldn't help but notice Darcy's dark, angry expression. At first Erin thought she was staring at Will, and she felt a momentary thrill of terror that Darcy might say something to him. Then, as they drew closer, Erin realized she was actually staring at Geo. She remembered then that same look in her eyes when they'd run into them after the Estes trip. Did Darcy and Geo know each other somehow?

But, before she could pull Darcy aside to ask her, the microphone gave a loud squeal. Everyone groaned and cringed, and the man onstage laughed.

"My apologies. I can never get these things to work right."

The master of ceremonies was a typical beer guy with a bushy, almost alpine beard, a thick flannel shirt, and corduroy slacks with suspenders. He wouldn't have been out of place in a logging town in the nineteenth century. He was accompanied on stage with the panel of judges, all of whom looked more or less like him, with varying degrees of beardedness or thick, seventies-style mustaches. The two women on the panel wore twee, vintage-style in terrible, gaudy patterns. The man at the microphone continued.

"I want to welcome you all to the closing winner's circle at the twenty-fifth annual Northern Colorado Brewing Festival!"

A loud round of applause and cheering broke out, and the man let it continue for a while before speaking again.

"I'm here to announce the winners of the competition for each style of beer. Second-place winners will receive a five-hundred-dollar gift certificate to a local brewing supplier. All first-place winners will, as usual, receive entry to the Western States Microbrewery Festival. Western States is being held this year here in beautiful Colorado, up in Aspen, in January. First-place winners also receive lodging and lift tickets at an Aspen resort, as well as entry to several brewers' parties."

Erin felt a tremor of anticipation, even though she knew she shouldn't get her hopes up. Most breweries couldn't even hope to be in the running for Western States until their fifth or sixth year, but the chance to go was a dream come true. For every brewery west of the Mississippi, it was the chance of a lifetime. Going to the festival meant a tremendous increase in sales and notoriety, as well as the chance to compete in the major competition. Prizes for winners at Western States had included expensive equipment as well as cash payouts. Even if they won today, they wouldn't have a chance in hell of winning at Western States, but the press they would get just for going would be incredibly good for business.

The man onstage started reading off winners of beers that BSB wasn't participating in, and as the names and prize-winning went on and on, Erin started to feel sick to her stomach. If they won today, or even came close to winning in one of their categories, regardless of whether they got a loan from their father or someone else, they could easily anticipate an increase in sales—maybe enough to stay open another year. For now, that would be enough.

Their gose came in second in its category, which was a genuine surprise and delight. She and Jen jumped up and down together, arms clasped, and Erin sent Jen up onstage to receive the gift certificate. The room fell silent at the sight of Jen, possibly out of surprise, as she was the first woman since the winners had been announced. She was, as always, beautiful, and Erin had to smile when she saw Charlie's face as he stared at her up there under the bright lights. He was visibly enchanted.

Jen rejoined them, and other brewers they knew and some strangers in the crowd in their general area congratulated them. One fan of their gose came up and told them that the other beer had stolen the category, that it really belonged to them. Erin thought that might be the nicest thing a stranger had ever said to her.

She was so delighted with the second-place win that she had completely tuned out what was happening onstage. Suddenly Jen went deathly pale, and everyone around them fell silent.

"What? What is it?" Erin asked, alarmed. Everyone looked stunned.

"We won, Erin," Jen whispered, eyes wide.

"Won what? I know we won—you're holding the gift certificate."

The guy at the microphone cleared his throat. "I repeat. The winner of the porter category this year is Bennet Sisters Brewing."

Erin's heart squeezed with shock. At best, she'd hoped to get third or fourth place and beat out their position from last year. She'd had real hopes for winning with the gose because it was so different from what the other breweries had submitted. She hadn't even hoped to win the porter category. Porters were ubiquitous to most breweries, which meant they had been competing with over fifty others. Yet somehow they'd won.

For a moment, she and Jen just stared at each other, too stunned to do anything. Then Jen's eyes teared up, and they leapt into each other's arms. By the time they pulled apart, Erin was crying too, and the crowd around them was hollering and screaming their approval. Charlie gave Erin and Jen a quick hug and pushed them, gently, toward the stage. They went up together. Erin was glad for Jen's presence, as her legs felt unsteady. After she took the envelope with their winner's certificate from the man behind the microphone, she and Jen shook hands with all the judges. Erin's eyes were so clouded she could hardly see, but she heard all of them congratulate her on a fantastic beer.

Just before she and Jen rejoined the others, her eyes met Darcy's in the crowd below them. She was smiling so widely, you might have thought she'd been the one to win.

CHAPTER EIGHT

Erin coasted to a stop, pausing at the intersection of the trail. From here, she could ride in one of two directions: farther north, toward Fort Collins, or back and around to where she'd started in South Loveland. The bike trail wasn't a perfect loop yet. Some sections still turned into regular roads for cars, but the two cities had promised to make one long bike path to share within the next couple of years. Erin hadn't ridden this far on the trail since last year, and the progress surprised her. She pulled out her phone to check the map, trying to decide if she had enough time to head up to see the trail in Fort Collins before going home. Technically, she had the day off, but she needed to go to the brewery once her assistant Javier got in to help him for a couple of hours later this afternoon.

She was near the Loveland Sculpture Garden, and with the sun beating down on her, the idea of resting in the shade for lunch was inviting. She climbed onto her seat and headed in that direction, a few blocks off the path. It was the middle of the week during the school year, so when she got off and locked her bike, she seemed to have the whole garden to herself.

Despite its size, Loveland has an enormous public-arts council, in part because of a large-scale bronze sculpture foundry in town. Erin walked by several of the sculptures she remembered seeing when she was younger, pleased to notice new works that had been added since the last time she'd visited. All of the large cottonwood trees were nearly leafless this time of year, but even so, their branches cast large patches of shade. Erin was searching for a particular spot she remembered sitting in before—a small picnic table was there—but she couldn't quite remember where it was. As she walked around, she paused, taking in several of the bronzes she knew and loved, not in any hurry to get where she was going. She'd already decided to head home after this stop, so she could take her time having lunch.

She came around a particularly large, life-sized bison and stopped short, so surprised she had to stifle the cry that rose to her lips. Darcy was standing a few feet away, talking on her cell phone. She hadn't seen Erin yet, as her back was partially to her, but it was obviously her. Erin debated for a long moment and then decided that, should she turn around and return to her bike, Darcy would possibly spot her anyway, and then it would be even more awkward than if she just said hello now.

Ever since Estes Park and the Brewing Festival, Erin had done her best to avoid Darcy any time she stopped by the brewery with Charlie. So far, she'd managed to get out of seeing her alone. Once or twice she'd noticed Darcy give her a funny look, as if she didn't quite understand why Erin didn't try harder to make contact with her, but she also never said anything about it.

Erin wasn't entirely sure why she was avoiding her. What had happened in Estes had certainly been awkward, but based on their ease at the Brewing Festival, they'd gotten past it. Her evasion was, however, in part because of what she'd told her about Will. Still, if Erin was honest with herself, it had less to do with the content of that conversation—which was embarrassing and still shameful— and more about how Darcy had made her feel: comforted and safe. Darcy had been tender, nicer than Erin deserved. So why did that make Erin want to run away any time she saw her? Erin shook her head. She didn't know.

Erin approached Darcy, shuffling her feet a little to avoid surprising her too much, and Darcy turned toward her, still on the phone. When she recognized Erin, her eyebrows shot up into her hairline. Erin gave her a weak smile and a wave, not sure if she should wait or if she could get away without saying anything.

"Hold on a minute, honey," Darcy said on the phone. She put her hand over the mouthpiece and then smiled at Erin. "Fancy meeting you here."

"Small world," Erin said lamely.

"Let me hang up, and we can see some of this place together," Darcy said, gesturing with her phone.

Erin moved away a bit to give her privacy. She couldn't help but wonder who Darcy had been talking to, especially with that "honey" thrown in. Her face felt hot and warm with embarrassment, and once again she was tempted to run away as fast as she could. She spent the next few seconds taking deep breaths, hoping she could make her excuses without acting like a complete idiot. She heard Darcy say good-bye behind her and made herself turn in her direction with a smile.

"Sorry about that," Darcy said, gesturing with her phone. "My sister."

"Ah," Erin said, strangely relieved.

"So what are you doing here? Shouldn't you be at work today? I thought you had Tuesday off, not Thursday."

Erin was taken aback. Darcy had clearly been paying attention to her schedule. "I had to switch days off with my assistant brewer. He's working on a special seasonal ale for next year, so he's sort of taken over the brewery this week."

"Interesting," Darcy said, and from her expression, Erin could tell she meant it. "I've reviewed a lot of breweries over the years, but I feel like I've learned more in the last couple of weeks than in the last few years, all thanks to you."

Again, Erin's face felt hot under Darcy's intense gaze, and she forced herself to look away. She gestured at the trail. "Shall we?"

"Yes. Please. Lead the way." Darcy joined her, and they started following the path. "Someone in town mentioned this garden, and I kept meaning to get over here. Funny we should bump into each other like this. Do you come here often?"

"No," Erin said, not looking at her. "I haven't been in years."

"What a strange coincidence."

Erin's throat felt tight and hot, and she nodded, unable to speak. They were walking side by side through the sculptures on a path narrow enough that their shoulders were almost brushing. Erin thought she could feel heat on Darcy's side, almost as if she was giving off some kind of internal warmth. A rush of electricity shot through her at the thought, and she struggled not to step farther away from what was undoubtedly an imaginary sensation. Imaginary or not, the feeling built the longer they walked in silence until it spread, first from that side of her body to her other and then throughout. She felt like she was humming with electrical energy, all of it somehow coming from Darcy.

Finally, she could take it no longer, and she stopped. Darcy seemed surprised, and Erin's stomach dropped when their eyes met. A hot flash of panic raced through her, and Erin, who had opened her mouth to make an excuse to leave, felt the words die in her throat.

Darcy lifted her eyebrows, waiting, and Erin snapped her mouth shut, shaking her head. "Nothing," she said.

"Do you want to have lunch somewhere?" Darcy asked.

"With you?" Erin couldn't help but convey some of her anxiety in the question, and she blushed after she'd spoken.

Darcy, however, laughed, her head thrown back. "Of course with me. What did you think I meant?"

Erin shook her head, still blushing, and thought up an excuse. "I meant with just you. Should we call Jen and Charlie?"

"Why would we?" Darcy asked. "Can't the two of us eat without them?"

Erin's face became even hotter, and she was once again forced to look away to avoid giving something away. Desperately, she searched her mind for an excuse but found nothing. She couldn't invent a single thing. She glanced at Darcy, ready to say almost anything, but her words dried up again when she met her eyes. Darcy was staring at her with open curiosity and interest, and for a moment, Erin felt as if she were slipping into the dark-gray depths of her eyes. She could feel herself letting go of the edge, and for the first time since she'd seen her on the path, she was happy they'd run into each other.

"I'd love to," Erin said.

Darcy's face broke into a beautiful, genuine smile, and Erin went warm from the toes up. It was an incredibly heady feeling to make a woman like Darcy smile at her like this.

"Great! Should we take your car or mine?"

"I rode my bike," Erin said.

Darcy grinned. "Of course you did. How stupid of me. We'll take mine then, and I can bring you back to your bike afterward. Sound good?"

"Perfect."

This time Darcy led the way, walking slightly in front of Erin, and Erin had a moment alone to watch her from behind. She caught her breath and searched her feelings. What on earth was going on? She still wasn't sure why she'd been avoiding Darcy. Beyond the fact that they'd had a couple of intense moments together, she barely knew the woman. So why did she feel like she was sinking into quicksand every time she saw her? She shook her head. Darcy was simply being friendly now, and the least Erin could do was respond in kind.

Darcy was driving a beautiful Mercedes sedan, a rental, judging from the plates. They climbed inside and just sat there for a moment. Erin felt a flash of panic again, wondering what Darcy was doing, but when she turned to her, she was simply staring at Erin, eyebrows raised.

"Where are we headed?"

Erin flushed with relief, not sure what she'd expected. Had she thought for a moment that Darcy would make a move on her? Here in the car? Ridiculous. Get yourself together, you idiot, she told herself.

Erin cleared her throat to disguise her anxiety. "Asian sound good to you?"

Darcy nodded, and Erin gave her the initial directions, still shaken from what she'd just imagined. Darcy started the car and reversed and then stopped.

"Oh, crap," she said, slapping the steering wheel lightly. "I forgot I have to stop by our place really quick. Is that okay? I need to pick something up. I have to do some work later on."

"That's fine. There's a good place we can go for Asian in Fort Collins, too."

"Great. Thanks. Sorry about that."

"No problem."

They rode in silence for a while as Darcy drove north, and Erin desperately tried to think of small talk. Once again she was struck by how little she knew the woman she was with, but on the other hand, Erin certainly knew her well enough to make simple conversation. Further, as a businesswoman, she was often required to talk to perfect strangers, sometimes for far longer than she would have liked. Why was it so difficult to talk to Darcy?

Erin looked over at her and then quickly away, her face once again heating up. Whether in profile or straight in, Darcy was gorgeous.

Oh, Erin thought. I'm an idiot. She was obviously having problems being around Darcy because Darcy was incredibly hot. Darcy's attractiveness simply drained all of Erin's suave and cool. Being around Darcy made Erin act like an idiot—that was all. Any time she or Jen had a crush, they used to call this feeling Being Hit with the Stupid Stick. Maybe, Erin thought, if she could just get used to seeing and being around Darcy, she'd regain her usual composure. Erin glanced over at her again and once again made herself wrench her eyes away. Easier thought than done. Her beauty drew her in and swallowed her whole.

Darcy and Charlie were staying in a house just past the southern border of Fort Collins. Their rental was larger than Jen and Erin's house, but, like their house, it was older construction and cute. Erin had pictured something huge and monstrous, like her father's place, but this house was charming, with large, developed trees in the yard and nice stonework. Like a lot of older homes in the area, it had likely been constructed in the early twentieth century, a functional if not beautiful era for houses.

Darcy seemed to see some of her surprise and gave Erin a wide smile. "Not what you expected?"

Erin shook her head. "Not exactly."

"We managed to get a good deal on it for the next month. Actually, the woman who owns this house is a distant friend of the family. She's on sabbatical here at the college, and it happened to line up with our visit."

Erin followed her inside after she unlocked the door. The house was dark, the curtains drawn against the sun, the wood a dark chocolate. It smelled like citrus and warmth, and the furniture was tasteful and midcentury. It was precisely the kind of place someone with taste and elegance would buy and design, almost as if it was actually Darcy's real house. Erin took a few steps inside, glancing into the living room and then stopping to wait in the little hallway by the stairs, too nervous to sit down.

Darcy excused herself and returned a moment later with her laptop bag slung over one shoulder. "Got what I needed. Sorry about that."

Erin's throat was tight, and her heart was racing again. Her nerves, which had settled a little in the car, had ramped up, and once again she wanted to run away and out the front door. She'd be safe if they left soon, but being here in this house was making her jumpy and tense. They made their way toward the door, and just as Erin reached out to open it, Darcy touched her shoulder from behind, making her jump.

"Sorry," Darcy said, her eyes wide when they met. "I didn't mean to startle you. I was just going to tell you that I have some nice salmon here in the fridge. What say we stay in for lunch?"

Erin wanted to decline, the instinct so strong she was desperate for any reason to leave. But it was too late for excuses now. She'd gotten herself into this…whatever it was, and saw no easy way out of it.

Darcy was frowning slightly, as if she could sense some of Erin's reluctance, but she looked confused as opposed to hurt. Again, Erin's mind went blank in the face of Darcy's guileless eyes. She opened her mouth to say something, anything, and then closed it again. She was done with excuses. Her relief as she accepted this situation gave her strength to smile at Darcy, and Darcy smiled in return.

"I'd love salmon." Erin's throat was still dry, but her terror had disappeared.

As hard as it was for her to believe, Darcy seemed oblivious to all of Erin's turmoil. She acted as if nothing was wrong and as if it wasn't blatantly obvious that Erin was acting strangely. She simply said, "Oh, good. It's fresh today, so I forgot I wanted to make sure I ate it right away. I was going to make it for dinner, but lunch is even better. Rice pilaf okay as a side?"

Again, Erin had to lick her lips in order to speak with her dry mouth. "Sounds delicious."

Darcy turned toward the kitchen, and Erin followed her for a few steps without saying or doing anything. Her defenses were falling, one brick at a time, as she walked behind this elegant, gorgeous woman.

They were by the stairs again, and Erin grabbed Darcy's hand. She turned, frowning a little, and Erin pulled her closer and into her arms before kissing her. Darcy returned the kiss as if she'd expected it. When they pulled apart a few seconds later, they were both breathing hard, Erin trembling all over.

Erin's fright was gone now, but she was still fraught with nerves. "I want you. Now."

As if she expected her to say this, Darcy, without replying, turned and led Erin upstairs to her bedroom.

❖

It was hard to hide what she and Darcy were doing together. Even the first time, Erin almost had to admit to Jen what had happened. She was so late getting back to the brewery that both Jen and Javier, the assistant brewer, were worried. They'd left countless messages on her phone, and she had no real excuse why she hadn't answered for hours. It didn't help that she was never late to work, and it definitely didn't help that she was so flustered and shaken she could hardly talk coherently. Luckily, just after she came through the door, claiming that she'd ridden too far north to get back in time, the phone rang, drawing Jen away and distracting her. Then another assistant came to tell them a transfer line had burst, and Javier left, cursing their old equipment.

She and Darcy started meeting almost every day. They varied the times and the places—one day at Darcy and Charlie's place, one day at Erin and Jen's, and once in Darcy's car when they couldn't arrange for a private tryst at someone's home. Erin had long since stopped her morning visits to the gym, mainly to avoid Lottie, so they usually met in the morning. They'd almost been caught several times, once by Jen and several times by Charlie, but so far neither Jen nor Charlie seemed to have cottoned to the fact that they were having what amounted to a sordid affair.

And that's precisely what it is, Erin thought: sordid. Nothing they were doing was above board. She and Darcy hardly talked about it except to plan the next time. The idea of telling anyone else about the affair was absurd.

The sex itself was almost angry in its intensity, always wordless and desperate. Usually by the time she saw Darcy, Erin was so worked up and her hands were shaking so much, she could barely unbutton her own clothes. They had ripped several of her shirts in their haste. A couple of times, she'd had to go home to get something new to wear, her clothes ruined. A similar number of times, she'd had to borrow Jen's makeup to cover up love marks on her neck and shoulders from Darcy's bites and scratches.

One Saturday they arranged to meet in the afternoon. Again, Javier had taken over the brewery, so Erin had an afternoon off, which was unusual for a weekend. Erin was lying on Darcy's bed, listening to Darcy shower. They had been spooning on the bed after sex, and Erin had drifted off. She'd awoken a few seconds earlier, confused and surprised to find herself alone. It was unusual for her to fall asleep like that. The affair had shaken up her sleep schedule. Most nights she tossed and turned, knowing she would see Darcy when she got up in the morning. Even on nights when they weren't meeting the next day, Erin's sleep was broken and restless. People at work had noticed her distraction and fatigue, but again, so far only she and Darcy seemed to know the cause.

She sat up when Darcy came into the room, pulling a sheet up to cover her nakedness. Darcy was in a silk bathrobe, drying her hair, and when she set the towel on her shoulders, she grinned at Erin.

"I've already seen what's under that sheet, Miss Bennet. You don't need to hide it from me."

Erin couldn't help but blush, and Darcy laughed. Darcy walked over and sat on the edge of the bed, taking Erin's hand in hers. Erin made herself relax and leaned back into the pillows, looking up into Darcy's beautiful face.

"This is nice," Darcy said, rubbing the back of her hand with a thumb.

"What's nice?"

"Having you here during the day. Almost like a normal couple."

Erin's eyebrows shot up. They never talked about what they were to each other or what they were doing. They simply slept together, or at least pretended that's all they were doing. Sometimes Erin wasn't so sure it was that simple. Most of their time apart, Erin was fantasizing about Darcy's body, and when they couldn't meet, she was almost frantic by the next time they saw each other.

Still, sometimes she longed for something more. They had a good rapport. Darcy seemed to be interested in Erin's work and she in hers, and they had other things to talk about when they did talk. They could, in fact, be friendly and companionable when they tried. And even if they couldn't turn into a "normal couple," Erin was starting to get a little tired of all of this sneaking around. It was exciting and made their desperate couplings seem somewhat dangerous since they could be caught, but Erin wouldn't mind giving up that part to come out to Jen and Charlie. Perhaps revealing their affair could mean taking a step toward meaning something more to each other than good sex.

For a moment, Darcy's eyes clouded over with emotion, but she broke eye contact, gazing outside the large bay window.

"When do you have to leave?" she asked.

The swift change in topic startled Erin, but she glanced over at the clock. "In about twenty minutes." She paused, watching Darcy's face. Her gaze was still averted, but her expression remained blank. Erin swallowed. "But I could call in."

Darcy's eyebrows creased. "Why would you do that?"

Erin's stomach dropped with dread and pain, but she managed to shake her head. "No reason. Just a thought."

Darcy still looked confused, and Erin shook her head again to dismiss the topic. A moment later she was sliding out of bed behind Darcy. She excused herself for a quick shower, and when she was alone in the bathroom, she glared into the mirror and shook her head at herself. This was no time for dramatics. After all, what they had was good enough—better than good enough. It was certainly the best sex she'd ever had.

Still, after she'd waved good-bye to Darcy in the kitchen—neither of them saying a word—she couldn't help but recognize that all of these thoughts and feelings were threatening to ruin what good they got out of each other. Erin apparently wasn't the only one with thoughts of something else, something more. Darcy had been thinking about being a "normal couple" too, no matter what she said after that. Soon, they would either have to talk about what they were doing and agree to simply have sex a few more times and leave it at that, or decide if they had something else—something more that they could bring into the open.

CHAPTER NINE

Erin knew something was wrong long before Charlie and Darcy broke the news that they were leaving. She and Jen had been so busy they were quite literally running around for over twelve hours a day. The *Denver Post* had announced the winners of the festival, and the *Loveland Reporter Herald* had a full-page spread on their story and success a week or so later. The crowds that started showing up were so intense, both of them had to help out in the taproom for hours every day, rotating with their normal duties. Even then, Erin was often at the brewery long after closing to finish tasks related to her actual work in the brewery, often crawling into bed in the middle of the night. Time off was temporarily canceled for everyone that worked at BSB, including Erin and Jen, but luckily most of their employees responded with good-natured grumbling. Everyone that worked for them knew the extra business could only be a good thing for everyone involved. Even Lydia made an effort the first couple of weeks after the festival, showing up early and staying late.

Erin barely saw Darcy. In fact, she suspected Darcy was doing everything she could to avoid her. They'd had a quick tryst once or twice after the awkward almost-conversation, and then nothing. Darcy's near disappearance the last couple of weeks was striking and unsettling in a way Erin didn't want to analyze, but she couldn't help but dwell on what they'd almost said. Had she given Darcy the wrong impression? Pressured her somehow? It had been awkward, yes, but hadn't they gotten past that? It was hard not to doubt everything she'd said, even though they'd barely spoken. Further, since she hadn't told anyone about the affair, she was locked in her own worries.

Still, she knew some of this absence and silence was due to how busy they were. Even Charlie and Jen had problems getting together during the last two weeks. If Charlie couldn't come by the brewery, Jen would hardly see him at all. At first, he was there every day for at least an hour or two, generally in the afternoon, when things were a little slower. He'd also stayed at their place a couple of nights, and Jen had stayed at his place perhaps as often. Throughout this period, Erin had seen Darcy twice in passing since she and Charlie shared a car, but they rarely said more than hello, and Darcy's coldness both times had shut down any further conversation.

Another week passed, and Charlie was absent a couple of days in a row, and Darcy disappeared altogether. Erin had to watch her sister talk to him on the phone, pretending she was okay with it. By the following week, two days without a visit turned into three, and by the week after that, even his phone calls were becoming spotty. Jen was putting on a brave face, but sometimes, when she thought no one was looking, Erin saw Jen simply staring off into space, her expression bleak and worried. Then Charlie showed up again for a couple of hours or spent the night, and everything seemed okay again.

Erin desperately wanted to talk to her sister about what was happening—she was starting to suspect what might come—but by late November, Jen seemed to be in some stage of deep denial. Any time Erin mentioned Charlie, Jen suddenly found something to do and ended the conversation. As for Darcy, with no phone calls and no more visits or meetups, Erin saw no real sign she was even in the same state anymore. Erin had to nurse a growing sense of loss about this all on her own, still wondering if she could have done something to make their affair last a little longer or become something more than an affair.

The Monday before Thanksgiving, Jen, Erin, and Lydia were on their own in the taproom, deep-cleaning the floors a couple of hours before opening. Normally they did this kind of cleaning once a week, usually at night, but with the madness since the festival, they'd only been able to do the usual surface-level cleaning they did every day. All of them were down on their knees, scrubbing the floors with hot, soapy water and scrub brushes, working their way back away from the front doors. Lydia had been bitching all morning, but at this point they were all so tired, all three were quiet.

The knock on the door startled them, and when they looked up, Erin was surprised to see Charlie and Darcy standing outside. The weather had finally turned this week, and both Charlie and Darcy were bundled up, huddled against the cold in their heavy wool coats. Charlie gave a little wave, and Jen leaped to her feet, almost rushing toward him. Erin grabbed her leg.

"Damn it, Jen! Don't walk on the floor."

"Oh, right." Jen motioned Charlie and Darcy toward the back entrance and then went behind the bar to meet them.

"Must be nice," Lydia said, shaking her head.

"What?" Erin asked.

"It's not like you'd let me stop and visit with Geo if he showed up."

Erin sighed and sat back on her feet, resting her knees. Lydia continued to scrub, angrily now, and Erin couldn't help but roll her eyes at her. Erin rotated her neck a little and then got to her feet, her knees popping with the effort of standing.

"Let's take a break. We're almost finished anyway."

Lydia sighed and met her eyes evenly. "It's okay, Erin. Go ahead. I'll finish up here."

Erin blushed. Lydia saw right through her. She wanted to go talk to Charlie and Darcy as much as Jen did, even if she was annoyed by them showing up like this unannounced.

"Thanks, kiddo."

Lydia shrugged and continued to work, and Erin moved quickly around the bar and down the hall to the back door. When she spotted Jen and the others, she stopped. Charlie and Darcy were standing, stiff as boards, watching Jen cry.

"But why?" Jen moaned. "You told me—"

"I said a lot of things, Jen." Charlie was near tears himself. "And I'm sorry. If it were up to me…" He shook his head, unable to go on, and turned to Darcy as if in desperation.

Unlike the others, Darcy's expression was impassive, bored even, and a shiver of something like horror passed through Erin. Darcy didn't care one bit about what was happening.

"It's not up to him," Darcy said. "Not if he wants to keep running his business. We have to get back to Boston today if that's even going to be a possibility."

"I thought you said you were leaving in December," Jen said, sobbing a little.

Charlie took a step toward her, lifting his arms for an embrace, and Darcy reached out to stop him. He looked at her, miserable, and she shook her head, firmly. He dropped his hands to his sides and stepped away from Jen, his face cloudy with pain and sorrow. Jen caught this whole exchange and sobbed even louder, raising her hands to her face.

No longer able to take it, Erin rushed down the hallway and drew Jen into her arms. Jen turned and started sobbing into her neck. Erin stared at Charlie and Darcy, so angry she couldn't say a word.

"I'm sorry, Jen," Charlie said. A single tear fell down his cheek. His expression was desperate, as if he hoped Erin could make it all better.

Darcy grabbed his arm. "Come on, Charlie. We have to leave now if we're going to make our flight."

He glared at Darcy, his expression almost angry, and then turned to Jen and Erin. Jen was still sobbing into Erin's shoulder, and this time Erin shook her head.

"Just go," she said. "You've done enough damage as it is."

The anger in her voice clearly surprised him. "I didn't mean—"

"I don't give a goddamn what you meant to do, Charlie. Just get the hell out of here."

"He's only doing what he has to," Darcy said, sounding angry herself.

"Good for him," Erin said. "Now go do it somewhere else and leave us the hell alone."

Darcy met her eyes, finally, and for a moment, Erin saw real emotion in them. Instead of the icy coldness she'd been putting on in front of Jen, true pain showed there. She opened her mouth to say something, but Erin shook her head. She didn't want to hear it.

Charlie and Darcy shared a look. Both of them hesitated, and their gaze met Erin's. Her stomach dropped at their identical expressions of resolve. A tiny part of her had been hoping Charlie would push Erin out of the way, take Jen in his arms, and never let her go. An even smaller part of her had been hoping Darcy would do the same. Instead, they did just what she'd asked them to.

They left.

❖

To say that Erin and Jen were not in the mood for Thanksgiving dinner with their father would be an understatement. Erin had only agreed to go to her father's some weeks ago because she and Jen still hadn't had an opportunity to talk to him about the loan they wanted. Getting a loan had been a long shot before Charlie left, but now, coupled with Jen's broken condition, it was likely impossible. Erin had been counting on Jen to make the case for them, for Jen to sweet-talk her father like no one else could, but obviously that wasn't going to happen now.

Beyond the fact that it was difficult to spend any time with her father, Erin wasn't in the best frame of mind for the holiday. While what she and Darcy had shared was nothing compared to Jen and Charlie's romance, Erin was still upset and hurt. They had distinctly avoided talking about romance and feelings with each other, but Erin had, at the very least, expected some kind of good-bye. Further, she was alone in her feelings. No one even suspected that anything had happened between them. As far as Jen knew, Erin still disliked Darcy, and telling her about the brief affair now wouldn't do her any good. In fact, it might make things worse. She'd been lying for so long. Jen would undoubtedly feel betrayed.

Jen had become a very different person in the three days since Charlie and Darcy had walked out of their lives. After crying almost nonstop for twenty-four hours, she'd finally stopped, as if a faucet was turned off. But, instead of becoming herself again, she'd shut down. Her movements were stiffer, her smile, if it came, false. She appeared beaten down, hollowed, as if emptied of life. She never spoke unless spoken to, and even then, she replied in one-word phrases.

All of this was, of course, understandable, and Erin did her best to be patient with her. But, as they'd scheduled to talk to their father, alone, sometime today, she couldn't help but wish Jen would pull herself together for a couple of hours. Much more than Jen and Erin's careers were on the line. While the extra business since the festival had done their bottom line a lot of good, unless they expanded their taproom and brewery soon, they would never be able to meet demand. Already, Erin was worried that they would have to close down for a couple of weeks in late January just so they could catch up. This would mean unpaid leave for all of their taproom counter employees. If this happened, some of them wouldn't be able to come back. They'd be forced to get new jobs, which would mean hiring new people and more expenses for BSB. She'd even looked into renting space to brew in larger local breweries to meet the demand, but, between rental and transportation fees, so far she'd run into a wall—it was just too expensive.

While she didn't want Jen to feel the same kind of anxiety she was wrestling with, Erin did long for someone to share her worries. Lottie was still avoiding her, Lydia had stopped coming in regularly again, and Erin didn't feel comfortable unburdening herself to anyone else. She had some other friends from college and elsewhere that she occasionally saw, but owning a small business meant most of them were distant friends at best. The three days between Darcy and Charlie's good-bye and Thanksgiving were a personal hell she had to suffer on her own. And now she would have to put up with her father on top of everything else, though "putting up" was stating it mildly. She needed to do some major groveling if she could even think of asking him for money.

Jen was silent on the ride to their father's house. Most holidays, she went over to his place early to help with dinner, but she hadn't even suggested doing it this year. Instead, she went where she was told to go, as if she had no will of her own. Erin glanced over at her a couple of times, wondering if it might be better to cancel altogether and claim illness. Jen certainly appeared to be ill. Her rosy cheeks were drained of color, and judging from the circles under her eyes, she hadn't slept in days. Her hair was greasy and poorly styled, her clothes threadbare and old. Their father wouldn't like this. He liked for everyone to dress up for dinner, especially on holidays. Erin decided that, scheduled or not, today was not the day to ask their father for money.

When they pulled into his driveway, several cars were already in front of them. Erin cursed silently. It would have been bad enough having only family around today with Jen the way she was, and now a roomful of people would be here. Anyone that knew Jen would be able to tell something was wrong, and Jen was just a few questions away from breaking down entirely. She was only holding herself together now by not talking about Charlie. If someone pushed her, she'd break open like a dam. They sat in the car for a moment, not saying anything.

"We could go home," Erin suggested.

Jen shrugged. "What difference does it make? Everyone knows I'm a failure anyway."

Erin touched her hand and waited until Jen met her eyes. "That's not true at all, Jen. You're a small-business owner and an excellent manager. That's not failure by anyone's standards."

Jen's face crumpled for a moment, and then she shook her head, hard. "But I can't hold on to a man, can I? First Jacob, and now this. Something must be wrong with me."

"Goddamn it, Jen, stop it. In both cases, it was *his* fault, not yours. Jacob was an unmitigated ass, and Charlie…"

Jen gave a bitter laugh. "What? What was wrong with him? Nothing, that's what. He's a wonderful person."

Erin shook her head. "That's clearly not true, Jen. He left you. He's a coward, if nothing else. He used you and he left." She had to swallow her own hurt, as it was precisely what Darcy had done to her.

Jen's eyes were leaking tears. "What was he supposed to do? I mean, Christ, he told me he was leaving when I first met him, for God's sake."

"He didn't have to leave, Jen."

"Of course he did!"

Erin shook her head, more firmly. "No. He didn't. You're special enough to hold onto, even if you don't believe it. And he knew how you felt about him. I'm pretty sure he felt the same way for you."

Jen was crying now, her shoulders shaking. "Then why? Something's wrong with me. What other reason could there be?"

Erin pulled her into an awkward hug. They were still in the car, and the windows of the little Beetle had fogged up. Surely someone had heard them drive up, but luckily no one had come out to investigate yet. Erin knew Lydia had told their father about the breakup, so she could only hope that had something to do with being left alone. They stayed there in each other's arms long enough for Jen to calm down, and when she pulled away, her face was a little more natural than it had been the last few days.

"I'm sorry, Erin," Jen said. "You shouldn't have to comfort me like this. It's my problem, not yours."

Erin laughed. "Of course it's my problem, Jen. I care about you. I don't want you to be unhappy. I'm so sorry it turned out this way."

Jen seemed to hesitate before she touched Erin's hand. "And I'm sorry. About Darcy. She left, too."

Erin felt a little flash of dread and looked away. "That doesn't matter. It isn't like we were dating or anything."

"But you were thinking about it. I could tell. The two of you seemed awfully cozy at the brewers' festival."

Erin felt a stab of guilt. She hated lying to Jen, but no way was she going to tell her about Darcy right now. She shook her head. "It doesn't matter. I'm fine. It's not the same thing as you and Charlie. And anyway, I hate her now."

They were quiet for a long time, staring at the foggy windows. Finally, Jen sighed. "I guess we better get in there. I'm sure everyone thinks I'm having a nervous breakdown out here by now."

Erin grinned at her. "Aren't you?"

Jen laughed and pushed her arm. "Fuck you."

When they opened the door to their father's house, the heavenly scent of truffle oil, turkey, and cornbread greeted them. The house was packed with people, and everyone shouted a welcome at them as they came in. Erin spotted some of their dad's brothers and their mother's sister, and she recognized several of her father's friends from the restaurant business. She was about to head over to her aunt to say hi, but their father suddenly appeared from the kitchen. He walked right by Erin and headed straight for Jen, his arms wide open. Jen launched herself into his embrace, and they stood there for a long moment, Jen's shoulders shaking with quiet sobs. Erin watched them with something like longing and pain, and her father's eyes met hers for a moment of concern before flickering away.

After Jen's sobbing seemed to stop, he held her out with his hands on her shoulders, looking her up and down. "Well, you look terrible. I was expecting that."

Jen laughed weakly, wiping her teary eyes. "Gee, thanks, Dad."

"But you're okay. That's all I can ask. You really are okay, aren't you, Jenny?"

She sighed. "I will be, Dad. I just feel so stupid. It's my own fault."

He tsked. "Somehow I doubt that. He just didn't know a good thing when he found it—that's my guess."

Jen shrugged.

Their father let go of her shoulders and clapped his hands once before rubbing them together. "Well, dinner will be ready in about an hour. Will brought some lovely wines for all of us to try. Go grab a glass in the living room, and he'll tell you all about them."

Jen gave him a brave smile. "Okay, Dad."

Erin turned to follow her, and her father touched her sleeve. "Just a minute, Erin. I want to talk to you."

Both Erin and Jen turned toward him, surprised. He hadn't voluntarily talked to Erin in years.

"Oh?" Erin asked.

"Yes. Please. In the kitchen, if you don't mind."

Erin and Jen looked at each other, and Erin couldn't help but widen her eyes to show her panic. Jen shrugged again and motioned for her to go, and Erin sighed, turning toward her father again.

"Sure, Dad. Let's talk."

Normally at a large gathering like this, their father commandeered people to work on some part of his culinary masterpieces. He'd clearly sent several people out of the kitchen, as abandoned projects in varying degrees of completion lay on several of the countertops around the room. Erin and her father were completely alone.

Her father raised his eyebrows, clearly amused with her confusion. He indicated an open bottle of wine on the counter, and Erin nodded. He poured them both a small glass, and Erin gulped hers down to cover her nerves.

Her father cleared his throat. "I know you find this strange, Erin. I do, too. But I need to talk to you about a couple of things. Can we put our differences aside for the time being?"

A retort rose to Erin's lips, but she bit down on her anger and nodded.

Some tension dropped from his shoulders as he visibly relaxed. "Thank you," he said. He set his glass down and rubbed his eyes, sighing. When he dropped his hands again, his expression had softened a little. "First of all, tell me. How is Jen, really? Lydia is so vague. I need the truth."

Erin shook her head. "She's not very good, Dad. Not good at all."

His eyebrows lowered. "That's what I thought. She looks terrible. I knew she was dating someone—she'd told me as much—and judging from her last choice, I was afraid something like this might happen, but she seemed happy with him, content even. Do you know what happened? I know he left for Boston, but I don't know the details."

Erin shrugged. "It was bad luck, really. He is a nice man—or was, I guess. I really thought he cared for her. He wasn't like Jacob, or any of the other guys Jen's dated. I think Charlie was in love with her. But it couldn't last—not without one of them changing cities. I guess it was too soon to think about something like that, and I suppose Charlie just decided to cut his losses rather than try to make something long-distance happen."

"So he's a fool?"

Erin shook her head and then shrugged again. "I don't know. Maybe. I liked him a lot, Dad, and even though he's hurt her, it's hard to hate him entirely. It was just a terrible situation, in the end."

They were quiet for a while. Her father looked troubled and upset, and for a moment, Erin had a flash of true affection for him. It was hard to resent anyone who loved Jen like he did. He seemed almost as upset as she was.

Finally he sighed and shook his head. "Another tragedy for Jen, I guess. She really can pick them."

They finished their wine, and as the awkward silence dragged out, Erin had an urge to run from the room as quickly as she could. This was as close to civil as the two of them had been in a long time, and she was afraid something would happen to ruin the feeling if she stayed longer.

Unable to stand the suspense anymore, she said, "Is that all you wanted to talk about?"

He frowned, his eyebrows knit with annoyance, but bit back a retort. It was the first time in a long time he'd even tried to hold his tongue.

"Not entirely. I wanted to discuss one other thing. I would have brought it up if you weren't so damn impatient, Erin."

He turned and rummaged around in a nearby drawer before pulling out a newspaper. Erin knew exactly what he was going to show her before he did: the full-page spread on their brewery from a couple of weeks ago. He held it up briefly before setting it aside.

"I wanted to talk to you about your business," he said.

Erin stiffened with anxiety and defensiveness. Every time they'd talked about the brewery in the past, the conversation had devolved into, at best, strong words and, at worst, a shouting match. The first time they'd argued about it, when she and Jen had finally gotten the business loan to open, he'd berated her for planning to open a brewery in a saturated market. He'd been convinced they'd go under inside a year. If Erin was honest with herself, part of the reason she was so desperate to keep her brewery open was to prove her father wrong. If they ended up folding, he'd be right, and he'd never give her the benefit of the doubt again. Knowing him, he'd likely lord it over her the rest of his life, taking every opportunity to remind her of her mistakes. They'd argued over the years since about other things related to the business, chief of which was that BSB was not a restaurant, just a taproom. He was convinced their business would be stronger if they sold food as well.

"What about it?" She was unable to keep a note of petulance from her tone.

Her father sighed before frowning deeply. "Look, maybe I deserve that tone, Erin, but could you hear me out for once before getting your back up?"

Erin made herself relax and nodded.

He tapped the newspaper article. "This is a really big deal. I asked some of my own brewery friends about Western States, and they told me simply getting invited is a major accomplishment. When I read this a couple of weeks ago, I could hardly believe it."

"So why didn't you say anything about it? Before now, I mean."

He shook his head. "I have no excuse, Erin. I should have called you right away to congratulate you—I know that." He paused, clearly troubled. "I had to think about it for a while to, uh, 'get my head out of my ass,' as your sister Lydia put it."

"Lydia was talking to you about this?"

He nodded. "She's the one that showed me the article. No matter how she acts, she's really proud of you." He paused and swallowed. "And so am I."

Erin was floored. Her father, in basically all of the years since her young adulthood, had never once told her he was proud of her. Not after she made team captainships in her high school sports teams, not after she was elected as her senior class president, and not after her countless scholarships and awards in college. The words had never crossed his lips until now.

Stunned, she didn't know what to say. She opened her mouth, but only a kind of croak came out. Her father was grinning at her, clearly amused, and then he did the unthinkable: he opened his arms wide for a hug. Despite all the pain and anger between them over the last twenty years, Erin didn't hesitate. She stepped into his embrace and hugged him.

A few moments later, when they stepped apart, both had red, teary eyes, and they shared an embarrassed grin. Her father poured them another glass of wine, and they drank it in quiet companionship. Erin was staring into space, still stunned, when she suddenly realized her father was looking at her. She met his eyes and gave him her first genuine smile in years. He smiled and touched her arm again.

"Can we put some of this," he gestured between them, "to rest now, Erin? I'm starting to become an old man, and being old makes you second-guess some of your decisions, especially the bad ones. I've been pig-headed over the years, and I know that you are too—that's part of why I've been so hard on you. You're just like me."

She nodded, still flushed with happy surprise.

"And while I may never agree with your lifestyle choices—"

She held up a hand to cut him off. "Dad, please. We were doing so well. Let's stop while we're ahead."

He shrugged. "Okay. Well, we may never see eye-to-eye on *everything*, but I want to be part of your life again, Éire, in some small way, before it's too late."

Erin's eyes welled up with emotion. Her father hadn't called her Éire since the days before they'd started fighting all the time. It had been his pet name for her during childhood. His parents were both Irish immigrants, and when Erin had started getting interested in Irish history, he'd explained that she'd been named after their ancestral land. Then, sometime in middle school, he'd started calling her by her real name, right around the time they'd cooled toward each other. She'd been so miffed, she refused to let anyone call her by her nickname and started insisting on Erin.

"I'd like that too, Dad. I really would."

They hugged again, and when they moved apart, Erin felt warm in every part of her body. She hadn't realized how much she'd wanted a conversation like this—or, even if she had, she'd never admitted it to herself. She'd been hurt for too long to even dream of it.

He was smiling when they pulled apart, and he kept his hands on her shoulders. "So that's that for now. We can talk again soon. I have some ideas for your brewery that I want to share with you, and maybe, for once, we can have a civil conversation about it. But not today. Today is for eating."

Erin laughed. "Okay, Dad. I'll try to hear you out. I can't promise to agree with you, but I'll try to listen. Just call me this weekend, and we'll set something up."

"Sounds good."

Afraid she might start crying again, Erin left the kitchen quickly and went outside for a moment to calm down. Her eyes and face felt hot and tight, and the cool November air was wonderfully refreshing. She took a few deep, shuddering breaths before she went inside to find Jen.

Jen and their Aunt Eddie were sitting next to the fireplace, deep in conversation. Eddie was their only living relative on their mother's side, and a favorite of all of her nieces. Aunt Eddie and their father had always been fond of each other, so it only made sense that he would keep inviting her for holidays even after their mother died. Seeing her there next to Jen, Erin was struck by her strong resemblance to their mother, and Erin felt that same old sick tightening in her chest at the memory of her loss. Their mother had died quickly and unexpectedly of breast cancer just shy of her sixtieth birthday. No one in the family had dealt with it very well then or since.

For one thing, without her mother's calming, peace-making presence, Erin and her father had been free to shout at each other as long as they wanted, driving them even further apart over the years. Lydia's sense of responsibility had disappeared at about the same time, and Erin had become somewhat more reserved in her affections with everyone. Their father, on the other hand, had become bitter and unforgiving, more so than ever. Seeing their aunt always brought back all that initial pain. Erin loved their aunt, deeply, but it was always hard to see her after an absence; for a moment, it was like seeing her mother again.

After dodging through and greeting several groups of people standing and sitting in the living room, Erin joined her sister and aunt, dragging a little ottoman close to them. Aunt Eddie got to her feet and gave her a hug before they both sat down.

Jen was looking at Erin critically, clearly seeing the tell-tale signs of crying, but Erin shook her head and gave her a reassuring smile. They'd talk about her conversation with their father later.

Aunt Eddie either didn't catch this exchange or pretended not to. She was grinning, her face a little red from the wine she was drinking.

"It's so lovely to see you, my dear." Like her face, Aunt Eddie's voice was almost identical to their mother's. Eddie and their mother had grown up being mistaken for each other in person and on the phone the entire time they lived together.

"It's good to see you, too, Eddie. It's been too long."

"Well, I was here last Easter, but you weren't. And the Christmas before that. If I hadn't come to the brewery when I was here for Thanksgiving last year, I'm not sure I would have seen you at all!"

Erin sighed. "I know. I'm sorry, Eddie. You know how it is with me and Dad."

She tutted and shook her head. "I do, honey, but I wish the two of you would work it out one of these days. I know you're both stubborn, but he's not getting any younger."

"We're trying now, Eddie. I promise."

She smiled. "Good. Maybe you girls and your father and I can finally have a meal just the five of us for once. It's always like Grand Central Station when I visit. I get the impression he invites all of these people here to act as a buffer."

"Not far off, there, I imagine."

"Anyway, I was telling your sister Jen here about this wonderful trip I'm taking next week."

"Oh?"

Their aunt was a travel writer and had spent almost her entire adult life in transit. She had a couple of small apartments around the world—including one about an hour away in Boulder—but she never stayed in one place very long. She'd never married, never had kids, and had been something like a happy ghost passing through their entire lives. She came for most major holidays and had stayed now and again in Colorado for a little longer, but generally the family saw her only on her way from place to place.

"Yes. I'm leaving on Monday and heading to Maine, New Hampshire, and Massachusetts for four weeks—a week in each state and then some extra time in Boston at the end."

Erin and Jen shared a quick glance. Charlie was in Boston by now.

"Not the usual exotic locale," Erin said. Their aunt spent most of her time in Asia and Europe.

Eddie laughed. "No—not exotic at all. In fact, quite ordinary. But I'm very excited about it. Did you know I've never actually been to any of those states? This will be a first for me. Sunny beaches and beautiful, ancient cities lose their glamour after a while. I asked my editor if I could do something in the US for once, and this is what we settled on. Doesn't it sound great?"

Erin laughed. "If you say so. I would never tire of sunny beaches, but that's just me."

Eddie raised her eyebrows. "You'd be surprised how quickly beaches start to blur together. Anyway, I wanted to see if you could spare Jen for a little while. I want her to come with me on the trip."

Erin was surprised. While her aunt had taken them both on trips in the past, most of those had been when they were teenagers or young adults. It had been over a decade since either of them had done a solo trip with Eddie. They had, over the years, occasionally met somewhere, usually domestic, and a few years ago, just after their mother's funeral, they'd all gone to Dublin together, where her father had some cousins.

"I don't know," Erin said, glancing at Jen. "Do you think that's a good idea?"

Eddie waved her hand dismissively. "I can't think of anything better than a trip to get her mind off things. Nothing like travel to lighten a loss, that's what I always say."

"Yeah, but Boston?" Erin continued to look at Jen.

Jen sighed. "I know what you're thinking, Erin, but you don't have to worry. Boston is a big city, and I can't imagine that Charlie and I would ever run into each other there. It's just a coincidence."

"Maybe a happy one, depending on how you look at it," Eddie said. "You could, after all, arrange to meet up with him."

Jen shook her head. "No, Eddie, that's the last thing I want to do. But I would like to go with you. I could use a change of scenery." She turned to Erin. "So can I? Do you think you could handle it at the brewery without me for a while?"

"Of course!" Erin tried to sound enthusiastic. The truth was, Erin was a little useless at some of the day-to-day business affairs at the brewery and had no idea how she would do without her sister to help her for the holiday season. On the other hand, this might be exactly what Jen needed to break out of her funk—even Erin could see that. And if it could help her, Jen was going.

Eddie clapped her hands with joy and gave Erin a long hug. "Oh, goody. I'm so glad you agreed. Jen was telling me how busy you've been lately, but you can handle things on your own for a while. You have a good head on your shoulders."

"When will you be back?"

"By Christmas, at the latest," Eddie said. "It works out perfectly, in fact, since I was planning to come back then anyway. We should be here on the twenty-first or second."

Erin's stomach dropped a little with dismay. Even beyond the difficulty this would put her in at work, it was a very long time to go without Jen. More than sisters, they were also best friends, and Erin had only rarely been apart from her that long. She made herself suppress these feelings, however, as for the first time in days, Jen looked excited and happy.

A few minutes later, dinner was ready, so for a while Erin was able to forget that she would be on her own soon. Still, when they drove home a few hours later, Erin couldn't help feeling a kind of low, lonely dread. Without Jen here and with the alienation between her and Lottie, she would be very much alone these next weeks.

CHAPTER TEN

Things at the brewery had gone from bad to downright terrible in the last few days. Three weeks ago, just after Jen left with their Aunt Eddie, Erin had actually fooled herself into thinking she could handle her sister's absence. The first day, she'd managed to pay the bills, order ingredients, and settle a scheduling conflict between two of their servers. Due to the season and other extenuating circumstances, however, things had quickly fallen apart.

First, several staff members came down with the same cold. This happened every year and was especially common in restaurants and breweries, where people worked in close contact. Erin saw it coming from the first sneeze and sent her newest server home almost the moment she recognized that she was actually sick. It was too late. By the next day, three of her servers were home sick, and a few days later, almost all of them were. Again, this would have been inconvenient but fine almost any other time. Technically, Jen, Erin, and the other brewers could cover the tasting room, if necessary, and had done so before. But, as it was the year-end, several accounting tasks needed to be handled, several beers were due to be kegged and bottled, and Erin needed to get her Valentine's seasonal ale ready for their city's biggest holiday.

A week before Jen was due home, the brewery was essentially falling apart. Since the Brewing Festival, they'd stayed busy nearly every day. While this was, of course, a good thing, the new business couldn't have come at a worse time. While most of the staff members were back after their illness, Lydia had caught the cold early and was still "at home" recovering, though Erin suspected she was fine now. Still, Erin was almost at full staff without Lydia, but everyone's cumulative absences had set back several crucial tasks.

The Valentine's seasonal was brewing and would be ready at the end of January as scheduled, but this evening they'd run out of kegs for three of their most popular beers. New batches were ready to be kegged and bottled, but those were all-day tasks. Unless Erin stayed up all night and made the other brewers and one of the general staffers or servers stay up most of it too, the tasting room would be short several beers tomorrow, as well. Most of the regulars knew the situation and had been extremely forgiving today when their favorite beer wasn't available. Still, they had new customers every day, especially since their festival win, and the people who had never been in or didn't come in often weren't so tolerant. Being low or out of stock was the best way to lose customers—new or old—in any business, so getting all their lines on by tomorrow was Erin's number-one priority.

It was just after closing, and everyone at the brewery was worn and tired. Erin hadn't slept more than a few hours a night since Jen left, and while she'd managed to avoid the cold everyone else got, she was starting to feel run-down. Generally, she had a bit of downtime most days, when she could sit with the other brewers and plan ahead and joke a little. Instead, they'd all been forced to work nonstop since Thanksgiving. The usual brewery cheer, which persisted even at their busiest most of the time, had dried up weeks ago. People were short with each other and unhappy. Erin was terrified that people would start walking out. While the counter staff was putting on a good face for the public, even their usual bouncy happiness had seemed strained for a while now.

The business had one good aspect, at least, and that was to keep her mind occupied. At first, after Charlie and Darcy left, she had been so wrapped up in helping Jen get through her initial devastation, she'd been able to suppress most of her own feelings about Darcy deserting her. After Jen left with Eddie, however, it wasn't so easy. She didn't know why she was so upset. After all—she and Darcy barely knew each other. They'd slept together and little else. Erin kept telling herself that she was being ridiculous. They hadn't been dating, after all, and Darcy didn't owe her a thing. But despite telling herself this over and over, she couldn't help but dwell on her, and not having anyone to share any of this with wasn't helping. Still, while she was at work, she could forget about this pain for hours at a time, so, despite feeling like her business was imploding around her, she was relieved to have so much extra work.

Soaking wet from the cleaning hoses and her own sweat, Erin paused for a moment, leaning heavily on her broom. The floors in the brewery in front and behind the counter were sticky and gross by the end of every day and had to be hosed down and mopped every night. They used big push brooms to get the excess water off the floor in order for it to dry by morning, and everyone was at this last sweeping stage. Erin was trying to figure out a way to ask four of her staff members to stay overnight and help her keg and bottle, but she'd been putting it off all day. She could tell everyone, like her, simply wanted to go home.

Two servers—Jonathan and Emily—were just around the corner from her, and she'd been listening to their banter for a while. Judging from their conversation, they'd likely forgotten she was here, but, as she hadn't really heard anything seditious or important, she hadn't announced herself again. Her broom would be visible to anyone in their position, so they clearly didn't care if someone overheard them. They were starting to perk up now that their shift was almost over, but Erin could hear the fatigue in their voices.

"Thank God it's almost payday," Jonathan said.

"No shit," Emily responded. "My landlord's been up my ass all week."

"I still haven't gone Christmas shopping."

Emily laughed. "Really? You're one of those guys?"

He laughed. "No. I just haven't had the time. Been stuck in this place every day. Can't wait until Jen comes back."

Erin was smiling throughout this conversation, and then she had a terrible, horrible thought. For a moment, her heart seemed to seize. She dropped her broom to the floor with a loud crack, and a moment later she was dashing, at full speed, toward the office. She ran across the clean floor she'd just mopped, passing several startled coworkers.

Her worst fears were realized when she saw the red leather envelope sitting on the desk under a pile of paperwork. She'd meant to take it to the bank a week ago, but it had slipped her mind then and every day since. Aside from being long overdue, which would create an utterly massive headache of paperwork later on, the money should have been deposited long before now, specifically for payroll.

Erin's legs liquefied with terror, and she had to lean against the edge of the doorway for support. Her ears started ringing, and she barely made it to the little desk chair before she collapsed. Since it was the end of the month, and since Christmas and New Years were looming, a lot of the bills she would normally pay at the end of the month had come due early. Moreover, yesterday she'd made several purchases to get them ready for January. Usually, if something like this happened, she could have simply transferred money from one account to the other, but she knew their accounts would be short for payroll. With everyone working extra hours, a lot of people had overtime coming to them, which meant that payroll was huge this month. The checks would be issued or deposited at midnight tonight—two hours from now—from an account with very little money in it.

One of her assistant brewers, Javier, poked his head into the office. "Hey, Boss! Do you want me and Craig to stay late and keg tonight? Emily was just saying that three lines are out in the tasting room." He became quiet, seeming to see something in her face. "Are you okay? You look like you've seen a ghost or something."

Erin was still rattled and unable to answer. She spun the desk chair toward him and swallowed a couple of times, her words dead in her mouth.

"I screwed up big-time, Javi," she said, her voice barely above a whisper.

Javi seemed to sense that she wanted to talk to him privately, but as the office didn't have a door, he simply walked over to her and crouched down.

"What's up?"

Erin quickly explained the problem, and she watched his face fall as she spoke.

"Shit," he said.

"Shit is right."

"What are you going to do? Isn't there anything?"

Erin started to shake her head and then stopped. Actually, she could try one thing, right now, and her spirit rose with hope.

"I need to make some phone calls," she told him.

Javi got to his feet. "Okay, Erin. I'll get some of the others to stay back and help me with the kegging and bottling. Don't worry about that end, at least. Let me know if I can do anything."

She squeezed his hand, too emotional to respond. She'd just told the man that he might not get paid a few days before Christmas, yet he was willing to cover her ass and help her out.

Seeming to understand her wordless thanks, Javi left the room, and soon she could hear several complaining voices out in the brewery after he'd told them what he needed. It would take at least five people to keg and bottle without her. She shook her head to dismiss the situation and turned to the computer and phone. Their current complaints were a problem for another day. If she didn't take care of the payroll problem right now, she might not have any staff members to appease. She'd be lucky if, in addition to losing her staff, they didn't sue the hell out of her.

She took a deep breath and picked up the phone. It was ten thirty, a little late for a phone call, but she couldn't avoid it.

Her father answered on the first ring. "Hello?"

"Hey, Dad. I have a big problem over here at the brewery, and I need a miracle." She explained the problem and then stopped, holding her breath to wait for his rebuke.

Instead, her father chuckled. "I'm sorry to laugh, Erin, but that's not a problem at all. I've done it myself so many times, I wouldn't even begin to try to count."

Immediately, Erin relaxed. She'd made the right call.

"You just need to get the money in before midnight, right?"

"Yes, Dad, but how can I do that when the banks are closed?"

"If you have the money in a personal account, you can transfer it over right now. It takes some paperwork to clear it up later when you pay yourself back, but you can do it temporarily."

Erin laughed. "I don't have that kind of money, Dad."

"Okay, I didn't think so, but I didn't want to presume. You can go to an ATM right now and deposit it yourself. It takes a while, but you just might be able to do it before midnight."

Erin had to think for a minute. Everything related to the business was done electronically now. In fact, generally the payroll was moved over electronically from the regular funds. She'd intended to use several checks she'd been paid by local restaurants and the register cash for payroll only because this month's register receipts had been so large. People apparently liked to stop by for a beer between holiday shopping trips. However, they'd never used the ATM debit card for the payroll account. She wasn't even sure where it was. But she did have a copy of the card for the general account, which meant that if she got the money deposited, she could transfer it over. She checked the clock and her heart sank. She had just over an hour to do all of that.

"Is there another option?" she asked.

He was quiet for a moment, and then he cleared his throat. "Well, I could lend you the money, temporarily. That creates even more of a headache to do it legally, but it can be done. I'm sure Jen will know how to clear it up when she comes home."

Erin flushed with pleasure. A month ago, if she'd asked for a loan even half the size of what she needed right now, he would have lectured her for hours and then likely only done it for Jen's sake. Things had decidedly changed since their conversation on Thanksgiving.

"Thanks, Dad, I really appreciate it. I'm going to try to do the ATM thing, I guess. It doesn't make sense to create more work for ourselves. If I leave now, I should be able to get the money in on time."

"Okay, honey, you do that. And let me know what happens tomorrow. I still want to talk to you about your business soon, but I'll let you go now." He paused. "Before you hang up, do me a favor, would you? I know Loveland's not a big city, but plenty of bad guys are out there, anyway. Take someone with you. For me, if not for yourself. I don't like thinking of you out there with all that cash all alone."

"I'll do that, Dad. Bye."

She grabbed the envelope, double-checked that she had the ATM card for the general account, and then went into the brewery proper. Javier and four other staff members were already wrapped up in the kegging process, and it would clearly take all of them to get the work done. Everyone was holding hose lines or other equipment, and not one of them could be spared. Erin was tempted to simply go to the bank on her own, but she suddenly remembered one person she could call this late at night. She pulled out her cell phone, hesitated, and then called Lottie.

"Hello? What's up, Erin? Why are you calling so late?"

"Lottie, I'm so sorry. I didn't know who else to call. Do you think you could meet me over at Chase Bank? On Seventh? I have a crap ton of money to deposit, and I don't want to be there by myself. I know it's a lot to ask, but could you?"

Lottie was quiet for a long time. Finally, Erin heard her sigh. "Sure, Erin. I'll meet you there in five."

"You're a lifesaver, Lottie. Thank you."

Erin told Javier she'd be back in half an hour to help, and he gave her a quick nod. She went to the alley door, where she kept her bike, and wheeled it into the alley. She crammed the leather envelope into her little fanny pack, strapped on her helmet, and turned on her headlamp. A moment later she was pedaling as fast as she could through the back alleys of downtown Loveland.

Lottie was waiting when she got to the bank. It was decidedly cold out, and her breath was steaming in the air. She was huddled into her long, down jacket, wrapped up with a scarf and hat. Erin hadn't even noticed the cold until now, but seeing Lottie suddenly brought her attention to the fact that she'd come here without her coat.

Erin stood astride her bike for a moment and then leaped off, running over to Lottie and pulling her into a tight hug. "I've been such an asshole, Lottie. I'm so sorry."

Lottie hugged her just as hard and then drew away. Erin could see tears in her eyes.

"Yes, you have, and I forgive you. I'm sorry I haven't tried to talk to you all this time. I was too angry."

"And you have every right to be. Let me make this deposit really quick, and we can talk about it more."

The process was actually quite fast. It took only one transaction to deposit all of the checks, and only a few to get all of the cash deposited. She used the ATM to transfer the money to her payroll account, dismayed to see that not all of the money was immediately available. This had been her fear from the beginning of this saga. The only thing she could hope for now was that, regardless of whether some of the money needed to be cleared, the paychecks would be issued tonight anyway. She didn't have any other options at this point, so she just had to hope this would do.

Lottie had stood nearby, quietly waiting, and when Erin finished, she explained what had happened with the money.

Lottie shrugged. "You're likely to run into some kind of problem, which might mean a bunch of fees, but I think the paychecks should be issued, or at least most of them—whatever the cash covers, anyway. The rest should be cleared up in a few days."

Erin sighed. "I'll be lucky if anyone is still working for us by the time Jen gets back. I'm a fucking idiot, Lottie. In more ways than one."

"Yes, you are."

The cold finally started getting to her, and Erin shivered, hard. Lottie grinned and came close enough to rub her arms with her hands.

"Where's your coat, you weirdo? You should get out of this cold."

"I need to get to the brewery. We have some bottling and other things to do tonight."

"You could use a good night's sleep."

"I could, but I won't get it tonight. It's almost Christmas, so at least we might have a couple of days off soon." Erin paused, and an overwhelming sense of sorrow and regret swept through her. Lottie had been her friend for almost three decades, and Erin had basically turned her back on her without explanation. She opened her mouth to say something to this effect, but Lottie held up a hand to stop her. "Let's talk tomorrow, okay, Erin? I'm too cold and tired to have a real conversation right now. Let's meet at the coffee shop for lunch. Noon okay?"

Erin agreed and gave her another hug before they parted. It was cold enough that by the time she got back to the brewery, her tears had frozen to her face.

❖

The other brewers had made good progress so that when Erin showed up, it took only another three hours to finish. By the time everyone left, little snowflakes were flying through the air. It was so cold that they were melting and freezing on the ground, making the sidewalks and streets slick with ice, so Erin was forced to walk her bike all the way home. She slept hard and deep for seven hours—the longest she'd slept since Jen left—and then went into work. Her staff, including the other brewer there, insisted that she leave for the day at noon, so when she went to meet Lottie, she had the whole afternoon off. Lottie had taken the rest of the day for shopping, so they decided to spend it together by driving down to Boulder.

Boulder, a beautiful little city in the foothills of the Rockies, is about forty-five minutes from Loveland and about the same from Denver, barring traffic. Colorado State in Fort Collins, where Erin had attended, and the University of Colorado at Boulder are rivals, and this rivalry had stretched from sports into a kind of competitive attitude between the two cities for some time. Erin had always considered Boulderites snobbish and clannish, in part because the City of Boulder was so wealthy, unlike the more middle- and working-class Fort Collins. It didn't help that a lot of trust-fund students were in Boulder, many of whom dressed like they were either homeless or going skiing year-round. Nevertheless, no one could deny that Boulder was beautiful, and now that she'd been out of college for over ten years, the snobbish chip on her shoulder had lessened, and she'd more or less allowed herself to accept that Boulder had its cute parts, too.

Their first stop in town was a brewery. Erin had heard that Avery Brewery had done a series of sour beers over the summer, and while they were out of season now, she was interested to see if they had any bottles she could try. One of the brewers ended up joining them, and before they knew it, they'd been there more than an hour tasting and joking around. After he excused himself, Erin saw Lottie was watching her, grinning.

"What?" Erin asked.

Lottie shook her head. "It's just funny. You get your first day off in God knows how long, and you basically end up talking about work."

Erin grinned. "I guess I love my job."

They were quiet for a while, finishing their tasters. Avery had several sours and a gose, and while they were all in bottles, Erin had been able to try them. She glanced over at Lottie to share her pleasure and felt her stomach drop a little with sorrow and something like dread. She'd missed Lottie a lot. Lottie had been perfectly pleasant to her all afternoon and on the drive down here, but a thick tension simmered between them. They'd avoided the conversation they needed to have, but if they didn't have it soon, things might be ruined between them forever. While she'd kept her distance these last few weeks, Erin couldn't picture her life without her friend long-term. She'd never forgive herself if she didn't try. They spoke at the same time.

"Listen, Lottie—"

"Erin—"

They both stopped and laughed. Lottie motioned with her hand to start first, and Erin swallowed. "Lottie, I'm so sorry. I really am. I shouldn't have turned my back on you. You're not Will and he's not you. I've been an asshole."

Lottie's face crumpled for a moment, and then she nodded, quickly, as if to dismiss her emotion.

"You have every right to be pissed at me, Lottie. I should have reached out to you to explain. I'm sorry."

Lottie took a deep breath, and then met Erin's eyes. "I told you I forgive you, and I do. But thank you for saying it again. I've needed to hear it. I've never been so...disappointed in someone, Erin. I mean, I guess you must have your reasons, but whatever happened between you and Will when you were kids—"

Erin's face twisted, and she suddenly found herself on the verge of crying. She closed her eyes and took a couple of deep breaths before looking at Lottie again.

Her eyebrows were knit, and her face had bleached of color. "Wait a minute," she said. "Did he do something to you? When you were younger?"

Erin couldn't help the tears that started leaking out of her eyes, and she nodded, quickly, once, and closed her eyes again. It had been one thing telling Darcy, but she had never told anyone close to her. For the most part, she'd suppressed the terror and disgust she'd felt that summer. She might have actually forgotten it altogether had she never seen him again. Erin made herself breathe in and out of her nose a couple of times and opened her eyes again to meet Lottie's. Lottie seemed scared now as well as horrified. Her lips were trembling, and she was gripping her glass of beer hard enough to make her hands shake. Erin put her hands over Lottie's on the glass.

"I'm going to tell you now. I've only ever told one other person..." She pictured the scene with Darcy at the festival. Darcy's eyes had been full of concern, and her hands had been warm and soothing on Erin's. She shook her head to dismiss the memory and met Lottie's eyes again. She had to swallow a few times first, but she finally managed to choke out her story.

Lottie's face was blank when she finished. Erin was so nervous to see her reaction, she shook all over now, but Lottie had gone completely still. Erin motioned to the floor staff and ordered them both a full glass of the seasonal ale, and Lottie remained quiet until it was delivered. The tap room was packed with shoppers between trips, but they had a little corner of the counter to themselves. Erin sipped at her beer nervously, but Lottie continued to stare, seemingly at nothing. Finally, too shaken to let the silence go on any longer,

Erin touched Lottie's shoulder, and she jumped, startled back into reality. Lottie's eyes were swimming, and the two of them reached for each other without another word, hugging fiercely. When they pulled away, their eyes were shining, and they both turned their attention to their beers to avoid breaking down altogether.

"Jesus, Erin," Lottie finally said. She took a little napkin from a pile behind the bar and blew her nose. Her eyes and nose were bright red from crying. "I'm so sorry. When you told me that he was a pest to you when you were kids, I just thought he was bratty or snobby or something. I never thought…Jesus. He was a monster. No wonder you reacted the way you did." She shook her head. "I just wish you'd told me sooner."

"I didn't want to. I was too embarrassed. Even now, more than twenty years later, I'm embarrassed. Disgusted, even. It's not as bad as it was then, but definitely not great now, either."

Lottie put her hand on hers and squeezed it once. "Now I know why you've been acting that way to him, though, Erin. Thank you for telling me. He and I are going to have to have a long talk about it tonight, and if I don't get a good explanation, I guess…" She shook her head. "I don't want to think about that right now. Can we change the subject?"

"Yes. Please. Otherwise I'm going to be sobbing into this glass all afternoon."

"Tell me about Jen, then. How is she doing? Have you heard from her? How is her trip going?"

The thought warmed Erin, and she smiled with genuine happiness. "I think it's going great. I've talked to her and Aunt Eddie almost every day since they left. They've been skiing, snow-mobiling, snowshoeing, and all other things snow-related. They've eaten mountains of lobster and clam chowder, and they've seen lots of cute little New England towns and villages. I've already had to wade through a thousand pictures online. Jen also sent me this postcard of downtown Portland, in Maine, and it was absolutely adorable. Looks a little like Fort Collins or Boulder, actually."

"When do they get back?"

"Christmas Eve or the day before, if all goes well. Aunt Eddie plans to stay with us for the holiday instead of here in Boulder. Usually she just comes up for the day, but I guess she wants to be near Jen a little longer. I've talked to Eddie a couple of times, just the two of us, and she's still pretty worried about her. I guess Jen's come out of her shell some and started behaving more normally, but she sometimes hears Jen crying at night."

Lottie set her glass down and wiped the foam off her lips. "Goddamn Charlie. That asshole. I can't believe he did that to her."

"Right? He seemed like such a nice person. I was halfway convinced he would ask her to marry him. I mean, I know it would have been premature and all that, but still. They really seemed attached."

"Do you think Darcy orchestrated everything?"

Erin hadn't had the opportunity to tell Lottie about what had happened between her and Darcy. That had all occurred after they'd stopped talking. For a moment, she was tempted to share the story, but she decided to let it go. Nothing had really happened, after all, and her first impression had apparently been the right one. Darcy was, after all, a bitch.

"It looked like it was Darcy's fault when they were leaving, but I don't know for sure." Erin took a long pull on her beer and then shrugged. "Hell, maybe it was for the best. If they'd stayed longer, it would have been even harder on Jen."

The same could be said about Darcy and Erin, but Erin didn't add that point. She still didn't want to talk about what had and hadn't happened and wasn't sure she ever would. Maybe if no one knew about their brief affair, Darcy's name would never come up again.

After she and Lottie finished their beers, they decided against driving for the time being and took the bus downtown to give themselves a chance to sober up. There were several mountaineering shops there, and Lottie needed to stop in just about every one for a different gift for family members. She was the only person in her immediate family who wasn't married and the only one of her parents' daughters without kids, which meant she had multiple couples and children to buy for. By the time they finished, both of them were carrying several large paper bags stuffed with presents.

They'd gone into the last store for the day on Pearl Street Mall, an outdoor pedestrian walkway with shops and restaurants. The day was bright and sunny, the snow from last night long gone. It was warmer than Erin had expected, and little rivulets of sweat were running down her back under her heavy down coat. She was shifting some of the heavier bags around to redistribute the weight from one arm to another when she heard Lottie gasp next to her. She glanced at her and then followed Lottie's gaze.

Darcy was walking directly toward them down Pearl Street Mall.

CHAPTER ELEVEN

It took Erin a long time to realize that what she was seeing was actually real. She would never have expected to see Darcy here. It took her even longer to realize that Darcy wasn't alone. She was with three people: an older woman in elegant clothing and two younger ones around their own age, one of whom slightly resembled Darcy.

She had spotted them before they'd seen her, and she was walking toward them, a determined grimace plastered on her face. Erin had just enough time to throw Lottie a panicked glance before Darcy was suddenly there, holding out her hand.

"Erin," she said. Her voice, like her expression, was cold and dour, and Erin wondered for a moment why she'd even come over.

"Darcy," Erin said, shaking her hand briefly. "You remember my friend Lottie?"

Darcy smiled at her, and then everyone stood there in awkward silence. Erin was unable to think of a single thing to say.

Finally, one of the younger women next to Darcy laughed out loud. "Christ, Darcy, aren't you going to introduce us?"

"Yes," the older woman said, staring at Darcy strangely. "Please. Introduce us, dear."

Darcy seemed to snap out of it, and her cheeks flushed slightly.

"Forgive me. This is Erin Bennet and her friend Lottie..." Darcy looked to Lottie.

"Lucas," Lottie said, grinning. She seemed to enjoy Darcy's clear embarrassment.

"And how do you know each other?" the older woman asked.

"We met at Erin's brewery. Up in Loveland."

"Oh, did you now?" the woman said, eyeing Erin. "You're a brewer? That's very interesting. I don't know that I've met any women brewers."

Erin gave her a strained smile. "We're a rare breed, it's true."

The woman smiled weakly, clearly just as unimpressed by this meeting as she was. Again, the group slipped into an awkward silence, and Erin found herself staring into Darcy's eyes. The expression there had turned from icy coldness to something like anger, but that wasn't quite it either. She seemed pained, almost hurt.

Suddenly, the younger woman who had spoken earlier stepped forward. "Since Darcy is clearly the worst person in the world to do this, I'll introduce the rest of us, Erin. My name is Wilhelmina, or Willie. I'm Darcy's cousin. This is my mother, Darcy's aunt Catherine," she indicated the older woman, "and this is our friend Anne." She indicated the other younger woman.

Erin and Lottie shook their hands and greeted them, Lottie much more warmly than Erin was currently capable of. She was still too surprised to do much more than stand there stupidly.

"We were just heading to dinner at the Oak," Willie said. "Care to join us?"

Erin almost shouted her refusal. "Oh, we really have to be—"

"We'd love to," Lottie said, grinning at her. "I'm starving."

"Great!" Willie said. "I was afraid it would be another dinner talking about politics or climate change or something else dire and awful. With you two along, maybe we can talk about something fun for once. I, for one, would love to hear more about your brewery, Erin."

"Wilhelmina, I'm certain that Erin was just about to decline," Catherine said. "Don't be rude. They seem to have things to do."

Willie stared at Erin, a clear hint of panic in her eyes, and Erin laughed out loud at the expression. While the resemblance between her and her cousin Darcy was slight, it was still there, and something about this woman's open friendliness coupled with a version of Darcy's cool beauty was disarming. It made Erin want to do whatever she wanted.

"Of course we'll come, if it's not too much of an imposition," Erin said.

"Great!" Willie said. She turned to Lottie. "So, Lottie, tell me all about yourself. We can let Darcy and Erin get caught up. Can I take some of those bags for you?"

As with the Brewing Festival last month, Erin and Darcy were left side by side, Catherine and Anne just in front of them. Erin knew that Lottie was only going along with this because she'd seen how embarrassed the whole situation made Darcy, so she was going to have to make the best of it. Darcy had silently taken some of the bags Erin was carrying so that both of them were only slightly encumbered, and Erin's shoulders felt much better for it. She turned to thank Darcy, only to find her staring at her, that same strange, pained expression in her eyes. She looked away quickly and scrambled for something to say.

"We're here for Christmas," Darcy suddenly said.

Erin turned, raising her eyebrows, and Darcy flushed a little. "I mean, we're in Colorado for Christmas. We're heading to Aspen tomorrow. My aunt has a place there."

"Oh?" Erin asked.

Darcy nodded, and they relapsed into quiet. It stretched, and again, Erin found herself scrambling for small talk just to ease the tension between them.

They spoke at the same time.

"How is Charlie—?"

"How is your sister?"

Erin gave Darcy a wry grin. "She's fine. At least I think she is. She's away right now with our aunt on a trip." She didn't want to elaborate, feeling a little like she was betraying Jen by saying even this much.

"Glad to hear it. And Charlie's fine, too. The board at the brewery has agreed to let him continue as interim chair for another six months. They were impressed with his new ideas and agreed to let him try to brew a couple of new beer ideas he picked up here on a trial basis. From what I could gather, it'll be a little like a test. If the beers market well, they'll keep him on more permanently."

"That's good," Erin said.

Their conversation dried up, and they walked in silence for another block. Lottie and Willie were talking rapidly in front of them, both of them pausing to laugh now and again and throw furtive glances their way.

"They must be talking about us," Erin said, sticking her tongue out.

Darcy sighed. "My cousin has always been the child of the family."

Erin looked at her sharply, surprised. "That's a little harsh."

Darcy shrugged. "I don't mean it in a derogatory way. She's simply a little less mature than the rest of us."

"I guess I should have known that you don't like to be teased."

Darcy glanced at her quickly and then away. After a moment, she nodded. "It's true. I don't have a tolerance for it. I've never liked being laughed at, even by people close to me."

"That's a shame," Erin said, meeting her eyes. "I do love to laugh."

Darcy's face underwent a series of shifting expressions, from hurt to surprise to again something like pain. After all, Erin thought, what difference does it make to Darcy what I like or don't like? Erin pretended to become absorbed in her bags to hide her own embarrassment. Why had she said that? It wasn't as if they would ever see each other again after this dinner. Something about Darcy always made her say and do stupid, impulsive things. She couldn't help but shift into the personal with her.

Their arrival at the restaurant saved her from an explanation, and Darcy had to speak with the host to see if they could arrange a different table for the larger party. A few minutes later they were seated, and Catherine insisted on making everyone sit in specific places at the table.

"I want to be able to talk to new people," she explained. "I want to hear all about your brewery, Erin. Tell me how you got into such a masculine business. How on earth did your parents let you do it?"

Erin choked on her water and saw Darcy staring at her aunt with something like horror. Willie, who was sitting next to her, laughed out loud and slapped Erin on the back.

"Yes, Erin, please, tell us what drew you to that manly business?"

"Uh, well, it's a very popular small business here in the state."

"Indeed," Catherine chimed in. "My niece Darcy has been doing an exposé of all the little places here in Northern Colorado. Some of them, as I understand, are quite good. I wouldn't know, as I never drink beer."

"Erin's place is the one I was telling you about, Catherine," Darcy said. "The review that's coming out tomorrow? The one I showed you?"

"Indeed!" Catherine said, looking surprised. "Well, that is shocking. I would never have guessed."

Darcy was smiling when Erin met her eyes, but before Erin could follow up, their waiter arrived for the drink order. Everyone at the table was wrapped up in their menus after this, and the moment slipped away. Erin couldn't bring up the review without giving away her newfound anxiety about it, and something in Darcy's smile had suggested that she didn't need to worry about it. After all, Darcy had nothing to say but good things about her beer. At the very least, the review shouldn't be outright terrible. Even if it was only middling, it shouldn't hurt their current boom.

As they waited for their food, Erin realized that she was more shaken by this meeting than she'd admitted to herself earlier. She'd been surprised to see Darcy, and her heart had been racing almost since the moment she'd walked over to them, but even here, sitting apart from her, her hands were shaking and her face and palms felt sweaty and cold. All of the feelings she'd suppressed this month were back, making her head whirl and her heart pound even harder. She could hardly look at Darcy for fear of saying something, doing something, to give herself away. She stood up, excused herself, and headed to the restroom. If she didn't get away for a few seconds she would do something rash.

There was a small washroom in front of the women's toilets, and Erin stopped at one of the sinks and splashed cold water on her face. She needed to figure out a way to get out of here soon without causing a scene. She desperately tried to think of an excuse—anything to get Lottie to understand that she needed to leave, but her mind was blank, still swimming in anguish. She met her eyes in the mirror and her pale, scared face.

"Get it together, Erin," she whispered. She had to leave.

The door opened a moment later, and Darcy stood behind her in the reflection. They met each other's eyes, and finally Erin turned toward her. Darcy continued to move closer, and then they were in each other's arms, Darcy's mouth meeting hers in a crushing kiss. Their embrace was desperate, tight, painful almost, and a moment later, Erin had to make herself push Darcy away. They both took a wary step apart, Erin shaking all over.

"Darcy, we can't," Erin said, still breathing heavily.

That pained expression passed over Darcy's face again, and she nodded. "I know. I'm sorry. I just couldn't…I mean, I needed to—"

Erin held up a hand to silence her. "I don't want to hear it, Darcy. Don't you get it? I can't do this. *We* can't do this. You must see that."

A moment later, Darcy nodded, but her eyes suddenly filled with tears. "I know. This is about Charlie and Jen, right?"

Erin nodded and then shook her head. "It is, but it isn't. I mean it's also us, isn't it? How could this ever work? What's happening between us?"

Darcy shook her head. "I don't know."

Erin took another deep breath and let it out. "We shouldn't be in here together. The others will wonder what's happening. I'll go out there and make up some excuse so Lottie and I can leave."

Darcy grabbed her arm. "Don't. Please don't go. I haven't told anyone, and I don't want to have to explain—"

"Don't you see I can hardly stand it? When I'm around you…" She shook her head. It was hard to explain, and even harder to say out loud. Being around Darcy made her feel unmoored, shaken.

Darcy took a step closer, and Erin held her breath. She had to stop herself from leaping into her arms again.

"Please stay. For me." Darcy's voice was barely above a whisper. "I won't ever bother you again."

Erin stared into her gray eyes for a long moment, and finally her heart rate slowed and calmed. She felt steadier now that they'd finally had it out, and she realized what it would look like if she and Lottie left now. It would cause more questions than she was willing to deal with.

Finally, she sighed in defeat. "Okay. I won't leave."

Darcy's shoulders dropped. "Thank you."

"I better go out there now. Give it a minute or two before you join me, or they're going to know we were in here together."

The dining room was bright and noisy after the quiet of the washroom, and for a moment Erin wasn't sure she could go through with this. Then she saw Lottie, happily chatting away with Willie at the table, and knew she must. If she didn't, the whole thing would come out right then and there. As calmly as she could, she walked toward their table, relieved to see that the food was arriving with her. No one even glanced at her as she sat down, giving her a couple of extra seconds to compose herself.

She kept her eyes fixed in front of her, only dimly aware that Darcy had rejoined them, too. Catherine turned her attention to Lottie as they ate, and Erin sagged with relief. The older woman's earlier attentions were a little hard to take. She glanced to her right and met Willie's smiling face.

"You are really quite striking," Willie said.

Erin couldn't help but blush, and she laughed uncomfortably. "Thanks." Like Willie, she kept her voice low enough that, in the relative noisiness of the dining room, none of the others at the table could hear them.

"When Darcy was talking about you before, I didn't think she was being quite honest with me. She has a tendency to exaggerate."

"She talked about me to you? Before this?" Erin's stomach dropped. How much had Darcy shared?

Willie nodded, turning to her food. "She said she'd met an interesting brewer while she was here." She was grinning as if she'd said something funny, but Erin didn't get it.

Erin's relief warred with something like hurt feelings. While she was glad she wouldn't have to talk about her affair with Darcy with this nice, but unfamiliar woman, she was a little hurt that Darcy hadn't told anyone. Then again, neither had she.

Erin swallowed a sip of water. "Interesting? That's all she said?"

Willie grinned at her. "That's why I thought she was exaggerating. That's the nicest compliment she ever gives someone she likes. She's a close one, our Darcy."

While nothing would ever come of it, it was still pleasing to know that Darcy had, in fact, been interested in her, not simply bored and passing time. The moment in the sitting room and now Willie's words confirmed this assumption. Like Erin, Darcy had felt something for her. She was incredibly beautiful, and Erin had seen what she could be like when her reserve melted that ice a little. Darcy would have gotten serious with her under different circumstances. It hadn't just been an affair after all—Erin could admit that to herself now. She cared about Darcy.

Trying to hide these feelings, Erin gave Willie a wide, if somewhat false, grin. "So you thought she was exaggerating when she said that I was interesting?"

Willie shrugged. "Hey. I've seen some of the women she called interesting before. And believe me, they weren't."

Both of them laughed, and Darcy, who was stuck chatting with Anne, looked at them suspiciously. They both laughed harder, and Darcy narrowed her eyes at them before turning to Anne.

"Who's she?" Erin asked, tilting her head at Anne.

"The woman my mother wants Darcy to marry."

Erin almost spit out her drink again and had to swallow painfully to keep from choking. She had a sudden flash of memory from several weeks ago. Charlie had mentioned this woman in passing to Darcy.

"Why?" Erin managed. "Why does she want her to marry her, I mean?"

"She might not look it, but Anne's a multimillionaire. She owns hotels all over the world. My mother met her at a charity function in Aspen last year, and when she found out she was a lesbian, she became determined to hook them up. I'm pretty sure she thinks lesbians are like pandas or something—just get two of them in the same room, and they'll fall in love. I think Anne's game, but Darcy is completely uninterested. Why she just doesn't tell my mother off is a mystery."

Erin watched Darcy and Anne for a while with horrified curiosity and soon reached the same conclusion as Willie. While it was clear that Darcy was polite enough to be civil to Anne, she was clearly just that—polite. Anne was gazing at Darcy with fawning appreciation, but Darcy's expression remained simply attentive. Erin was pretty sure she could recognize Darcy's attraction now, and this wasn't it. The thought gave her a stab of embarrassment, and she looked away quickly, only to find Willie grinning at her.

"Do you find Darcy interesting yourself, Erin?"

Erin guffawed and then put a hand over her mouth when everyone turned her way. "Sorry," she said to the others. She lowered her voice again and spoke to Willie. "I'm not going to answer that question, Willie. God knows what you'll do with the answer. I've known you less than an hour, and I can already tell you're a gossip."

They shared a conspiratorial smile and then ate in silence for a while. Just when Erin had convinced herself that the dinner could end without more personal questions from this woman, Willie set her silverware down and sighed.

"That was really wonderful. I don't know what I expected from the restaurants out here, but they've all been great."

Erin shook her head. "Not you, too. I thought your cousin was the snob. Guess what. Even people in 'flyover country' know how to cook."

Willie held up her hands. "Sorry, sorry. I deserve that." She leaned forward a little, lowering her voice again. "Hey, I wanted to ask you something you could probably answer."

"Sure, what?"

"Darcy was telling me about this other woman brewer here in the state."

"Another interesting one?"

Willie grinned. "Not interesting to Darcy, no, but to her friend Charlie. He apparently had some kind of fling with her when he was here. Jane or Jackie, something like that. Do you know her?"

Erin's stomach dropped. Darcy had clearly not told Willie about her connection with Jen, if that's who Willie was talking about. Erin decided to make sure. Her throat felt suddenly constricted, and she swallowed with some difficulty. "Do you mean Jen?" She almost whispered.

Willie pointed at her. "That's it! That's the name. Darcy said this Jen was taking Charlie for a ride. Just wanted his money. Darcy decided to step in and save him before it was too late. The guy was actually thinking of buying her a ring, if you can believe it."

Erin was staring at Darcy now, her stomach now reeling with sorrow and disappointment. "But Darcy stopped him?"

"Yes. Luckily Darcy said she talked Charlie into leaving while he was ahead. He's out the dinners he bought her and some overnights at hotels, but nothing more serious. Anyway, since you know Jen, could you do me a favor?"

Angry tears rose to her eyes, and she looked down at her plate to hide them from Willie. She took a calming breath. "What kind of favor?"

"If you see her, could you sock her in the eye for me? Charlie Betters is about the nicest person in the world. I hate to think of someone trying to take advantage of him."

Later, at home in bed, Erin wasn't really sure how she made it through the rest of the dinner, but she managed to pass off her altered behavior as a headache. She and Darcy avoided each other as they said their good-byes. Erin was glad for the earlier awkwardness that allowed her to keep from meeting her eyes. She was pretty sure Darcy would see her anger there, and she didn't want to say anything in front of the others.

She kept the news from Lottie on the drive home, rolling Willie's words over and over again in her mind.

Only when she was alone, sitting on her bed with the lights off, did she let herself feel the depth of Darcy's betrayal. She had known in her gut that Darcy was the reason Charlie had left so abruptly, but she had never once thought it had anything to do with money. Bile rose in her throat with the heat of her anger, and she jumped to her feet, fists clenched, almost ready to track Darcy down and punch her in the face. She paced around inside her dark house long enough to let the anger pass, and when it did, she felt drained and depressed. She sank down on her bed, still clothed, and passed out from fatigue.

She'd never been as disappointed in someone as she was in Darcy. What she'd done was unforgivable. And she would never forgive herself for getting involved with her.

CHAPTER TWELVE

With only a few days left before Christmas, the brewery was packed the next day with tired shoppers and out-of-towners home for the holidays. Thankfully, Erin was too busy to think about anything but the next task for most of the morning and afternoon. She wanted to give all of her employees the evening of Christmas Eve and the day of Christmas off, but it was going to be tight to see if that was even possible. The brewery would be closed to the public at that time, but if she and the rest of the staff didn't manage to take care of several things before then, she would have to ask some of them to come in on Christmas Day. Just about everyone who worked for her was waiting for the announcement of their vacation, but she didn't want to disappoint anyone by telling them prematurely. They would be closed, so most of the front counter staff knew they had the time off, but everyone else was still waiting.

Luckily, she still had a full staff. Two or three had grumbled about late paychecks, but the bank had sorted everything out by that afternoon. The people who hadn't been paid yesterday had gotten their deposit at midnight, and everyone had been warned beforehand in a staff-wide email. Even the fees Erin owed were nominal, considering what could have happened. On the whole, she was lucky the disaster hadn't been worse.

During a lull in the late afternoon, Erin let Lydia and the other counter staff go home early before the evening shift arrived. A lone pair of drinkers sat in the corner—two men—but they kept to themselves, talking in hushed voices and bent over their beers. One of them was clearly upset about something, and they both gave the impression of wanting to be left alone. Erin did just that.

However, for the first time all day, Erin had nothing immediate to do. In her current mood, this was bad. She needed to stay busy, or the bleak, angry darkness that had come over her last night would take over again. She'd been so upset that her entire evening, from the drive home and afterward, seemed like a bad dream. She couldn't help but think of Jen, and a wave of anxiety and sorrow washed over her again.

The counter staff used a couple of tablets as the cash register for credit-card transactions, but, as the brewery was so quiet right now, one of them was available. She detached it from the stand and opened her Facebook account, hoping to see more pictures from Jen and Aunt Eddie. Sure enough, another huge batch of photos showed up, all of them from Boston, where they were now at the end of their trip. Uninterested in the pictures of places and things, Erin scrolled through them, searching for some of Jen. For the most part, she had remained absent from the series her aunt had posted these last weeks, with, at best, a side profile or a shot from behind; however, there was an occasional shot of her entire face, as there was in this batch.

Erin's heart sank when she saw the photo. Jen's smile was weak and strained. Her face was pale, with dark circles under her eyes, and she looked as if she'd lost some weight. During their almost-nightly phone calls, Erin had detected a note of phony happiness in Jen's voice from time to time. She'd said all the right things, but something had been off in Jen's tone. These pictures proved it. While she might pretend to be better now, over Charlie and the heartbreak, she clearly wasn't. The two or three times Erin had talked to their aunt on the phone over the last weeks had also seemed to confirm exactly that. Aunt Eddie had suggested things were a little better, but she'd also told her that Jen was certainly not back to normal. Sighing, Erin put the tablet away.

Too agitated to stand there waiting for a customer, she decided to polish the high tables in the center of the tasting room. The sides of the tasting room had smaller, more intimate tables, but the center of the room contained three long, group tables that stretched nearly its length. They were tall and, like all of the wood in the brewery, made of beetle kill pine, all a shiny warm yellow. Tall metal stools were set up along each side, and Erin pushed moved these aside to give herself room to work.

Jen had long ago insisted on using all-natural products for as many of the cleaning and upkeep tasks as possible, and after Erin began rubbing the first long table with lemon oil, she sent Jen a silent thought of thankfulness. No customer should smell harsh cleaners in a brewery, and the lemon, mixed with the heady odors of yeast and hops, was delicious and cheering. It was just one more example of Jen's wisdom and good sense.

Erin had known she would miss her sister during this time, and it was more than simply needing her here at work. Jen was her best friend, and it was difficult to be without her for so long. Not since college had they spent so much time apart, and her absence had been trying and depressing.

The polishing task absorbed and pleased her so much that she barely noticed when the door opened behind her. The jingle bells they'd hung for the holiday chimed merrily, but she didn't immediately turn around. She sent out a general greeting and told the customer she'd be right there, but continued polishing the table, nearly finished. When she finally looked up, smiling, it took her a long beat to realize that Darcy was now sitting at the front counter.

Erin froze in place, clutching the little rag and bottle of lemon oil she'd been using. The smile died on her face, and pure fury rose up from within. She flashed from hot to deadly cold and clutched the rag and the bottle so hard she started shaking. With careful, quiet calculation, she set the bottle and rag down on the table she'd just polished, afraid that if she continued to hold them, she might throw them.

Erin took a couple of steps closer and then stopped, afraid to approach Darcy in her current fury. "What do you want?"

Darcy seemed surprised at her tone, her eyebrows shooting up. "I'm sorry. Have I come at a bad time?"

Erin closed her eyes and took a long, deep breath. If she was going to get through this without flying off the handle, she needed to control her anger. It was always better to be civil during an argument. She'd learned this over the years with her father. It was always smarter to be the better man, as it were, than fly into a furious rage. She opened her eyes and calmly walked around behind the bar counter. She wanted to have a kind of barrier between them, for Darcy's safety and her own. Darcy turned in her stool to face her, and they stayed there, staring at each other in total silence.

Again, Erin took a deep breath, let it out, and finally relaxed a little. "How can I help you?"

As before, Darcy seemed confused, but she shook her head and changed her expression to something like natural before speaking. "I wanted to talk to you before my family and I head up to Aspen. I wasn't sure if I would get another chance to see you this trip, so I just drove here from Boulder. I couldn't let things stay how they are."

Erin didn't reply.

Darcy flushed a little, but she continued. "You see, the thing is, I've been thinking about us. A lot. I mean, even before we ran into each other yesterday…I don't know how to tell you…" There was a long pause as she sat there silently. Darcy's face darkened further, and her eyes darted away from Erin's. She swallowed a few times, and for the first time, Erin could see that she was agitated, nervous about something. With someone so generally placid and calm, Darcy's nervousness, which might go unnoticed in someone else, was striking. Darcy looked at her with something like panic in her eyes, clearly hoping for some kind of help, and still, Erin didn't say a word.

Darcy took a deep breath and let it out. "Okay. I'm just going to say it. God knows what you'll think of me when I do, but I feel like if I don't tell you, I'm going to lose my mind."

Erin's curiosity rose a little, piercing her cold anger, but she wasn't curious enough to overcome her hurt and resentment. She kept her mouth closed but nodded slightly.

Darcy seemed relieved to see that Erin was willing to listen to her, and her face regained some of its normal color. Darcy sat up a little straighter, folded her hands, and said, "I have been fighting this for a while, Erin, but I can no longer repress my feelings. I have to tell you, and like I said, if I don't do it now, I don't know when I'll ever get the chance. I admire you."

In her surprised confusion, Erin couldn't help but respond. "Admire me? What does that even mean?"

Darcy paled this time and swallowed. "I admire your passion for your work, your love for your sister, your success despite all odds. I admire your business, your dedication to your chosen craft, but most of all, I admire you. This has caused me to feel certain things for you—things I've struggled against but no longer wish to. I want..." She met Erin's eyes for the first time since she began. "I want to get to know you. I want us to start seeing each other. More seriously, I mean, than before."

Erin was so stunned, this time she couldn't reply.

Darcy clearly saw some of this shock in her face, but, obviously reading her lack of reply as happy surprise, she went on. "I know the odds are against us. My family, for example, will be horrified. You won't believe the kind of garbage that came out of my Aunt Catherine's mouth last night about you after you left. She has other plans for me, as Willie no doubt told you, and even Willie seems to expect that I'll follow her plan and start dating Anne.

"And you live in this backwoods little town. I mean, now that I've been here a while, I can see some of its charms, but I don't understand why you would want to stay here. I know your family is here, and that you have some kind of sentimental attachment to this place, but it's hard for me to understand. I mean, God—are there even people of color here? And I can't imagine what the gay nightlife is like.

"But I don't care what it takes. If it means finding a place here for a while, I'll do it. For you. I don't want to go back to Boston without you."

Throughout this diatribe, Erin's anger had transformed from something initially volcanic to a deeply rooted, frozen rage. She let Darcy continue purely out of curiosity. Could the woman keep on insulting her with every word out of her mouth, or would she eventually realize the depths to which her words had horrified and disgusted Erin? Apparently, she hadn't. Now finished, Darcy grinned with smug satisfaction, as if she were waiting for Erin to leap across the bar and into her arms. Erin detected nothing like regret or even doubt in Darcy's face to suggest that she understood what she'd just done and said.

"Are you fucking kidding me?" Erin finally said. She'd just managed not to shout, but her voice was loud enough to carry across the room. The two drinkers in the corner turned their way.

Darcy reacted as if she'd been slapped, visibly flinching.

Erin leaned forward onto the bar, merely to put her hands somewhere. She was once again afraid she might slap this woman. She'd never been physical with anyone in anger before, but that didn't mean she wouldn't be.

"You come in here, you say these things to me, and you expect what—a prize? You have insulted everything I care about. You couldn't have said things in a way that would have hurt me any more than you just did."

"That's not what I meant—"

"I don't care what you meant! You just told me that, against your better judgement, you've basically decided to make the *sacrifice* to be with me. How on earth do you think that makes me feel?"

"You're misunderstanding—"

"And beyond that, how on earth do you think I could ever get involved with someone who, ruined, perhaps forever, the happiness of my sister?"

Darcy's mouth, which had been open to interrupt her again, snapped closed. She had looked incredulous and stunned, but now her expression closed down into an icy fury.

They stared at each other, each fuming, until Erin could no longer stand it. "Are you going to deny it? You separated them, didn't you?"

Darcy shook her head. "I don't deny it. From the beginning, right after they met, I did everything in my power to keep them apart, but Charlie wouldn't listen. For weeks, I told him he should stop, for Jen's sake as much as his. He was smitten, and he dismissed every warning I gave him. He finally listened to me, but I basically had to beg. It helped that we had to go to Boston that day regardless, but I've talked him out of coming back here. Ever, I hope."

Erin's anger dried up. Instead, the sorrow she'd felt last night returned in full force. For a moment, tears threatened to spill from her eyes, and she turned away abruptly to hide them. She refused to give Darcy the satisfaction of seeing how much she'd hurt her. She blinked rapidly and took a few deep breaths, but, still shaken, she kept her back turned.

Erin swallowed a couple of times. "Was it because of the money? Is that why you drove them apart?"

After a long pause, Darcy finally replied. "How can you even ask that? Is that what you think of me?"

Erin whirled around, ready to defend herself, but when she saw Darcy's expression, the words died on her lips. The defiant, angry coldness from Darcy's face was gone. Instead, she seemed pained again, hurt. Like Erin, her eyes were brimming with tears.

"You give me no choice," Erin finally managed. "Without explanation, that's all I'm left to believe. My sister loves Charlie. Even now, she's off nursing a broken heart, and I'm afraid she'll never get over him."

A single tear splashed down Darcy's cheek, then another. She continued to stare at Erin, her eyes flickering over different parts of her face. They said nothing, and watching Darcy cry made Erin feel like she might start again. Finally, Darcy got to her feet. She hastily wiped her eyes and turned to leave. She started walking toward the door and then paused a few feet away. Erin watched her dig around in her oversized purse for a moment. She pulled out a magazine and then came and laid it on the counter.

"I meant to give this to you yesterday. It's an advance copy. It's on newsstands today."

With that, she turned again and left the brewery without saying another word.

Erin started shaking all over. The extent of her emotion actually made her weak in the knees, and it was all she could do to make it to one of the small tables and collapse into a chair. She was crying, and she couldn't seem to hold on to one thought as they whirled around in her head. She continued to hear Darcy's words and see her hurt expression. Erin's anger, however, quickly overcame her pity, and fury raced through her again.

She might have sat there all night, emotions warring between sorrow and anger, but she snapped back into reality at the sound of the evening shift arriving in the brewery. She looked around, almost guiltily, and realized she was alone. Somewhere amidst her conversation with Darcy, the two remaining drinkers had departed without notice.

She wiped her eyes and carefully rose, afraid that if she moved too quickly she might collapse in a heap on the floor. She was about to go into the back room and hide long enough to regain her equilibrium for the night ahead when she remembered the magazine on the counter. She grabbed it, unwilling to read it right then, and went into the back office to calm down.

Several hours later, after another busy night, she was safely at home. The brewery was catching up, finally, and, in addition to getting everyone home before midnight, everyone should be able to take the holiday off, including her. She'd made the announcement at closing to a series of cheers from her staff. It was the first time in a long time everyone seemed to go home happy.

She'd brought the magazine home with her, intending to read it, but once she'd taken it out of her backpack, she couldn't make herself do more than open it to the table of contents. She paced around her house for a while, sitting down at the table to read only to get up again and pace around some more. She didn't know why she was so nervous. Clearly, it was going to be a good review. Darcy would never have declared herself otherwise—even she didn't have the gall to do that. But of course, it was more than the review. Opening and reading Darcy's words would be like seeing her again, or at least a part of Erin had convinced herself of that possibility. She didn't want to see Darcy again. As far as Erin was concerned, if she never thought of her again after today, all the better. Still, Erin knew she wouldn't sleep tonight if she didn't know what Darcy had said about BSB.

Shortly after midnight, she decided to call Lottie. She couldn't help herself. Like the last time she'd called this late, Lottie answered on the second ring, almost as if she'd been waiting.

"What's up, Erin?"

"I'm so sorry. I know I shouldn't be calling this late—"

"Don't worry about it. It must be important. What's going on?"

Erin paused. "Listen. Could you look up something on the Internet for me?"

"Is yours down or something?"

"No. That's not it." Erin couldn't think of anything that would explain her request without giving herself away, so she decided not to try. "I know it sounds strange, but I can't make myself do something. I'll explain this all to you later. In fact, I probably should have said something sooner, but I couldn't."

"You're not making any sense, Erin."

She sighed. "I know. I'll stop blubbering. Anyway, I need you to look up a review for BSB in *Food and Beverage*. Could you read it for me and tell me what you think?"

"*Food and Beverage*? Really? That sounds important."

"It is. At least I think it is. Could you? Please? I know it's a lot to ask."

Lottie yawned, loudly, and Erin could picture her stretching in bed. "Sure. Just give me a few minutes to read it, and I'll call you back. Try not to freak out. It sounds like that's what you're doing."

"I am."

"Well, try not to. BSB is the best."

"Thanks, Lottie."

The wait was infinite. At first, Erin thought that if she paced around her house, she'd feel better. Instead, her nervous pacing seemed to make her more anxious. Her heart was racing, and her palms and forehead were slick with sweat. She was tempted to get out the tequila and take a shot, but she decided that would only make matters worse. She sat for a few minutes, stood up, paced around, and sat down again. She was surprised, when she checked the clock, to see that it had been only twenty minutes since the phone call.

Another twenty endless minutes later, and Erin was starting to believe that Lottie must have accidently fallen asleep again. She was just about to call her and check, when the doorbell rang. Erin couldn't help but let out a yelp of surprise, but she wasn't surprised to see Lottie when she opened the door.

Lottie immediately came in and into her arms, and they hugged, hard, for a long moment. Lottie eventually drew away and put her hands on Erin's shoulders.

"It's really, really good, Erin."

Erin's tension, which had built up into something hard and tight in her stomach, finally let go, and she felt weak with relief.

"Oh, thank God."

"Let's sit down," Lottie suggested. "You look like you're about to fall over."

They made their way into the little living room and sat next to each other on the couch. Erin left the lights off as the came into the room, but the streetlights from outside were enough to avoid banging into things. Erin was glad it was dark. She was afraid that if Lottie saw her face, she'd see something in there Erin would have to explain.

As if sensing that Erin was incapable of speech right now, Lottie began talking. "The review gave you the highest points possible on every single beer except one."

"The lager?"

Lottie laughed. "Exactly. But we both know lager isn't your strong suit. Anyway, in addition to praising the beers to the skies, it also praised the brewery, though it did suggest that it needed to expand."

"Which is only the truth."

"She said," Lottie continued, emphasizing the word *she* a little, "that your brewery was by far the best in the state, and possibly in the entire region."

"She said that?"

"She did."

They sat in silence. Lottie had taken Erin's hands, and they were close enough that no space was between them.

Lottie finally broke the silence. "I could tell last night that something was going on between you two. I'm sorry I forced us to go to dinner with them. I didn't know until I realized how upset you were. I just wanted to piss her off." She paused. "What happened? Do you want to talk about her?"

The story boiled up in her, threatening to come out, but Erin forced it back down. Even if she admitted to having had, and possibly still having, some feelings for Darcy, what difference did it make now? All of that was over, and they'd never see each other again. Darcy would go home to Boston, and Erin and Jen would have to get on with their lives as best they could.

"I want to tell you, Lottie. I do. But I just can't. Not right now. Ask me again in a month or two."

Lottie peered at her critically for a moment, as if deciding whether she should wait. She finally sighed. "Okay. I'll let you sit on it for now, if you need to—forever, if that's how you want it. Just tell me one thing. Did she hurt you, Erin?"

Erin thought about this for a long moment and then nodded. "Yes. But I think I hurt her, too. And I feel worse about that than my own hurt. How stupid is that?"

"It's not stupid, Erin. It's just human. What kind of world would it be if we didn't feel badly for other people?"

Erin hugged her again and couldn't help but start to cry again.

Much later, Erin still lay awake, twisting around in her bed. Was Darcy awake now, too? Was she thinking of her?

CHAPTER THIRTEEN

Jen and Aunt Eddie returned the morning of Christmas Eve. Erin still had to work for a few hours in the late morning and early afternoon, and Jen and Eddie surprised her by stopping by the brewery for a few minutes once they were in town. The last she'd heard, they'd been forced to fly in Christmas morning, but Aunt Eddie explained that they'd wanted to surprise everyone. Erin couldn't have received a better present, and when she and Jen saw each other, both of them starting crying and hugged each other fiercely.

"Jeez," Lydia said, rolling her eyes. "I didn't get that kind of greeting when you saw me in the tasting room."

"I'm sorry, Lydia," Jen said, laughing and wiping her eyes. "I didn't mean to make you feel left out." She gave their younger sister a similar hug.

"God, it's good to see you, Jen," Erin said. She was still blinking back tears.

"You, too. I had such a nice trip, but I was ready to come home ages ago."

"You'd have thought I was keeping her locked up in a dungeon," Aunt Eddie said. "She couldn't wait to leave New England."

Jen threw her a sad grin. "I'm sorry, Eddie. I know you were hoping for a better companion."

Eddie raised her palms. "Not at all! I'm not complaining. I'm so glad you could get away for so long. Goodness knows the next time we'll be able to do anything like that."

Erin had used this exchange to give herself some time to observe her older sister, and, as she'd suspected, she didn't like what she saw. Rather than revived and energized, Jen look tired and worn. Her normally rosy face was still pale, still wan, and her sweater was hanging on her frame in an alarming manner. Her smiles were slow to surface and obviously forced. She seemed to have closed in on herself a little, her shoulders hunched and small.

Jen, sensing Erin's stare, met her eyes and gave her another weak smile. Erin's heart wrenched at the sight. They made eye contact and Jen nodded slightly, as if following Erin's thoughts. She wasn't over Charlie. If anything, the trip had made things worse. Erin was desperate to get her sister alone and talk it out, but with everyone else here, this simply wasn't the time. They were both staying over at their father's place tonight and sharing the guest room, so perhaps they'd get an opportunity a little later.

"Are you ready to head over to Dad's?" Jen asked.

"Yes. Just give me a minute to get my stuff. I brought an overnight bag."

"You can ride with us in my car," Eddie offered. "We picked it up in Boulder on the way here."

By the time they'd made it to their father's place, his house was warm and heady with the scents of Christmas Eve dinner. He greeted them briefly before disappearing into the kitchen, and Erin helped Jen carry one of her suitcases upstairs. Erin and Jen rejoined Eddie and Lydia in the living room, chatting and catching up for a few minutes as they relaxed.

Jen suddenly rose to her feet. "Between traveling and getting up so early this morning, I feel disgusting. I'm going to take a bath before dinner."

Erin couldn't help but notice the concern that flashed across her aunt's face, but it was quickly suppressed. Eddie squeezed Jen's hand.

"Sure, honey. You do that. I could use a shower myself when you're done."

Without another word, Jen left the three of them alone, and Erin and Eddie shared a long, silent look. Eddie clearly knew that things were not yet right with Jen. Erin opened her mouth to ask about the situation, but Lydia suddenly starting talking to their aunt about a band, and, too polite to cut her off, Eddie turned her full attention to her. Erin decided that, like her talk with Jen, she'd have to wait to grill her aunt for details about the trip. She excused herself and left the living room.

Their father had been in on the early surprise return, in part because he was cooking the meal. Tonight, unlike Christmas Day, was for family only, and this was Erin's first time at this dinner since their mother died. Rather than avoid him as she would any other time she'd visited in recent years, Erin went into the kitchen on purpose to talk to him. He set down his spatula, grinned at her, and gave her a solid hug.

They pulled apart, and he shook a finger. "You've been avoiding me this month, little lady."

Erin laughed. "I know, Dad, but not on purpose." He'd called once a week or so to arrange the talk she'd promised to have with him after Thanksgiving, but she'd been too swamped this month to find the time.

"That's good to hear," he said. He maneuvered around her and, like the last time she'd been here, held up a bottle of wine. Erin nodded, and he poured them both a glass.

"A nice crisp white this time to go with the fish. Will recommended it, and I've almost gone through a whole case this month on my own."

Erin made herself ignore Will's name and took a glass. It was perfectly chilled and tasted like citrus and sunshine. "It's really good."

"I think so. Anyway," her father said, setting down his glass, "now that you've seen your sister, what do you think?"

A lump in her throat suddenly made her speechless. She turned away to hide her upset.

He looked at her evenly and took another deep drink of his wine. He cleared his throat. "I see we're in agreement. I don't like it, Erin, that's for sure. She's a wreck. She seems more upset now than when that good-for-nothing Jacob left her at the altar."

Erin rolled his eyes. "He didn't 'leave her at the altar,' Dad. He cancelled the wedding weeks in advance."

"Potayto, potahto. Anyway, that whole thing with Jacob really messed her up, and it seems like this Charlie guy has done the job again. I was halfway convinced she might try to meet up with him in Boston again and mend fences, but, from what your aunt said, she refused to even consider the idea when they were there. And, apparently, he didn't bother calling on her, either."

"Did he know she was in town?"

"According to your aunt, yes. She sent him an email or something."

Erin raised her eyebrows and then continued drinking her wine. Despite everything, this news still surprised her. With Darcy here in Colorado, Charlie would have been out from under her influence and free to visit Jen, yet he hadn't. It appeared that all her earlier worries about him had, in fact, been real. He'd used her sister and was done with her now.

Erin shook her head. "At this point, there's nothing we can do about it. Once she's back to work, things should be better. They are—I mean they always are for me." Erin flushed with the little slip. As far as anyone knew, the Bostonians had hurt only Jen.

Her father raised an eyebrow but clearly decided to let it go. He turned to the food on the stovetop, and Erin watched him silently for a while. Many of her childhood memories resembled this moment—watching her father cook as they talked about her day and whatever else was on her mind. Those times had taken place in their childhood home, in a much older and smaller kitchen, but the setting was still similar enough to give her a deep sense of calming nostalgia. They talked a little about the food, but the rest of their conversation was light. Erin didn't want to discuss Jen any more than he did. It was too painful.

Jen eventually joined them. She was dressed in a thick bathrobe and bunny slippers, her wet hair up under a towel on her head.

"Sorry, Dad," she said. "I'll get dressed in a minute for dinner. I just need a glass of water."

"Hey—no apology necessary, pumpkin. We can keep it casual this year, if you want. You and your aunt must be exhausted."

She nodded but didn't say anything, sipping her water and staring into space with faraway eyes. She was so distracted, she didn't notice Erin and her father, who shared a pained glance.

"Say," her father said, "this rice dish needs to simmer a while longer, and I wanted to talk to the both of you while it was just the three of us."

Jen looked confused. "What about?"

Her dad walked across the room and rummaged around in a pile of papers on a small credenza in the corner. A moment later, he pulled out a magazine, and Erin knew what it was immediately: the recent edition of *Food and Beverage*. He waved it around once and then came over to their side of the kitchen.

"What's that?" Jen asked.

Their father was shocked. "You haven't seen it?"

"I was waiting until she got home," Erin explained.

Their father opened the magazine to the review and handed it to Jen. "Read that."

Jen's eyebrows shot up when she read the title of the article, and a moment later, she was completely absorbed, her brow knit in concentration. Erin had managed to make herself read the review on her own yesterday, and she knew exactly how it felt to see those words the first time.

When she was finished, Jen seemed even more surprised than before. "This is incredible!"

Their father gave them both a hug, and when he stepped away he had tears in his eyes. "I've never been prouder of the two of you in my entire life. I know I was probably your biggest skeptic when you told me you planned to open a brewery, and I regret that now more than I can say."

Jen opened her mouth, and he held up a hand. "Let me finish, honey. It's hard to eat crow, and I want to get through it. It's not just that you won the Brewing Festival and now this review." He cleared his throat. "It's also that I should have supported you from the beginning. I should have remembered what it was like to go out on a limb for your dreams. My first restaurant almost didn't get off the ground, and my father was a complete ass about it at the time. I should have known better than to treat you the same way. I'm sorry I did."

Tears were streaming down Jen's face, and she gave him a hug. "Thanks, Dad. It means a lot to hear you say that."

Erin was fighting back her emotion, her vision blurry. "Yes, Dad. It really does."

"I think I was even more unfair to you, Erin. I blamed you for getting your sister involved in the brewery to begin with. I'm so very glad it's a success."

They hugged tightly, and a weight that had been dragging down Erin's heart was finally lifted for good.

"Let's rejoin the others," their dad suggested. "I have an announcement to make, and I want to tell them, too."

They followed him into the living room, and Aunt Eddie looked up at them with seeming relief. Lydia had obviously been talking this whole time, and she clearly needed a break.

"Girls, please sit down for a moment," their father said, gesturing.

Erin and Jen shared a confused glance and then sat down on the love seat. Everyone was waiting on their father now. He'd brought his wineglass in with him and twirled it nervously in his hands.

"As you all know, I'm moving toward retirement now. Will is set to take on management starting, well, now, in the new quarter after the holidays."

Everyone nodded. None of this was news.

"What you don't know is that I decided to sell one of my restaurants after all. Will is a great kid, and an excellent manager, but like anyone in a new field, he has some kooky ideas. I'm all for kooky, myself, most of the time, but there was one restaurant I decided I simply couldn't let him get his hands on. He wanted to change just about everything about it, and I thought it was a bad idea. It's popular as it is. At most it needs some updates to the dining room, but very little beyond that. I'm talking about The Steak Lodge, of course."

Erin sat up a little in pleased surprise. The Lodge was her father's first restaurant and his pride and joy. She'd been stunned that he'd thought of letting someone else change and manage it, so it made sense that he'd kept it separate from the negotiations.

"Anyway, I purposefully left The Lodge out of my initial contract with Will until he pitched his ideas to me, and I'm glad I did. I told him a couple of weeks ago that I'd found a seller that plans to renovate and keep it running as is, and the sale was finalized yesterday."

"That's great news, Daddy!" Lydia said, rocketing to her feet. She gave him a long hug and shook her fists in the air. "The Steak Lodge will live on!"

He laughed and patted her shoulder. "Thanks, honey. I don't know how it will feel to go there when I no longer run it, but I'm very pleased to have found the buyers I did. They might, in the end, decide to change things, and I'll have no control over that, but that should be years down the road. Hopefully, by then, I won't care."

Everyone got up and hugged him in congratulations, and Aunt Eddie offered to open one of the bottles of champagne she'd brought from her most recent trip to France.

"That sounds lovely, Eddie, but hold on a minute, everyone. I have some more news to tell you. Please, sit back down again."

Everyone shared a look, but they sat, waiting expectantly.

"Professionally, I've been a lucky man. My restaurants have all thrived in a difficult market in a pretty small city. People have always seemed to like what I cook for them."

"Hear, hear!" Eddie shouted. Everyone laughed.

He grinned. "The point is, I've made a lot of money, and since I'll be more or less retired now, my expenses are getting smaller. This house is paid off and I have no other debts. I like to travel as much as the next man, but my savings will easily cover the trips I still plan on taking." He paused and held up his glass to Erin and Jen. "Erin, Jen, I want to take the money from the sale and invest it in your brewery."

Erin felt like she'd been dropped from a tall building. Her stomach flopped and her face heated with emotion. Jen clasped Erin's hands and squeezed them so hard it hurt. Erin barely noticed.

"Are you serious?" Erin asked. She could hardly get the words out of her mouth.

"I'm completely serious, Erin," her father said. "I want you girls to have the kind of success I've enjoyed, and from what I've seen of the place and the crowds, you need to expand. I had one of my lawyers look into it, and you should be able to expand right where you are on either side of the current brewery."

Erin nodded. "That's what we've been wanting to do for over a year now."

"Well, good! I was hoping you'd say that."

Jen finally seemed to snap into reality, and when she got up to hug their father, she was sobbing. Their father rubbed her back as she cried into his shoulder, and he and Erin shared a wide smile.

They might have had one of the nicest holidays they'd shared since childhood if Lydia had been capable of being an adult, but she wasn't. After Aunt Eddie, Jen, Erin, and their father had all hugged and cried themselves out, Erin realized that Lydia was still sitting down, scowling.

"What's up, Lydia?" she asked, trying not to sound annoyed.

Lydia jumped to her feet so suddenly everyone flinched in startled surprise. "So you finally noticed me? I know it's hard to remember you have another daughter, Dad, but I am actually still here."

"What's this, now?" their dad said, scowling.

Lydia was crying freely now. "I can't believe you. How could you?"

"How could I what?" His voice contained some heat now.

"How could you do that in front of me? You had to know how much it would hurt me. Don't you care about me at all?"

"You're not making sense, Lydia. What are you talking about?"

"Giving them all that money! What about me? Don't I matter to you at all?"

He shook his head. "I'm not giving them the money, Lydia. I'm *investing* my money in their business. I'd do the same thing if you had your own successful business."

"But I don't! What I am supposed to do, work as a barmaid the rest of my life?"

Erin was already out of patience and couldn't keep from breaking in. "You could have plenty of roles in the brewery that would lead to advancement, Lydia. I'd be happy to steer you that direction if you were a better employee."

Lydia's face closed in anger, and she went rigid. "I never wanted to work in a brewery, Erin. It's stupid. I only did it to make Dad happy."

Erin shook her head. "That's not true, Lydia. You begged to work with us, and it was *Jen* who convinced me to give you a chance. You've done nothing but blow it since you started."

"That's fine, then, 'cause I quit."

"Lydia—" Jen said.

"No, really, Jen. I don't want to work there anymore, and no one can make me."

"It's fine with me," Erin said.

Jen threw her a dirty look and then grabbed Lydia's arm. "Honey, listen to reason—"

"I don't want to."

"You're acting like a child, Lydia," their dad said. "And you're not helping, Erin."

Erin sighed and then nodded. She shouldn't have risen to the bait.

"What are you going to do if you don't work there?" their dad asked. "You have to have a job to live under this roof."

"Then maybe I won't live under it. Geo asked me to move in with him. I was going to tell you all about it tonight before you stabbed me in the back."

"That seems like a really bad idea, Lydia." Erin turned to her dad. "Tell her, Dad."

He shrugged. "She's an adult. Everyone gets to make their own bad decisions."

Lydia nodded. "See? It's not your decision to make, Erin, or Dad's."

"You barely even know this guy—" Jen said.

Lydia held up a hand. "I met him the same day you met Charlie, Jen. Don't tell me not to fall for someone when you just did the same thing."

It was a low blow, and everyone stared at her in stunned silence. Lydia smiled at their expressions, self-satisfied.

"In fact," she said, "Geo and I are planning a little trip. We were going to leave in a couple of days, but maybe I'll call him and see if he'd like to go sooner. Like now."

If she was expecting them to argue with her, none of them gave her the satisfaction. Seeing that they were no longer playing her game, Lydia stormed out of the room and upstairs.

"I'm sorry, everyone," their dad said when she'd left. "You all know she's always been temperamental, but I didn't expect that. I guess I should have told you about the money when she wasn't around. I thought, perhaps naively, that she'd be happy for you."

Erin shook her head. "You don't have to apologize for her. She's just being a pest. She can't stand it when the attention isn't on her."

"But egging her on certainly doesn't help, Erin," he said, his brows lowered.

Her temper rose, and she made herself take a deep breath. "You're right, Dad. I'm sorry."

He shrugged. "I appreciate the apology, but maybe you should apologize to her. See if you can get her to listen to reason—have dinner with us, at least, before she leaves."

She looked at Jen. "Can you help me?"

"Sure. Let's go talk to her together."

They went upstairs and were surprised to find Lydia's bedroom door wide open. Normally if she stormed off in a huff, she'd slam it behind her. They both paused in the doorway, and Erin wasn't surprised to see her packing a large suitcase.

"What are you doing?" Jen asked.

"What does it look like, genius?"

Erin sighed. "Lydia, come on. I'm sorry. I like working with you. Well, sometimes. I think if you gave even a little more effort, you could really go places with BSB."

She laughed. "In a brewery? As if. That's the last thing I want."

"Then what do you want?" Jen asked. "Maybe we can help you. Or maybe Dad can."

Lydia laughed again and shook her head. "You really are blind, Jen. Dad only likes you. It's always been that way. Even Erin knows that's true." She zipped her suitcase and picked it up. "Anyway, I've got to go. Geo's already waiting outside."

"Where are you going at this hour?"

"To Geo's place. He lives with his brother and sister. Then we're heading off on our trip tomorrow morning."

"Where are you going?" Jen asked.

"Far away from both of you." Lydia walked toward them, and when neither of them moved, she used her suitcase to push through them and kept going.

Jen and Erin watched her. A moment later, they could hear their aunt downstairs pleading with Lydia to stay, at least for the holiday, but the front door opened a moment later and then slammed shut. A car engine revved in the driveway, followed by the squeal of tires as it pulled away.

Erin and Jen shared a long look, and then they moved toward each other, arms open. They hugged, and Erin knew Jen felt as badly as she did about all this. Pest or not, Lydia was their sister. Jen and Erin had always been closer, in part because they were nearer in age, and Erin knew Lydia often felt left out. They pulled apart, eyes red and guilty.

"Merry Christmas, Jen."

"Merry Christmas, Erin."

CHAPTER FOURTEEN

A few days before Western States Microbrewery Festival, Jen dropped a bombshell: she wasn't going to the festival with Erin. She claimed that the cause was work-related, and while it was true that they'd been even busier than before the holidays, their perfectly capable staff could handle the business for a few days, especially with their help over the phone or through Skype. Jen claimed that phone calls and Skype wouldn't be enough, but Erin knew better. By mid-January, Jen was acting almost like her old self again, certainly with their customers. She'd also thrown herself into the plans for the brewery's expansion with even more dedication than Erin, if that was possible. But again, Erin could see through her phony happiness and cheer. Jen was still in pain and doing her utmost to hide it. She refused to listen to Erin's pleas or talk about anything besides work.

Two nights before she planned to leave, Erin finally decided to force the issue. She went home a little earlier than Jen and set the scene, arranging their living room for a heart-to-heart. By the time Jen finally walked through the door, just after midnight, Erin had a pot of tea sitting under a cozy, a plate full of shortbread cookies, and a fire crackling in their rarely used fireplace. Jen took in the setup and sighed, clearly understanding that she couldn't avoid a conversation. She unwound her scarf and took off her coat before sitting across from Erin on the second armchair.

"Look, I know what you're going to say, Erin, so you can save it."

Erin raised her eyebrows. "Oh, really? What is it?"

"You're going to tell me that I have to go. That you can't do it without me. But you're wrong—you can. In fact, in some ways I think it's better if you do go alone. It's a brewers' festival, not an accounting conference. What do you need me for? I'm just the money person."

Erin shook her head. "There you go again, Jen, selling yourself short. You know you're more than 'just the money person.' Without you, we wouldn't have a brewery. You're more important than I am, in fact. If I left, you could hire a new brewer with no problems."

Jen opened her mouth to interrupt, and Erin held up a hand to stop her. "Listen, Jen, and listen closely. I know you're in pain. I know the only thing you want to do right now is work so you don't have to think about Charlie or anything else that's bothering you. I also know you don't want to hear his name or even talk to me about him anymore, even if I wish you would. But this festival is a major deal for us, and I mean *us*—both of us. I don't think we have a chance in hell at winning, but we need to be there. We're both the face of Bennett Sisters Brewing. How would it look if it was just me?"

Jen sighed and picked up her teacup for the first time. She held it in her hands, clutching it as if for warmth despite the overly hot room. Erin was relieved to see that she was clearly giving her arguments some thought, possibly for the first time since she'd refused to go.

Still, after a long, quiet minute, Jen shook her head and set her cup down, appearing determined. "I'm sorry, Erin, but I just can't."

This time Jen held up her hand when Erin opened her mouth. "Please listen to me before you say anything more. I already feel guilty enough. You really don't have to make it worse. I'd love to go. Or at least part of me *thinks* I'd love to go. I thought the same thing about leaving at Thanksgiving, but when I was in New England with Aunt Eddie, I could barely take it. All I thought about was Charlie, every minute of every day. The whole time I was away, I was afraid I might lose my mind. It didn't help that Charlie was nearby and I couldn't do anything about it." She paused, her eyes distant at the memory, and shook her head again. "I don't need downtime. I need work to keep my mind occupied. I'm not ready for another break right now."

Erin could see that Jen had made up her mind, but she tried once more anyway. "We'll be working almost the whole time! All those parties and schmoozing can only help promote the brewery. How is that not work?"

Jen shook her head, her eyes serious. "I'm not going, Erin."

They were quiet again. Erin was silently fuming—she couldn't help it. Even if Jen seemed sad and broken, she was making a mistake letting her feelings get to her like this. Erin wasn't sure who she was angrier with at this moment—Charlie for breaking her sister's heart, or Jen for taking it the way she did. Their lives were in shambles thanks to two people from Boston, and she couldn't do anything about it right now.

"Look," Jen said, meeting her eyes again. "How about we compromise?"

"How?"

"I'll come for the final party on Saturday, when they announce the winners. My car won't make it up there, but I'll ask Dad to loan me his for the day. That way, I can stay busy this week, but I'll be there for the announcements."

Erin felt a little better. At this point, it seemed like the only concession she would receive. "I guess if that's the way it has to be, I'll take it. But Jen, if you change your mind and decide to come up earlier, please just do it, okay?"

They got to their feet and hugged before sitting down again. Erin could see that Jen was just as unhappy as she was about the situation, but, if anything, that made her feel worse. She didn't want her sister to feel guilty on top of everything else.

She tried to lighten the mood. "I still don't know how I'll go to all those parties by myself. I'm an absolute idiot when it comes to small talk."

Jen laughed. "God, you are." Suddenly she sat upright. "Hey! I just had an idea."

"What?"

"Why don't you ask Aunt Eddie to go with you? I know she's between trips right now, but I'm pretty sure she told me last week she's planning to come to Colorado tomorrow or the day after. I mean, I know it's not totally ideal to take her, since she doesn't know a lot about beer, but at least you'd have someone with you. I'm sure some of the other brewers are taking their families, so you won't be the only person like that there. She'd love to go. She was just saying at Christmas that she hasn't been skiing in Colorado in ages."

"You're right. She would like it, and I could definitely use the company, even if she doesn't go to all the parties with me. I intended to ask her if I could use her car to get up there, anyway."

"I'll call her tomorrow and see if she'd be interested, but I'm sure she will."

"Okay. It's settled."

Erin stood up to pick up their tea things, and Jen touched her wrist. "Erin? I'm sorry. You don't deserve this. You're caught in the middle of my drama, and it's not fair."

Erin's eyes filled with tears. The comment was so typical of Jen. She was heartbroken, yet she was apologizing to Erin.

"You don't need to say that. I'm disappointed that you're not coming, but it's not your fault. Really—it isn't."

Jen blinked and wiped her face, and they stayed that way for a moment, Erin standing, Jen sitting, having a silent conversation with their eyes. Jen finally nodded, acknowledging what Erin had said if not accepting it yet.

Soon after Erin finished washing their dishes, Jen joined her in the kitchen, and they hugged fiercely. They wiped their eyes when they pulled apart, neither of them interested in taking up the conversation again.

"Oh, hey, I almost forgot," Jen said.

"What?"

"The private detective is coming to the brewery tomorrow to talk to us about Lydia."

Their father had told them a few days ago that he'd hired someone to track Lydia. She'd been missing since Christmas Eve, and while she'd taken off with friends and boyfriends in the past, this was the first time she hadn't bothered to check in with them every other day or so. No one in the family had heard from her in almost three weeks.

"Goddamn Lydia," Erin said.

At this point, Erin was more angry than worried, though even she acknowledged to herself that her anger stemmed from her worry. Mostly, she was angry with how much the whole situation had upset her sister and their father, when, in fact, Lydia was probably somewhere sunny and fun, living it up on the beach or in Vegas.

Jen shook her head, her face clouded. "I just hope she's okay."

"I'm sure she's fine," Erin said, this conversation a word-for-word repetition of the one they'd had several times since Lydia ran away.

Jen's brows were still knit with concern. Erin gave her another rough hug and then rubbed her back a few times. "Try not to freak out about her too much right now, Jen. It's late. I'm sure the PI will have some ideas how to track her down."

Jen looked a little relieved, but she was clearly still worried. Erin cursed to herself silently. The last thing anyone needed right now was more of Lydia's drama.

❖

Two days later, Erin and Aunt Eddie were in Eddie's car heading to Aspen via Denver. The drive is one of the most spectacular stretches of interstate in the entire United States. While Denver, the Mile High City, is already at a significant elevation, the roads from it to Aspen occasionally took the two of them to heights of over 10,000 feet. The interstate was clear, the mountains gorgeously snow-capped, and every time they got out of the warm little car for a stretch, the air was thin and bitterly cold. While the entire drive is stunning, the stretch of interstate designated as Glenwood Canyon is by far the most spectacular, with deep-red rock stretching far above the winding road below.

They stopped for lunch and a long walk in the charming little city of Glenwood Springs, about an hour northwest of Aspen. Despite not having Jen with her, Erin was starting to feel excited and happy. Aunt Eddie was excellent company. She could prattle on and on about almost anything, but she was also interesting and often very funny. Of course, the idea of being at Western States Microbrewery Festival was exciting, if scary, but it had also been ages since Erin had been out this far west. The last two months had been so busy that, for the first time since her childhood, she hadn't yet gone skiing a single time this season. Even when she had the time, she usually hit the slopes closer to Loveland, but most winters she went as far as Vail for a weekend or two. She'd been to Aspen only twice in her whole life, both times with friends when she was much younger. It was too far away and too expensive to go casually.

As they drove into Aspen in the early afternoon, Erin saw that the city had changed a lot since the last time she'd been here. For one thing, high-end restaurants and designer chains had replaced all the quaint stores and cafes. While Aspen had been growing in popularity with celebrities ever since people like John Denver and Hunter S. Thompson had made it famous in the 1970s, during the last twenty years it had become a kind of haven for the ultra-rich. It was not generally the kind of place most people in the middle and lower classes could now afford, and that didn't seem to bother anyone who lived there. Nevertheless, the city was breathtakingly beautiful, and Erin was excited to see the transformations. Also, this trip gave her a chance to hit the excellent slopes at the ski resort, something she might never have done again with the usual cost of the lift tickets and hotels here.

With Western States Microbrewery Festival more or less taking over the little city this week, Erin didn't think they'd see many—if any—celebrities, but her aunt was already peering intently out the window at every person they noticed on the street, her camera ready for a sighting like a member of the paparazzi. When they drove up to the gorgeous hotel they were staying in, Eddie actually looked put out that they hadn't spotted anyone famous yet.

An efficient bellhop helped Erin and her aunt remove their bags from the car and directed them to the official registration desk for the festival. While it appeared that some of the guests here weren't involved in the festival, almost everyone they passed in the lobby was a brewery representative. Erin recognized a few of them on sight from brewing magazines and found herself a little starstruck, much to her aunt's glee.

"You have your celebrities, and I have mine. Do you want me to take a picture of some of them for you?"

Erin glared at her aunt in reply, and Eddie laughed out loud. "Don't worry, Erin. I'll snap some pictures of the lobby while you check in, and maybe I'll get a few of them in there 'by accident.'" She made scare quotes as she said the last part.

"Don't you dare!"

Eddie just laughed and left the line, taking pictures of everything. Erin decided to ignore her to avoid drawing attention to what she was doing. She could only hope her aunt was teasing.

When she reached the front of the line, the registration attendee handed her keycards and a folder stuffed full of tickets and maps to the various functions this week. There was a gathering every evening for tastings, as well as several keynote speakers from some of the larger, more famous microbreweries on topics ranging from hops to the best methods for brewing different beer varieties. Erin was disappointed to realize how many of the sessions overlapped, as she would have happily attended every panel. It would be difficult to choose which ones to attend and still make time to ski every day.

One of the bellhops offered to carry her luggage up to her room, and she turned around to find her aunt. She was no longer in the lobby, as far as Erin could see. As she scanned the small crowd, she saw a set of doors at the far end of the lobby. Even from where she stood, she could hear loud, happy voices from inside. Two weeks ago, she'd been asked to send a smaller, pony keg of her porter for this bar, which was promoting beer from all the festival attendees. It was supposed to be one of the largest tap houses in Colorado, with over a hundred taps of local beer. She'd been excited to visit it since she'd read about it, and she knew immediately that her aunt was likely in there trying to get a glass of BSB beer.

She swung the door open and immediately spotted Eddie chatting happily with someone, a glass of dark beer in her hands. Her aunt spotted her and waved at her. "Erin! Get over here. I was just bragging about you to Anne here. She just *loves* your porter."

The woman with her aunt turned around, and Erin's heart seized. She'd met Anne before when she and Lottie had run into Darcy and her family in Boulder. Darcy's cousin had suggested that this was the woman Darcy's Aunt Catherine wanted to set her up with.

Suppressing her shock, Erin approached and extended a hand. "We've actually met before."

Anne was clearly taken aback, but she took Erin's hand and shook it. "Yes, we have. Under somewhat unusual circumstances."

Aunt Eddie looked back and forth between them, clearly sensing something. "Oh? How strange! What a small world."

"What brings you here to the festival?" Erin asked.

"I own this hotel," Anne said simply.

A long, awkward silence stretched out as Erin absorbed this information. The hotel was one of the nicest Erin had ever been in. Even having just seen the outside and the lobby, Erin could tell it would cost a small fortune to stay here. The smallest rooms would likely cost more than anything Erin could ever afford on her own. The idea that this woman owned it all was humbling, to say the least. Anne seemed to find her shock amusing. She was grinning, almost gloating.

Erin made herself smile. "It's incredibly beautiful." She turned to her aunt. "Shall we go up to our room? I'm sorry, Anne, but it was a long drive."

"Of course!" Anne's expression was still smug. "By all means."

Aunt Eddie still seemed confused, but she set her half-finished beer down and followed Erin out of the bar without any questions.

When they'd returned to the safety of the lobby, Aunt Eddie touched her arm to stop her. "What on earth was that all about?

When you saw her, you looked like you'd swallowed an egg! Who is she?"

Erin shook her head, too shaken to think of something to explain herself. "It doesn't matter." Seeing her aunt's stricken face, she gave a weak smile. "Really, Eddie, it doesn't. And I don't want to get into it right now, okay?"

Her aunt gave her a long stare. "Okay. I'll let it drop. I'm sorry if I made some kind of mistake talking to her."

"You couldn't have known. Don't worry about it." She squeezed her aunt's hand. "Now let's go up to our room and relax for a while. There's an opening reception in a few hours, and I want to have a long nap and a shower first."

Their room was stunning. A large gas fireplace with huge, comfortable-looking couches and oversized armchairs dominated the living room. One side of the room was entirely glass, with sweeping views of the town and mountains spreading out in front of them. She and her aunt stood there, simply staring, for a long moment, too stunned to do anything but stare.

"Wow," her aunt finally managed.

"You said it."

"What do you suppose a room like this costs on average?"

"More than I could ever afford, that's for sure."

They were quiet a while longer, still staring out the window, and then her aunt seemed to shake herself awake.

"If you're going to take a nap, I think I'll go out and explore the town a little. Do some shopping, poke around. I'll be back before dinner. You don't mind, do you? I know you're not much of a shopper."

Erin shook her head. "You go ahead. I want to lie down for an hour or two. I'm worn out."

Each of them had a small bedroom off this main room, one on the far left and the other on the far right, the living room separating them for privacy. Each bedroom had a large en suite bathroom and a small gas fireplace. The bedrooms boasted similarly glorious views of the surrounding mountains, and once again, Erin simply stood and stared out the window for a long moment, too captivated to do anything else.

Finally, she sighed and flopped down on the bed. She hadn't slept well last night, and they'd gotten up early to avoid traffic in the canyon. Her face felt hot, almost feverish, from her fatigue, but she no longer felt sleepy. Now she was in that awkward liminal place between exhaustion and the effects of a second wind. Having pushed herself many, many times in her life, she knew it would be difficult to fall asleep now with the jittery anxiety coursing through her veins. Still, she closed her eyes, hoping to will herself to sleep if she couldn't get there naturally.

Something about seeing Anne had shaken her. Erin kept steering her mind away from dwelling on the encounter, but she couldn't help but remember how she'd felt seeing her again. It had almost been like running into Darcy, but she didn't know quite why. Certainly the woman reminded her of Darcy a little, but it wasn't just that.

After a long hour stewing and tossing over the encounter with Anne, Erin finally sighed and sat up, knowing she wouldn't get any sleep now no matter how much she might need it. She rubbed her face, hard, and the beginnings of a pinching tension headache built in her temples.

She climbed off the huge bed and went out into the little living room in search of coffee. A tiny kitchenette had a single-serving coffee machine and a mini fridge. Erin put a pod into the chamber of the coffeemaker and set it to brew before going back to gaze out the large living-room window again.

With the city of Aspen stretching out around beneath her, and the mountains rising behind it in majestic, cold beauty, Erin couldn't help but feel a little twist of envy in the pit of her stomach. People like Anne and Darcy could afford these kinds of views, these kinds of trips, any time they wanted them. Perhaps this realization, more than anything, had shaken her when she'd seen Anne. Like Darcy, Anne was part of all of this. Indeed, she owned the very view Erin was now enjoying. How could Erin ever hope to compete?

Erin shook her head, disgusted with herself. Ever since her last encounter with Darcy, she'd been very careful not to allow herself to think in these terms. There was nothing between her and Darcy now, and never would be. No competition existed between her and Anne, because Erin wasn't in the running for Darcy's affections. Why should she care how little she stacked up against the other woman? Yet, even as she made these claims to herself, she knew she did care. She couldn't help it. She simply didn't like the idea of Darcy ending up with a woman like Anne. In fact, she didn't like the idea of Darcy ending up with anyone except her.

She felt a little sick. Even admitting this fact about Darcy to herself seemed like betrayal. She didn't want to have these feelings anymore, yet suppressing them these last few weeks seemed to have made them stronger.

She thought about calling Jen. This last few weeks, ever since Jen had returned from her trip, Erin had desperately wanted to talk to her about Darcy. In the past, when Erin had girlfriend problems, she discussed them with Jen first. Her problem with Darcy was more complicated than any relationship that had come before it. For one thing, as far as Jen or anyone else knew, nothing existed between the two of them—not now and not before. If she told Jen now, she would be admitting that she'd lied about Darcy all of those weeks they were in town. She couldn't make herself do that now, since Jen apparently didn't suspect a thing. Lottie clearly suspected, and even Charlie had seemed to sense something was going on before they left, but only Erin and Darcy knew the truth.

She'd avoided telling Jen in part because she knew that bringing up Darcy would remind her sister of Charlie, and that was the last thing Erin wanted to do. As far as Erin was concerned, the sooner Jen forgot Charlie, the better. If that meant never telling Jen about her and Darcy, so be it, even if her lie of omission made her feel guilty about it forever. She probably deserved that. She should have told Jen the day after the first encounter in the cabin in Estes. It was too late now.

Still, she couldn't help but feel a little lonely with this decision. She didn't have anyone to talk to about any of this. Tears prickled her eyes, and she cursed herself for being so weak.

Hearing a sound at the door, Erin quickly wiped her eyes. Her aunt bustled in, carrying several bags, most of which appeared to be from various food stores. Erin's smile felt tense and phony as she attempted to greet her aunt's excitement with enthusiasm, but luckily Eddie was too wrapped up in her purchases to notice that Erin was faking it.

With something like relief, Erin finally excused herself to go get ready for the opening reception, and when the door to her bedroom closed behind her, she shuddered with dread.

Sighing, she shook her head, once again disgusted with herself. This was going to be one of the most important weeks of her life. She needed to get her shit together and forget about Darcy. Determined now to do just that, she headed for the shower, hoping the hot water would revive her enough that she could get through the evening.

CHAPTER FIFTEEN

Erin woke up just before sunrise the next day. She was determined to get as much skiing in as possible this week, and only her mornings were free from festival activities. While Snowmass Resort wouldn't open until later in the morning, several state-owned cross-country trails didn't have opening hours, and she was headed to the nearest one just outside of the city.

Last night's reception had been a nice surprise. She hadn't realized how nervous she'd been about being here until she and her aunt had headed downstairs. In the elevator, her hands had started shaking, almost as if she were about to give a speech. Then, when they'd finally walked into the bar where she'd found her aunt earlier, she'd almost instantly realized that just about everyone here was like her—small-time brewers trying to make a name for themselves. She'd agonized about what to wear for weeks now, only to realize upon seeing everyone that she needn't have bothered. In fact, in her nicest button-up shirt and slacks, she was overdressed in a sea of denim and flannel.

Someone had immediately called her and her aunt over to talk about BSB beer, and the rest of the night went smoothly. She'd had a little too much to drink, trying to sample something from everyone she met, but that was to be expected at a brewers' festival. On the whole, the night had been easy, and she expected the rest of the week would be similar. Making contacts and friends with other brewers would be straightforward, and even if some of them were her competition, everyone here had the right to believe that they could win. Each beer she'd tried last night had been excellent. If the competition was up to her, she'd never be able to choose.

The morning air was bitter and brisk, and the slight hangover she was nursing cleared as she waited for the valet to bring her aunt's car. She and her aunt had brought downhill and cross-country skis as well as snowshoes, ready for anything they might feel like doing while they were here. Her aunt had decided to sleep in today, which was, to Erin, for the best. She needed a couple of hours to herself before the panels and receptions started for the day.

Despite being the only person out here this morning, she had to wait a long time for the valet to finally bring her aunt's Subaru around to the front, and as she drove to the trail, the sun was already starting to peak above the mountains around her. She was surprised to find another car parked at the trailhead, and when she climbed out of her aunt's battered, muddy car, she saw that the other car was a very new-looking Mercedes SUV. It was jet-black and so clean, it might have been washed of mud and snow here in the parking lot. Erin grinned to herself. Only in Aspen could you expect to see a car like this parked at a trailhead.

She took a few minutes to put on extra layers, check her backpack, and snap on her skis, but she was soon gliding up the long, sloping hill that started the trail, her breath frosting in the morning air. By the top of the hill, she had warmed up and was thrumming with exertion. Here, she had three directions to choose from, left and right and straight ahead. She paused to catch her breath and look down at her car before choosing a path to the left. She decided on that direction primarily because someone had been skiing here recently—probably the person with the Mercedes—and it was always easier to ski in someone else's tracks than to break new ground, even in soft snow like this. She didn't have a good trail map, either, so following someone else's trail would also help her avoid getting lost.

Her troubles began to fall behind her as she skied. It was always like this, and one of the reasons she loved spending time skiing and hiking. Outside, with this kind of natural beauty, her problems seemed small and insignificant, and the simple joy she felt seeing the snow and the trees lifted her spirits from her everyday life and heartache. It was, in fact, heartache she'd been feeling. She could admit that to herself, now. She hadn't wanted to let herself fall for Darcy, but she had—she couldn't deny it anymore. That, coupled with her worries for Jen, and now Lydia, had made it seem like she was falling apart lately. Even the good news about the loan her father was giving them hadn't made things better, which was telling. As recently as last October, the money had been the only thing she thought she needed, and now it wasn't enough. She didn't know how her brewery would ever be enough for her again, and it would probably take longer for Jen to think that way again, too.

She let her mind wander as she skied, her remaining worries dropping away with the pleasant warmth that coursed through her. It had been entirely too long since she'd been on a trail like this— hiking or skiing. Why didn't she do something like this every chance she got? One of the biggest benefits to living in a state like Colorado was having access to beautiful places, and she'd been squandering the opportunity all winter. She vowed to at least go hiking every week for the rest of the season, no matter how busy they were at the brewery.

As she relaxed into a smooth rhythm of motion, she found herself absorbed in memories of her earliest ski trips as a child. Her father had dragged all of them into the mountains as often as possible. It had been a disaster when they'd first started going, with both Jen and Erin complaining nonstop. Once they'd grown a little better at skiing, it had been much more fun, and then Lydia had started coming, too, and it was awful again. Still, their dad persisted, and eventually all three of them accepted that skiing and hiking were part of their lives. Whether they camped, hiked, or skied, depending on the season, the whole family did it together.

Considering that they rarely saw their father during the week, these outings became a big deal to her as a little girl. No matter how busy he was at the restaurant, he always made time for at least two or three activities a month. This, more than anything, had eventually made their trips into the mountains something she looked forward to rather than dreaded. And when her sisters were old enough to refuse to go, just she and her father went together. Very likely that was why she'd fallen in love with all of this to begin with. Of course, that had changed with their estrangement, but luckily the love for nature had settled in her heart, and once she and her father stopped doing anything together, she'd simply gone on her own or with friends.

A tiny part of her had realized somewhere along the trail that rather than one person, at least two had made the trail she was following in the snow. Occasionally, she saw two sets of ski tracks, and in several places the pole tracks indicated the same thing. She only noticed in part because she was still surprised to find anyone out here this early in the morning. Also, though it should have been obvious, it hadn't occurred to her that she might run into the other skiers. She rounded a corner and saw them up ahead, peering over the side of a steep cliff on the left. They were absorbed in whatever they were staring at and, with the slight breeze, had neither heard nor seen her yet.

Erin paused, startled, and then continued toward them. Trail etiquette dictated that she stop and say hello, at least, but on the other hand, neither she nor they would want to ski together, so this was her opportunity to get ahead of them a bit to put some distance between them. Both figures were slight, but tall, with the farther one a little taller than the one closer to Erin. Both of them were dressed in sleek, black ski gear, so new and nice it was reminiscent of their car in the parking lot some miles behind them.

As Erin got closer, she opened her mouth simply to call out a greeting before moving on, but before she could, one of the figures turned toward her and touched the other person's arm. The second head turned her way a moment later. They were both looking at Erin now, not saying a thing, and Erin realized they were waiting for her to stop. She sighed and turned a little to meet them. They'd skied a bit off the trail for the view. As she got within a few feet of them, she reached up to remove her goggles, and when she came to a stop, her heart almost stopped.

The taller woman was Darcy.

Erin felt the friendly hello she'd been about to give die in her throat. Darcy was clearly struggling to make herself say something as well, her face contorting with emotion. Both of them were gaping like fish.

Erin finally wrenched her eyes away from Darcy's and met those of the other woman standing next to her. She was young and pretty, with large, dark-gray eyes like Darcy.

"Hi?" the younger woman said. She frowned back and forth at them, clearly confused.

Erin made herself break eye contact and held out a gloved hand to the younger woman. "Hi. Nice to meet you."

The woman took her hand in hers. "Nice to meet you, too. I take it you and Darcy know each other from somewhere?"

Erin kept her eyes on the younger woman, too afraid to look at Darcy again.

"Yes," Darcy said. "Erin, this is my sister. Georgiana, this is Erin, the one I told you about."

Before Erin knew what was happening, Georgiana had thrown her arms around Erin in a tight hug, their skis crossing beneath them.

"Really?" she said. "How cool! I'm so happy to finally meet you! What are the chances we'd run into you up here, of all places?"

Erin couldn't help but laugh, and some of the tension between her and Darcy seemed to magically disappear. Darcy was smiling now, too.

"It is a pretty big coincidence," Erin said.

"I mean, I suppose it was bound to happen this week at some time," Georgiana said, still grinning. "You're here, we're here, and it is a small town. But up here on the trail? Too weird." She turned to her sister. "You have to invite her tonight, Darcy."

Darcy started a little and then shook her head before giving Erin a quick grin. "I'm sure she has plans, Georgiana."

Georgiana turned to Erin, eyes pleading. "Do you? Have plans? Because if you don't, I insist you come."

"Come where?" Erin asked.

"It's my eighteenth birthday today, and we're having a little party. That's why we're here—in Aspen, I mean. Darcy sprung the whole trip on me a couple of days ago, and here we are! Isn't she the best?"

Georgiana turned and hugged Darcy, and Darcy gave Erin an embarrassed grin again. Erin couldn't help but laugh. This was a side to Darcy she'd only rarely seen, and it suited her. She was clearly completely devoted to her younger sister.

"I'd love to, Georgiana, and happy birthday. Unfortunately, I already have plans."

The girl's face fell, and so did her older sister's. Erin's heart lifted at the sight, and she couldn't help but feel almost as disappointed as they looked.

"I'm here on business, actually," Erin said. "And I have a work thing most of the evening."

Georgiana slapped her forehead. "Oh, that's right! Darcy and I saw the announcement about the festival." She glanced at Darcy and then winked at Erin. "Once I saw it, I kind of thought the festival might be part of the reason we came here this week. I'm sure she wanted to see you again."

Darcy's face flushed with color, and she opened her mouth, but Georgiana cut her off. "Don't deny it, sister of mine. I know how you operate. And I don't mind. I love Aspen, and I wanted to meet Erin anyway."

"That's not really the case, Erin," Darcy said, meeting her eyes. "I would never presume—"

Erin held up a hand. "It's okay. You don't have to explain."

They were all quiet for a while, Georgiana looking back and forth between them as they simply stared at each other. Erin couldn't wrench her eyes away. All these weeks, when she'd tried to stop thinking about her, she barely stopped even for a few minutes. And now here she was, in front of her, and she was clearly here at least in part to see her. Erin finally made herself turn to Georgiana, and she was surprised to see that the girl's expression had fallen a little in that long, awkward silence. She must have sensed the tension between them.

"Look," Georgiana said, shaking her head. "I know you're busy, but maybe you could stop by? Just for a little while? I really want to get to know you better, and I'm sure Darcy would love it if you came, even if she's too stubborn to ask."

Erin was about to give the girl a firm no, but as she looked into her eyes, which were, in fact, a replica of Darcy's, her resolve drained away. After all, she didn't have a good reason to attend the entire reception at the festival tonight. She could duck out a little earlier than last night with no problem.

"I'll try, Georgiana, but it will probably be kind of late, like nine or nine thirty, before I could get away. Would that be all right?"

Georgiana let out a loud whoop and hugged her again. "Thank you, thank you, thank you! You just made my day. And come as late as you want. We're all night owls in our family. We'll be up until at least midnight. Please promise me you'll be there. Don't try—just do it! That's what our dad always says."

"Okay. I promise. I'll be there by ten at the latest. Is it all right if I bring my aunt with me?"

"Bring anyone you like! The more the merrier. And no presents! I just want to see you, and I know Darcy does, too."

Darcy's face was a rosy red again, and not from the cold. She gave Erin a quick, embarrassed smile and pulled her goggles down over her eyes again. "And on that note, I guess we'll see you later."

"Unless you want to ski with us?" Georgiana asked, gesturing at the trail.

Erin shook her head. "I have to head back, actually. I have another work thing in a couple of hours." This was only partially true, as she'd planned to keep going another half hour, but Erin refused to ski with them.

Georgiana seemed put out, but she smiled a second later. "Okay! Well, we'll see you tonight then."

"Bye," Erin said.

She stood there for a while, watching them ski away up the trail. Georgiana was in the lead, and Erin had a long moment in which to watch Darcy from behind before they disappeared into the trees. In her daydreams, after Darcy had told her all those months ago that she liked to ski, Erin had pictured her doing just that, but the fantasy version she'd imagined was not nearly as impressive as the reality of Darcy's firm body moving with easy grace across the snow. It was a sight to warm anyone from the inside out.

"Goddamn it," Erin said.

CHAPTER SIXTEEN

At nine thirty that night, Erin and her aunt were slipping and sliding on the icy sidewalks of downtown Aspen. To Erin's surprise, Darcy wasn't staying at the hotel. This afternoon, she'd texted Erin an address a few blocks away, and rather than drive over there, Erin had decided that the walk would help give her time to center herself before what would likely be an incredibly awkward encounter.

"Can you explain this to me again?" her aunt asked, breathing heavily. Despite the ice, they were moving quickly to get out of the cold night air. "I still don't understand why we're going over there. Isn't this the same woman who helped break your sister's heart?"

Erin looked at her, surprised. When Erin had told her this afternoon that they were invited to Darcy's for a party, it had taken Eddie a moment to remember who she was. As Erin had never told anyone what she'd learned about Darcy driving Charlie and Jen apart, she'd thought that as far as Eddie knew, Darcy was simply Charlie's friend. Eddie had known Darcy was in Colorado with Charlie before they left, and that they left together, but Erin thought that was the extent of Eddie's knowledge of her.

Seeing her confused expression, Eddie continued: "When your sister said that Charlie left with his friend Darcy—his *female* friend Darcy—I assumed she had something to do with the breakup, if you catch my drift."

Erin kept staring at her, puzzled, and then realized what her aunt was suggesting. She laughed out loud. "No, Eddie. It's not like that at all. Charlie and Darcy aren't a couple."

Eddie raised her eyebrows. "I wouldn't be too sure about that, Erin. I've seen how some women work. They buddy up to a man, get rejected by him, and then sabotage all of his relationships until they get what they want."

Thinking of her conversation with Darcy in the brewery last month, Erin couldn't help but laugh again and shake her head. Her aunt still looked doubtful. Erin stopped and put her hands on her shoulders. "I can assure you, Eddie, that Darcy is not interested in Charlie that way. I promise."

Eddie wouldn't let it go. "You can't be sure about anything in this life, Erin. The whole thing seemed very suspicious to me when Jen told me about it. And it makes perfect sense." She paused. "Even if she and Charlie aren't together now, don't you think she might have had something to do with the breakup?"

Erin had no response, since it was true. As they walked the last couple of blocks, she mulled over this fact again. Darcy had helped break up Charlie and Jen. Shouldn't she hate her for it? Shouldn't she do everything in her power never to speak to the woman again?

"We're here!" Eddie said, getting her attention.

Erin had gone a few feet beyond the set of stone steps that led up from the street, and she turned around, shaking her head to clear it. Her aunt was gaping up at the house, and Erin immediately saw why. Rather than a simple ski chalet, or even a large townhouse, the house on the hill was fantastically large. From down here on the sidewalk, it loomed above the whole street, dwarfing all nearby buildings. For a moment, Erin was confused. Darcy wasn't staying in a hotel, so why were they having a party at one? As she stared at it, however, she realized it wasn't a hotel. It was, in fact, a tremendously large, stone house. It had been designed to resemble an English country house, and, even beyond the size, the architecture clashed with the mainly wooden ski chalets around it.

"Who on earth is this woman?" her aunt asked.

Erin shook her head and shrugged. "I don't even know, Eddie."

They climbed the long set of stone stairs up to the door, and the house seemed to grow larger and larger the closer they got. Most of the windows were blazing with light, and once they were close enough, they could hear lots of voices and music inside. Erin took a deep breath before ringing the bell, which chimed loudly inside. Someone flung the door open a moment later, and suddenly Georgiana appeared in the square of light, her face bright with happiness.

"You came!" she said, and threw herself at Erin.

Erin laughed and returned the hug. "Happy Birthday!"

"Darcy said you wouldn't be able to make it. I'm so glad you proved her wrong."

"Georgiana, this is my aunt, Eddie," Erin said.

Eddie was thunderstruck, clearly confused by the whole scene. Erin had told her they were attending a birthday party, but she'd neglected to fill in the blanks.

"So nice to meet you," Eddie said, holding out her hand.

"I'm so glad to meet you!" Georgiana took her hand in both of hers and squeezed it. "I'm sure Darcy will be excited to meet you, too. Erin was about the only thing she could think about today."

Eddie threw Erin a surprised look just before Georgiana grabbed Erin's hand and dragged her inside. Erin should have told her aunt a little more about what to expect, but she hadn't been able to make herself talk about it. Her past with Darcy was a secret for a reason. She'd been afraid that if she started telling her aunt about it today, she'd get emotional, so she'd avoided bringing it up. Erin cursed her own cowardice now.

The room was crowded and overly warm. Erin had expected a small family affair, maybe with a friend or two, but at least thirty people were here. Two servers inched through the room, one with glasses of champagne and another with hors d'oeuvres. The furniture was tasteful and modern, and expensive-looking art hung on the walls. Like the house itself, it didn't really seem like a living room that belonged in Aspen.

"Darcy said I could have champagne tonight," Georgiana said, taking a glass off the tray.

"I said you could have *a glass* of champagne," Darcy said, appearing suddenly from the side.

Georgiana pouted and turned to give her glass to Aunt Eddie. "You're no fun at all, Darcy."

"I just don't want to see my eighteen-year-old sister get drunk, birthday or no birthday."

Darcy was breathtaking tonight. She was dressed simply, in a dark-gray sweater that matched her eyes and slim, dark, form-fitting jeans. Her hair was down, kissing her shoulders in pale, golden waves. Her face was open and flushed a little, the corners of her mouth lifting in a loose smile. Erin's throat caught, and she was momentarily incapable of speech.

"I didn't think you would make it," Darcy said.

"I didn't know if I would."

They continued to stare at each other, and Erin felt for a moment as if the rest of the world had dropped away. Darcy's eyes were the only thing in the room. The chill from the walk disappeared in a wave of pleasurable heat the longer she stared into those dark depths.

Movement to their right snapped Erin back to reality, and she looked over at her aunt and Georgiana, both of whom were grinning like fools.

Darcy shook her head as if to clear it. "I'm so sorry." She held out her hand. "I'm Darcy. You must be Erin's aunt?"

Eddie was still grinning as she took Darcy's hand in hers and shook it. "Yes, I am. You can call me Eddie." She released Darcy's hand and turned to Georgiana.

"Say, honey, why don't you show me around? I've never been in a big house like this before."

Georgiana looked like she was about to object, and then she smiled and winked at Eddie. "Oh yeah, okay. I'll give you the tour. I'm sure these two won't mind being left to their own devices for a while."

Darcy and Erin were alone a moment later, their companions giggling as they left them alone. They shared a smile.

"Now I'll never hear the end of it," Darcy said.

"Me neither. God knows what Aunt Eddie thinks now."

They were quiet for a while, still smiling at each other, but some of the humor gradually died out of Darcy's eyes.

"Can we talk?" Darcy asked.

"Isn't that what we're doing now?"

Darcy sighed. "I mean alone." She gestured at the crowded room. "Could you come upstairs, just for a few minutes?"

"Okay."

Erin followed Darcy across the room and over to a wide staircase. Heads swiveled their way as they crossed the room, and she could only imagine what everyone was thinking as they disappeared upstairs together. Following Darcy from behind was an exercise in self-control, however, as she wanted to reach out and touch her the moment they rounded the corner out of sight from the others. She balled her fists and kept them at her sides to stop herself.

Darcy led her to a room at the end of a short hallway, and when Erin walked in, she stopped, surprised. The light from the hallway illuminated an enormous piano taking up one side of the room and a harp in the other corner.

"Do you play?" Erin asked.

Darcy shook her head. "My sister is the musician. She's at Julliard, actually. I can do some simple melodies, but I never had the discipline to get very good at it."

Darcy closed the door behind them, and the room plunged into darkness. The only light was ambient from the outside streetlights. Erin could see silhouettes, however, and when Darcy moved across the room to stand in front of the large windows, she followed a moment later. She stood close enough that she could feel the warmth from Darcy's shoulder. It was also lighter by the window. Streetlights reflecting on the snow outside cast both of their faces in pale light, and the longer they stood there, the clearer details became as her eyes adjusted.

They continued to stare outside, not at each other, for a long, quiet pause. This was better. Erin lost her train of thought any time she looked at Darcy's face, so maybe in this dark, quiet room, they could say what they needed to and be done with this. She started to shake with nerves and took a long breath before speaking.

"It's a beautiful house."

Darcy laughed. "You think so? I disagree. It's ostentatious, and it sticks out like a sore thumb here. It's my aunt's."

Oh, Erin thought. That explained things much better.

"She keeps a music room here? For your sister?"

Darcy nodded. "She's devoted to her. I think she likes Georgiana almost as much as her own daughter. She's easy to love."

Erin could sense the unspoken follow-up—that Darcy was not. Her heart started pounding, and she took a deep breath to steady her nerves. It was time to start the real conversation they needed to have.

"What did you want to talk to me about?"

During another long pause, Erin could hear Darcy breathing quickly. She finally cleared her throat and said, "First of all, I wanted to apologize."

Erin's breath hitched. "For what?"

"For lots of things. First, for my presumption. I know that… well, my feelings are my own. I should never have assumed that you shared them."

Erin looked over at her. "Darcy, I—"

"Please let me finish."

Erin turned to look out the window again and waited. Darcy was clearly nervous, and Erin wanted to let her have her say.

"Second, I need to apologize about Charlie. And your sister."

Darcy finally turned, and Erin turned with her, both of them reaching out wordlessly and taking each other's hands. Erin could feel Darcy trembling now, though she might simply be feeling her own hands shaking.

"I drove them apart, and I regret it very much. You accused me of doing it because of money, and I denied it. At the time, I thought I was telling you the truth. And on the surface, it wasn't because of the money. I *was* afraid she was playing him. She didn't seem to actually love him, and I wanted him to break it off before things got too serious." She paused, swallowing. "But then I saw her. After the breakup, I mean."

Erin was surprised. "You did? Jen never mentioned it."

"She didn't see me. It was right before Christmas. My family was already up in Aspen, but I stayed in Boulder a little longer. I told them I still needed to do some shopping, but I couldn't make myself go up there without seeing you again. We'd had our...conversation at your brewery a couple of days before that."

Erin laughed. "That's a nice way of putting it. Argument is probably more accurate."

"Right. Well, anyway, I couldn't let it go. I needed to talk to you again, or at least see you, so I drove up to Loveland. I parked in front of the brewery, and then I saw Jen outside, waiting for something or someone. You, maybe."

Darcy was quiet again for a long moment, her eyes troubled and inward-looking. "When I saw her, she looked absolutely wrecked. She was so forlorn and empty. I knew exactly what she was feeling and that I'd done that to her. I knew then that I'd been wrong. She loves Charlie just as much as he loves her. I've never felt worse about anything in my entire life. I was so guilty, I immediately left without talking to you or to her."

Darcy paused, wetting her lips. "But that's not the worst part. I've been thinking about what you said, about the money, just about every minute since I saw you in the brewery. And I think you're right about that, too. I was afraid Jen was planning to use him for his money. She told us several times that your brewery was in trouble, and I think part of me—maybe even a big part—thought she was angling for a loan."

Erin's heart wrenched, and Darcy squeezed her hands.

"But I was wrong, Erin. I can admit that now. I know better. I was arrogant and I was wrong. They loved each other, and I drove them apart."

They were quiet as Erin absorbed this confession. Darcy's admission didn't necessarily make what she'd done any better—it certainly wouldn't erase Jen's pain—but it did make Erin feel a little better.

"Thank you for saying that," Erin finally said.

"I know it doesn't do Jen or Charlie any good, but I couldn't take it if you thought of me that way anymore. I'm so sorry." Erin pulled on one of Darcy's hands, and a moment later they were hugging, fiercely. The scent of her perfume, that light, citrusy odor, filled Erin's nose again, and she inhaled, deeply, as if for the last time. And it would have to be the last time—Erin knew that. The whole situation was too confused now to salvage. She was glad it was ending this way, though, with some of the hurt feelings behind them.

Darcy pulled away a little, still holding her, and met her eyes, and suddenly Erin's decision a moment before seemed ridiculous. Darcy's eyes were shining, happy, and Erin didn't want to give this up. Even if it would be better for everyone—Jen, Charlie, Darcy, and herself—she wanted to hold on to this woman, maybe forever. Despite the dim light, she saw Darcy's eyes start to shine, as if she too were thinking precisely the same thing.

The kiss nearly undid her. Darcy's lips were soft at first, and then, meeting no resistance, they became more and more insistent. Erin's knees threatened to unhinge, and she grabbed Darcy's shoulders in order to kiss her back and not fall to the floor. Darcy grabbed Erin's waist and squeezed her closer, as if trying to pull her inside. It was a long time before Erin pulled away for air, and when she did, she thought at first that Darcy was angry. A moment later, however, she realized her expression was actually something like hunger. The thought sent fluttering waves of heat coursing through her veins, and she had to make herself step back and away or risk letting go.

"Darcy, I—"

Darcy shook her head and raised a hand. "It's okay. I understand. I shouldn't have kissed you again."

Erin touched her arm. "It's not that I don't want to, Darcy. I like kissing you—maybe more than you know. But doing this here, now…It's not the right time."

Darcy laughed and then touched her face. "You mean you think we shouldn't make out at my little sister's birthday party?" Her fingers were warm and soft, and they sent shivers of pleasure racing up and down Erin's back.

Erin laughed and took her hand in hers. "Well, that too, yes. What I meant is that, well, with Jen and everything…I'm just not sure how she'd take it. I mean if she knew you and I were seeing each other. I haven't told her anything, and I don't like hiding things from her. I've already lied to her too much, and it's making me feel like a complete jerk. I just can't make it worse than it already is."

Darcy released Erin's hand before taking a step away. "It's okay, Erin. I understand. I blew it."

"You didn't 'blow it,' Darcy. It's just—"

"Believe me, Erin. I blew it. I have to live with that now, and again, I'm sorry."

Erin opened her mouth to argue again but closed it. Despite wanting to reassure her, Erin knew what Darcy said was true. They couldn't do anything about their situation now. What might have been had died weeks ago.

They continued to stare at each other, and once again Erin almost gave in. She wanted this woman, and when she was younger, she would have taken what she wanted, consequences be damned. Even now, old enough to know better, she nearly closed the distance between them again. The nagging reminder of her older sister stopped her. Jen was so brokenhearted that she couldn't be here tonight. This thought stopped Erin from making what would undoubtedly be a mistake, and she turned away to gaze out the window again.

Out of the corner of her eye, she noticed Darcy still looking at her, but before long, she let out a sigh and joined Erin at the window. Once again, her shoulder was close enough to Erin's that she could feel the warmth of her skin, and she had to suppress a shudder of longing. Erin wasn't really seeing anything besides her own reflection. She was so rattled she could barely think straight. She needed to get out of here.

Desperate for an excuse, she was about to invent a reason to leave the room when her phone in her pocket rang.

"Sorry," she said after she pulled it out. "It's Jen."

"Don't worry about it. Go ahead," Darcy said, and took a few steps away.

"Hello?"

After a long pause, then Erin heard sobbing on the other end of the line.

"Jen? Are you there? What's going on?"

Jen snuffled a little, took a deep breath, and started sobbing again.

"Jen? What is it? What's wrong? Are you okay? Is Dad okay?"

"It-it's not us," Jen said, choking on her words.

"Then what is it? Is someone hurt?"

It took Jen a moment to calm down enough to talk again. "It's Lydia, Erin. She's in trouble."

"Trouble? What kind of trouble?"

She was dimly aware of Darcy coming closer at this point, but she was too focused on the phone to look at her.

Jen was sobbing again, too upset to talk, and a moment later their father was on the line. "Sorry, Erin, it's your dad. Jen can't talk."

"What's happened, Dad?"

"Lydia is in some big trouble out in California. She was at the scene of a crime."

"What?" Erin shouted.

"The private investigator I hired managed to find some leads, first in Las Vegas and then in Southern California. The trail went cold for a while, but he's been circulating her photo among his connections down there until he finally found something. A cop friend of his found some video footage of a gas-station burglary just outside of Los Angeles. Your sister was there."

"She robbed someone?"

"She didn't, but her boyfriend did. Still, she could be considered an accessory."

Erin had moved closer to the piano and found herself sitting down, hard, on the bench. She put a hand to her mouth, so horrified she thought she might scream.

"Is she in jail?"

"No. They're on the run, and the police are hunting them. We're still looking for her. If we find them first, we might be able to convince them to turn themselves in. Maybe the cops will be more forgiving that way. I'm going to fly out to California tonight and help the investigators. I can't take just waiting around."

"I'll come too," Erin said, and got to her feet.

"No, honey, please don't. Jen needs you more than I do right now. Can you come home? I don't want to leave her here alone."

"Of course. Whatever she needs."

"Thanks, Erin. I'll see you in a few hours."

They hung up, and Erin burst into tears. Darcy was there in seconds, pulling her into an embrace. She let Erin cry without saying anything, simply soothing her. Erin finally got control of herself and stepped away.

"Thanks, Darcy. Sorry for crying all over you."

"It's okay."

"Could you go get my aunt for me? It's about my little sister— Lydia. I don't think I can go downstairs with all those people right now."

"Of course."

Erin was left alone for a moment, and she took the opportunity to turn on the lights. By the time her aunt joined her, she'd managed to calm down considerably, but Eddie was clearly upset at her appearance. They walked directly toward each other and gave each other a long, solid hug.

Darcy was hovering in the doorway, and Erin motioned her in. "Come on, Darcy. It won't be a secret for long, and the least I can do is let you know why we have to leave."

Eddie seemed surprised but said nothing. Darcy and Eddie were both waiting, expectantly, with a similar worried expression in their eyes. Her voice was caught in her throat, and she opened her mouth several times to speak, but nothing came out.

Eddie prompted her. "Darcy said it was something about Lydia?"

Erin nodded, surprised to be tearing up again. Darcy reached out a hand and Erin took it, squeezing it gratefully. Eddie raised her eyebrows at this exchange but said nothing.

Erin took a deep breath and let it out. "Lydia was seen in California. She's on video while her boyfriend is robbing a gas station. The police are looking for them."

She managed to get through this explanation without breaking down, but once she'd finished, she started crying again. This time her aunt held her until she calmed down, and when they finally pulled apart, Darcy had taken a few steps away from them, her expression troubled and upset.

Darcy shook her head, now clearly angry. "This is my fault. I should have said something earlier."

Erin was stunned. "What do you mean?"

Darcy met her eyes. "A few days after we met, I saw Lydia and Geo outside of your brewery, in the alley. They were with someone else, and your sister's boyfriend sold a little bag of something to the third person."

"Drugs?" Eddie asked, pale.

Darcy shrugged. "I can't be sure, but yes, that's what it looked like." She turned to Erin. "I should have said something."

Erin shook her head. "It's okay, Darcy. It's not your fault. Lydia is constantly making bad decisions. She should have known better."

Darcy wouldn't let it go. "Still, maybe if I'd mentioned it to you—"

"I would have said you were being nosy," Erin said, shaking her head. "Really, Darcy, don't blame yourself." She looked at her aunt. "Eddie, I have to get back to Loveland. Can I borrow your car?"

"I'm coming with you," Eddie said. "We can go right now."

Erin turned to Darcy again. "I'm sorry, and please tell your sister we hate to have to leave her party."

"I will," Darcy said, "and no need to apologize to me or to her. She'll understand."

They stared at each other for a long beat before Erin wrenched her eyes away. She was vaguely aware of her aunt saying her own good-byes behind her, but she kept her eyes averted. She didn't want to look at Darcy anymore. Her aunt and Darcy talked far longer than seemed necessary, just far enough away that Erin couldn't hear them. She didn't know what they could possibly be discussing, but strangely, they quickly embraced before Eddie rejoined her. She and her aunt left soon after, rushing downstairs and out into the chilly night.

Only as they walked the last block to the hotel did Erin realize she might never see Darcy again. But perhaps it was for the best. Even if Jen could recover from the whole nightmare with Charlie, after what had happened with Lydia, Erin couldn't imagine Darcy being interested in getting involved.

CHAPTER SEVENTEEN

The ride home was a blur of looming dark mountains and snow. Erin drove much too fast for mountain roads at night, but Eddie never suggested that she slow down or take it easier. She too was upset and didn't seem to notice Erin's speed. Eddie continued to suggest that everything would be okay, but even she didn't sound like she believed it. Lydia might very well end up in jail if she was caught.

They drove straight through without stopping, the usual four-hour ride taking less than three. As they pulled into her driveway, Erin saw her father's car in front of their house. She parked and saw him coming out the side door, a small suitcase in hand. He appeared surprised to see them and checked his watch before coming over and giving them both a quick hug.

"You must have flown here!" he said. "We didn't expect you for another hour at least. I'm glad you're here, though. I have to go to the airport now, and I didn't want to leave Jen by herself for long. I tried calling Lottie a while ago but didn't get any response."

"I'm coming with you," Eddie said.

Her father's eyebrows shot up, and then he quickly shook his head. "I can't let you do that, Eddie. Let me get settled out there, and you can join me later today. After all, you've been driving all night. You must be exhausted."

"On the contrary—I'm wide awake. And I can do more good with you than staying around here. I have a lot of friends in the hotel business in California, and I can ask them to start looking for Lydia."

"Well, I can't imagine she and Geo staying anyplace you might have written about, Eddie. They're probably holed up in some bed-bug motel or sleeping under a bridge, for all we know."

Eddie shook her head. "It doesn't matter. We'll find them together."

Her father, seeing he couldn't dissuade her, finally sighed. "Okay, Eddie. I'll appreciate the company, anyway. Grab your things and we can get going. The least I can do is drive us to the airport." He turned to Erin. "Like I said earlier, Jen is very upset. Do what you can to keep her calm. I'll call when we get to California, and I'll update you as often as I can."

All three embraced, and Erin stood in the driveway to watch them leave. Once they'd disappeared down the street, she sighed and went inside.

Jen stood in the living room, in front of the fireplace. She seemed haggard and tired and was wearing an ill-fitting set of pajamas that hung on her body. She smiled when she saw Erin, and they held each other tightly for a long moment.

Erin sat down heavily on the sofa, her fatigue finally catching up to her. Jen was clearly hyped up and started pacing.

"Come on, Jen, sit down. You're making me nervous."

Jen frowned and stopped walking, but she didn't sit. She shook her head. "I should have done something."

"What do you mean?"

"We both noticed something was off with Lydia. I mean, even more than usual. Didn't you think she'd been acting strange the last few months?"

"Well, yes, but I couldn't imagine her getting herself into this kind of trouble."

Jen gave her a level stare. "You can be honest, Erin. Didn't you see any signs that something was going on?"

Erin opened her mouth to protest and then closed it. She remembered seeing Lydia and Geo together at the Brewers' Festival in Fort Collins. They'd both been pale and bedraggled. Erin had known something was up, but she'd dismissed her suspicions, thinking maybe they had a hangover. Even after that, Lydia had been acting strangely—secretive and furtive, even for her.

Jen nodded when she saw Erin hesitate. "Exactly. She's been missing work—"

"Which she always does—"

"She looks terrible—"

"Which is not exactly something new, either."

Jen shook her head. "No, Erin, it was different, and we both knew that."

"So what if she was different, Jen? How is that our fault?"

"We could have done something, said something. Maybe if we'd intervened, she wouldn't be in this position now."

Erin laughed, bitterly. "Do you honestly believe that? Since when has Lydia ever taken our advice?"

Jen didn't let it go. "We still should have tried. I'm so mad at myself, I could spit. I've been so self-centered, so focused on my own stupid drama, that I let it blind me to a real tragedy taking place right in front of our eyes."

Erin sighed and got to her feet. She hugged Jen again, but her sister remained stiff and withdrawn, her eyes dark and worried.

"Goddamn it, Jen. You can't blame yourself. Lydia is always doing dumb things and running around with stupid people. She always has. This isn't anyone's fault but her own."

Jen's face contorted as if she couldn't believe what she was hearing. "You don't feel bad for her? For ignoring her?"

Erin shook her head. "I feel bad, yes, and I'm worried, but I genuinely don't think we could have done anything before she ran away or stopped her from running away. Anyway—that's all in the past. We need to worry about what comes next—how to find her and how to help her."

Jen was still upset. Her face got paler and paler as she stared at Erin. "You sound heartless, Erin. You know that?"

"I'm not heartless, Jen. I'm just being realistic. What do you want me to do? Get down on my knees and beg for forgiveness? I don't think either one of us did anything wrong."

"Well, that's how we differ, I suppose," Jen said, her voice icy and quiet. She turned and left the room.

"Jen!" Erin called. She started to go after her and then stopped. It was rare for Jen to be angry enough to storm out of a room. She needed time to calm down.

Erin sat down heavily on the sofa again and thought about the conversation they'd just had. Was she being heartless? Was she cruel? She shook her head. If they'd approached Lydia about anything before she ran away, she would have blown up, just like she did Christmas Eve. She might have run away even sooner or done something else equally stupid. Ever since their mother died, Lydia had been one step from falling apart or throwing her whole life away, and it looked like it had finally happened. She needed therapy, not just sympathy and attention.

Wanting to rest her eyes for a moment, Erin nestled into the sofa, letting the warmth from the fire seep through her. A moment later, she was asleep.

❖

The next few days passed with rigid iciness between Erin and Jen. Jen refused to talk to her and did everything she could to avoid being alone with her. Erin initially tried to be patient. A lot of people coped with sorrow and worry by blaming themselves. Jen had acted very similarly right after their mother died—wishing she could turn back time. Erin coped by being pragmatic, making plans and being realistic. She did what she could to help her father from afar, in addition to keeping up with the search. Jen wanted nothing to do with reality, and after a while, Erin's annoyance with her turned to anger. Hiding in hurt feelings did no good for anyone, least of all Lydia, and let alone Jen. By the third day of the silent treatment, Erin resented Jen's pity-party, as it meant Jen didn't have to do anything but feel guilty.

Because of the upset with Lydia, they of course missed the announcement of the winners of Western States in Aspen. By the time Erin read the email about it, she'd almost forgotten they'd even been in the running. Two breweries from Oregon were the winner and runner-up—BSB's porter came in tenth out of eleven states, winning over only Arizona's entry. In her current mood, she didn't even bother trying to tell Jen about their loss. She simply forwarded the email to her, and Jen didn't say a thing about it.

Erin tried to restrict the story about Lydia to people within their family, but by the fourth day of Jen's silent treatment, she finally called Lottie, desperate to hear a friendly voice.

"Christ, Erin. I'm so sorry to hear it. And there's no news yet?"

"Nothing. My dad and Eddie split up a couple of days ago so they could cover more ground, but they haven't found any sign of Lydia anywhere. Last I heard, they planned to stay in Southern California for a while longer, and then they might actually leave the state. Lydia and Geo could be headed back to Nevada after the robbery. But that was yesterday's rumor, so I'm not sure."

"Crap. How's Jen taking it?"

Erin smiled. Lottie would remember how she reacted to their mother's death. "About as you would expect."

"So you're not talking to each other?"

This time Erin laughed, the first time she'd done so in days. "How'd you know?"

"Lucky guess. Want me to come over?"

"Would you?"

"Sure. I just have to stop by my place first." She paused. "I'm at Will's right now."

"Okay, Lottie. No problem. Just come over when you can."

A few days after Christmas, Lottie told her that she and Will had a long, painful heart-to-heart discussion about what had happened when Erin and Will were kids. Will had immediately confessed to what he'd done. Lottie explained that this had helped her decide to give him another chance. Had he dismissed it or pretended it hadn't happened, she would have walked out on him forever. As an apology, Will had written Erin a letter, of all things, apologizing for his behavior when they were children. It was long and heartfelt, and seemed genuine, but Erin wasn't quite sold on him yet. Lottie seemed content with him, maybe even happy, and Erin didn't hate him anymore, but she didn't see the appeal, either. He would have to prove himself worthy of Lottie somehow, and he hadn't done that yet. Lottie was still awkward about bringing him up around Erin, despite the fact that they had essentially moved in together. Erin hoped they could both reach a place where it wasn't like this, but they weren't there yet.

Erin paced around the living room as she waited. The brewery was between big projects right now, so she was home before midnight for once. Jen was still at work. She didn't have any real reason to be there, which meant she was simply hiding out. This was, for the moment, however, convenient, as it gave her and Lottie a chance to catch up, and Erin could bitch about her sisters without Jen around to hear her.

Strangely, two sets of headlights flashed across the darkened windows, and when Erin pulled the curtains aside, she was surprised to see that two cars had pulled into the driveway, almost simultaneously. The lights blinded her for a moment, and even after both cars turned them off, she didn't recognize the car farther away until her father got out. She raced for the door and opened it, just as Lottie and her father were hugging hello. She ran over to them, and all three of them hugged again.

"What are you doing here?" Erin asked him. "Did you find Lydia?"

"Unfortunately, no. I'm just here for a day or two to take care of some business I can't put off, and then I'm going to meet your aunt in Las Vegas. She went there yesterday with one of the private investigators we're working with."

"Well, come in, both of you," Erin said, motioning toward the door. "It's freezing out here."

"I can't stay long," her father said, following her. "I'm beat, and I have to get up early in the morning so I can head back as soon as possible. I just wanted to see you and your sister before I went home."

All three of them were inside now, and the house seemed overly warm after the chilly night air. Erin couldn't help but grimace at the mention of her sister, and her father caught the expression.

"What's the matter? Is Jen not here?"

"No. She's hiding at work. We're not really talking right now."

He raised his eyebrows. "Did something happen between you two?"

"No. She's just being Jen. Blaming herself, blaming me, blaming everyone but Lydia."

Her father stopped removing his coat and fixed her with a stern stare. "Is that fair of you, Erin? Blaming Lydia?"

"Who else am I supposed to blame, Dad? She got herself in this mess, as usual."

Again he shook his head. "I don't know why Lydia did what she did, Erin, but I can promise you she's not entirely to blame. I've seen the security video of the robbery, and one thing that's completely obvious is that she was surprised when Geo pulled that gun."

Erin's face heated with shame, but anger immediately replaced the emotion. "If that's the case, why hasn't she turned him in? Why keep running? She has to know it'll only make things worse."

Her father sighed and shook his head. "I can't answer that, Erin, but I have to give her the benefit of the doubt. She could have a lot of reasons. At the very least, I imagine she's scared to death right now."

Lottie agreed. "She's probably terrified."

Erin's anger warred with her sympathy, but again, her anger won out, in part because the two of them seemed to be ganging up on her.

"But again, how is that my fault? Or Jen's fault, or yours?" Erin was almost shouting now.

Her father grabbed her shoulders. "Erin—it's not anyone's fault. I agree with you. But blaming Lydia isn't the solution, and staying angry with Jen won't make things better. We need to help each other get through this."

Hot tears prickled Erin's eyes, and she almost relented. Shame and terror were beginning to overcome her anger, and she didn't want to let those feelings win. It was easier to be angry. She threw Lottie a searching look, hoping for someone to recognize and appreciate the justice of her reaction, but Lottie simply seemed sad, much like her father.

Before she could say anything, the door behind them opened, and Jen strode in. She must have seen the cars outside, but she looked startled to find them all standing just inside the door.

"What's going on? Is it about Lydia? Is she okay?"

Erin opened her mouth to fill her in but started sobbing. A moment later, Jen was hugging her, fiercely.

"I'm so sorry, Jen," Erin said.

"Shhhhh. It's okay. I haven't exactly been the best sister in the world, either. I'm sorry, too."

When they pulled apart, Jen was smiling, tears spilling down her cheeks. They both turned to the others, and everyone hugged again. The remains of Erin's anger disappeared, her sympathy and pity now warring with terror for her younger sister.

"My God," she said when they'd all pulled apart. "What's going to happen to her?"

Her father shook his head. "Nothing good. At best, we can hope she'll get an accessory-after-the-fact charge. At worst, she'll be tried for armed robbery. I've been calling all my lawyer friends to start looking for some representation for her in California. We can only hope now that she'll turn herself in, and soon."

Everyone jumped at the sound of ringing from her father's pocket. It was almost midnight now, so an unusual time for a call. He reached in and showed them the number phoning him—Aunt Eddie's—before answering.

"Yes, Eddie. What is it?"

Whatever Eddie had said was obviously important since her father staggered a little. Jen immediately grabbed his elbow and steered him over to one of the chairs at their kitchen table. He sat down heavily and covered his eyes with his spare hand.

"Thank God," he said. When he removed his hand, Erin saw that he was crying. "She's okay," he finally told them.

Erin and Jen immediately started talking, but he held up a hand to silence them, still listening to Eddie on the phone. He agreed with her a few times, shaking his head in clear disbelief. Finally, he said good-bye and hung up, still shaking his head.

"I can't believe it," he said.

"What happened?" Erin said, pulling out the chair nearest him. He was clearly stunned. He looked at all three of them and smiled widely, and Erin felt as if a thousand-pound weight had been lifted from her shoulders.

He had to swallow a few times and wipe his eyes before he could start talking. "Lydia turned herself in this morning. She also helped the police find Geo. According to your aunt, because she did this, she's in a much better position to be charged with accessory-after-the-fact than be charged as a principal. We'll just have to wait and see. She'll have her first court hearing in Los Angeles next week. Your aunt is going to bail her out in the morning after the arraignment."

"I thought they were in Las Vegas," Erin said.

"They were, but they went back to Los Angeles together so she could turn herself in."

"How?" Jen asked.

He shook his head. "I don't know the details. Your aunt's going to call in the morning once she has Lydia in a safe place. We owe Eddie a huge debt. I can't even imagine how she did it."

Everyone stood or sat in stunned silence. Ten minutes ago, Erin had been half-convinced that her sister would stay on the run for as long as she could—maybe forever—and now it looked like she might have a chance of making it out of all this without ruining her life. It was a slim possibility, but however slim, it was still a chance. She started shaking all over, crying again. She couldn't remember the last time she'd felt this relieved.

She and her father were on their feet again, and everyone was hugging and crying, but as the happy moment continued, Erin couldn't help but feel like something—someone—was missing. It was a strange sensation, and certainly not a welcome one. She'd been suppressing the feeling for days: a kind of desperate yearning for someone not here. Jen took an old bottle of cheap sparkling wine from the fridge, opened it, and poured everyone a glass, but

Erin was fighting something rising from within the deepest, darkest regions of her heart.

For the last few days, ever since she'd left Aspen, she'd done everything she could not to think about her conversation with Darcy in the darkened music room of that beautiful house. Now, however, as everyone around her gushed with relief and jubilation, she couldn't help but think about her. Maybe it was because Darcy had been there at the beginning of all of this mess with Lydia, but that wasn't the whole truth.

No. She simply wished Darcy was here with her, with them. Darcy would be just as happy as everyone here to think that Lydia was, if not yet saved, at least safe again. Erin had to stop herself from finding her phone and calling her. She should, at the very least, text Darcy the news, as she would no doubt be wondering what had happened to Lydia, but she should wait until tomorrow. It was late now, and Darcy would undoubtedly be surprised to get a message this late at night.

She saw Jen watching her strangely, one eyebrow raised, and shrugged off the deep longing as best as she could. After all, it didn't matter now, anyway. Darcy was in the past—for good this time. All that mattered was doing what she could in the present to help support her family. She lifted her glass for a toast and soon managed to suppress the feeling as they celebrated.

Still, lying in bed later that night, Erin wondered what would have happened if she'd called Darcy. Where was she? What was she doing? Who was she with? Despite her exhaustion, she couldn't fall asleep for a long time.

CHAPTER EIGHTEEN

Erin stood behind the counter in the tasting room and watched Lydia wash tables. Lydia seemed distracted, going slowly through the motions and not doing a very good job. All the tables she'd already wiped down still looked a little dirty. Erin and Jen needed to have a frank conversation with her about her job performance soon, certainly before the expansion project began in earnest next month. If Lydia couldn't get her act together, it might be better for her to find work somewhere else. Still, today wasn't the day for that conversation. It could wait a while longer, until Lydia found her equilibrium again.

The last three weeks had been a whirlwind. Erin and Jen had asked some of their brewing friends in the area to help cover their work in the days leading up to Lydia's preliminary trial. They'd flown out to Los Angeles with her father and were soon reunited with their aunt and Lydia, who'd been bailed out the morning before they got there. Lydia, of course, had to stay in California, and the whole family rented a house as they waited. The arraignment had been fast, but the preliminary trial was delayed several times that week. Just when it seemed like it might be delayed again over the following weekend, Lydia and her lawyers were called in on Friday. It was an open court, so the whole family was allowed to attend.

When the charges against Lydia were dismissed, everyone in the courtroom seemed to hold their breath in disbelief. It was a rare thing for a judge to dismiss charges at any time, let alone for armed robbery, accessory or not. Until that point, the family had been hoping for a quick turnaround between the preliminary and jury trial. No one had expected the charges to be dropped.

After she was dismissed, Lydia stood there for a long time, clearly too stunned to react. The rest of the family started crying and hugging each other. Even after their dad and aunt led her out of the courthouse and onto the street, each of them holding an arm, Lydia still seemed confused, almost as if she couldn't believe what was happening. Erin didn't blame her—she hardly believed it herself.

They'd been back in Loveland for a little over a week now. Lydia had been quiet all the way home and after they got her to their dad's place. Jen and Erin had been over once or twice to check on her and their father, but nothing had really changed. She was still silent, unwilling to talk about what had happened. Jen had argued that this was natural—clearly she was upset by what had happened, but Erin was starting to lose patience. She wanted some answers—or at least some version of a story—but Lydia seemed to think she didn't need to say or do anything now that she was out of jail. Further, as far as Erin knew, Lydia had never thanked their aunt for doing what she had to save her, and while she was quiet now, Lydia's silence seemed sullen rather than apologetic, almost as if she was angry about how things turned out.

Lydia had showed up at BSB a couple of days ago asking for shifts, and Jen had immediately put her into the schedule, thinking it would be good for her to have some structure to her life again. Erin had her reservations about having her here, and now, seeing her mope around the tasting room, Erin knew she'd been right. Lydia might be here in person, but clearly her mind was somewhere else. It didn't matter now, when the tasting room was quiet, but it could turn into a problem when more customers arrived later in the evening.

Erin set down the glass she'd been cleaning and walked around the corner of the bar. Lydia didn't notice her approach until Erin touched her shoulder, and even then she hardly reacted beyond turning around. Her face was blank and still pale, her hair greasy and lank.

Her lifelessness immediately quelled Erin's impatience, and she made her voice as gentle as possible. "Do you want to go home early? We're pretty dead in here, and it's going to be crazy this weekend."

The following weekend was the Loveland Valentine's Day Fire and Ice Festival. Valentine's Day is a major holiday in the City of Loveland, and the downtown festival had developed into a significant party over the last few years. There would be fireworks, ice sculptures, food vendors, and a huge number of people, many of whom would be ducking into BSB and other breweries and restaurants downtown to warm up. BSB was a sponsor this year for the first time, which meant that their name would be on all the programs and in the newspaper. She and Jen had taken a calculated risk and spent the money for a sponsorship, hoping to draw some out-of-towners a little distance from the main festival area to their brewery. They'd been fairly busy at last year's event, but they expected to be swamped all weekend this year.

Lydia shrugged. "I don't have any reason to leave early today or any day. Not like I have anything to go home to."

Erin's stomach dropped. Lydia's depression was starting to seem serious. Erin grabbed her shoulders. "Hey. Don't think like that. You have your whole life in front of you. You're still in your twenties, for God's sake."

Lydia gave a bitter laugh. "It's over, Erin, and you know it. The only thing I ever wanted—the only man I ever loved…" She shook her head, suddenly choking up. "It doesn't matter anymore."

"Of course it does, Lydia. You still have so much to look forward to. I know you don't like working here, but Dad, Jen, and I are willing to help you find a career you're interested in. Maybe you can go back to school—"

Lydia laughed again and shook her head. "You're all so deluded. Can you see me going back to school? Really?"

Erin's patience snapped again, and she dropped her hands. "So what are you going to do? Mope around Loveland for the rest of your life doing nothing? Do you know how ridiculous that sounds?"

For the first time in weeks, some life flared into Lydia's eyes. "Hey—fuck you, Erin! If anyone's pathetic around here, it's you and Jen. At least I went after my dreams!"

"What they hell are you talking about? I have my dream. You're working here!"

"I'm talking about Geo, you dummy. I left with him because I love him. And now…" She fought a sob and shook her head. "Well, he did something stupid, but I still love him. We were going to get married later that week." Her face hardened again. "And like I said, at least I tried to make it work. Jen just gave up when Charlie left. And you—well, you're not much better."

"What are you talking about?"

"I'm talking about Darcy! Who the hell do you think I'm talking about?"

Erin felt as if she'd been slapped, and she flinched in surprise. As far as she knew, Darcy and Lydia had never even spoken to each other. They'd met once or twice, and seen each other in passing more than that, but Erin thought that was the extent of their contact.

"Wh-what?" Erin asked.

"You know what I'm talking about, Erin. You drove her away."

"How did you—how could you—"

Lydia shook her head. "I know because Aunt Eddie told me, stupid."

"Told you what? What could she have possibly told you? Darcy and I aren't anything. I mean, we barely—"

"Oh, save it, Erin. Aunt Eddie told me everything."

Erin still couldn't believe what she was hearing. What on earth could Aunt Eddie have told her? She didn't know anything about their affair. How could she?

"I don't understand, Lydia. I really don't. What did she say?"

Lydia sighed, rolling her eyes. "Christ. Do you really want it spelled out? I told you I know everything."

"Tell me what you know." Erin could barely keep the impatience from her voice.

Lydia sighed again. "Fine. I'm in Vegas, right? With Geo?"

Erin nodded.

"We're minding our own business. We got this great suite at the Flamingo because Geo is so good at poker. He's like a high roller, or whatever."

"Okay," Erin said, making a rolling motion with her hands. "I get it. Geo's a swell guy."

Lydia glared at her. "As I was saying, before you interrupted me: we were in Vegas. I was still pretty mad at him after the whole robbery thing, but he kept saying he would be fine—that there were no witnesses or anything. I didn't even know I could get into trouble, too. Anyway, we're just hanging out, watching TV, and there's this loud knock on the door—almost pounding. We both freeze. I'm sure we were thinking the same thing: it's the police. Then I hear Aunt Eddie calling my name, and when I open the door, there she is."

Erin nodded again. She'd been wondering about this part of things. Her aunt had been evasive about how she'd found Lydia and gotten her to California, but Erin had thought she was simply being modest, not wanting to give herself credit and to save Lydia some embarrassment.

"Go on," Erin said.

"The thing is, Aunt Eddie wasn't alone."

"Oh?"

"Two other people were with her. One was a little guy wearing a swear-to-God fedora hat and trench coat. He looked like an extra in a bad detective movie. The other person was Darcy."

"What?" Erin couldn't help but shout.

Lydia laughed. "That's what I said. I was like, 'What are you doing here?' And Aunt Eddie was like, 'I could ask the same thing,' and I said, 'Not you, her!' and pointed at Darcy."

She was quiet after this, grinning. Erin finally couldn't take it. "And? What was Darcy doing there?"

"I'm not supposed to tell you. I wasn't even supposed to tell you she was there. She and Aunt Eddie made me promise not to say anything."

"Goddamn it, Lydia. Stop screwing around already. Just tell me the whole story."

Lydia laughed. "Well, let me ask you this. Who do you think bailed me out?"

Erin's heart seemed to skip a beat. Some of her surprise must have shown on her face, since Lydia laughed. "Exactly! It isn't like

Daddy or Aunt Eddie have that kind of money, not in ready cash like that, anyway. California seriously jacks up the cost of bail."

"You mean Darcy paid for your bail?"

"Yes, she did. Right before you, Jen, and Dad got there. She also tracked me and Geo down. She hired some people in Vegas while Daddy and Eddie were still in California. Anyway, she and Eddie flew me back to California, and then Darcy bailed me out the next morning. She disappeared before you got there, but she must have stayed in town, working her magic. No way were the charges dropped without some serious help."

Again, Erin was shocked. "You mean like bribes? That can't be true. Things like that happen only in the movies."

Lydia shook her head and then shrugged. "I guess. I don't know for sure, but I do know that one day I'm looking at ten-to-twenty, and the next I'm on a plane home."

"Jesus," Erin said. Her legs felt weak, and she pulled out one of the stools nearby and sat down on it heavily. Her head was whirling. If all of this was true, they basically owed Darcy Lydia's life.

Lydia seemed guilty now, her eyes darting around. "Don't tell Darcy I told you though, okay? Or Aunt Eddie? I'm supposed to keep it a secret." She glanced away and set her rag down on the table. "Anyway, I think I will go home to Dad's place, if you don't mind."

She paused, seeming, finally, to realize how upset Erin was. She touched Erin's shoulder, making her meet her eyes. "That woman loves you, Erin. You're really stupid if you don't go after her."

Erin didn't respond, and a moment later Lydia walked out the door.

❖

Erin spent the new few days in a daze. Jen noticed she was acting strangely, but Erin managed to blame it on stress related to the festival and their impending expansion. Truthfully, she could hardly keep her mind on work. She was still in shock over what Lydia had told her.

She was tempted to call and ask Aunt Eddie to confirm what Lydia had said, but she also didn't want Lydia to feel like she'd betrayed her trust. She'd promised not to say anything, which meant she needed to think of a way to get Aunt Eddie to admit it on her own. Once or twice, between tasks in the brewery and sitting alone at home, Erin was tempted to call Darcy, but that was the last thing she should do, even if she was desperate to hear her voice.

Erin was also thinking about what Lydia had said—about going after what you wanted. Lydia had clearly fallen for and gone after the wrong guy, but she did have a point. Maybe if Jen had chased Charlie, gotten him alone, and admitted how she felt about him, the two of them would have had a chance. And maybe if Erin had been honest from the beginning about her feelings for Darcy—admitted them to herself and to everyone else—she could have had a chance with Darcy, too.

It seemed too late now to do anything about Darcy. It had been too long since they'd seen each other, and it was so complicated now. Erin would figure out a way of thanking her for Lydia, something that wouldn't embarrass her too much, but that would have to be it. It was too much to rake up all that pain again. Darcy hadn't contacted her since Aspen, and it was clear she wanted to stay away. Erin had decided that Darcy had done what she'd done for Lydia out of guilt over Charlie and Jen, a kind of parting gift. Helping Lydia had been an apology, even if, as far as Darcy knew, no one knew about her involvement but their aunt and her little sister.

Unlike Oktoberfest, the first morning of Valentine's Day Fire and Ice Festival dawned with bitter, biting cold. It was, however, sunny and bright out, and the sun woke Erin from a deep sleep. Like Lydia, she'd been moping around a little the last few days, her moods vacillating between elation and depression, but today she would have to put all that on pause. They would be busy from tonight until Monday, and she still needed to double-check that their Valentine's Ale tap was up and running. She'd let an assistant brewer, Javi, set it up last night without her, knowing he could handle it, but he would want her to check his work. Once the expansion was completed this summer, she planned to promote him to full brewer. She and Jen had already decided this would be a natural next step for him, and no one deserved it more than he did.

Erin dressed carefully in thick, burgundy corduroy pants and a heavy, yellow flannel shirt under a dark-blue sweater. Because the street in front of their brewery would be closed to traffic for the festival, they'd received permission from the city to set up a small beer garden right in the street. There would be tables and heat lamps for guests, but it would still be very cold once the sun set. Erin would be inside and outside all night tonight, and she would have to stay as warm as possible despite the chill. Even with the cold, the city was expecting record attendees, and the last thing Erin needed to worry about was the weather. More than likely, she'd get overly hot from running around all day and night, but that was always better than freezing. Lydia had volunteered to be a secondary outside runner, which was no small task, and Erin was a little worried that Lydia would bungle it. When Lydia volunteered, she seemed eager to help, and Jen was convinced she'd turned over a new leaf in the last couple of days. Maybe she was starting to realize how much people had done for her to get her back home. Erin wasn't convinced, but maybe, at the very least, Lydia was hoping for some good tips this weekend, which meant she would have to work harder than usual.

The morning and afternoon of the first day passed in a blur of last-minute activity. Once they had checked and double-checked the beer lines, with backup kegs at the waiting, they had to wait for the city to close the street outside, which ended being much later in the day than anticipated. Customers were already starting to come in the door before they had a chance to set up their beer garden outside, and once again, Erin was forced to call Lottie for assistance.

She showed up with Will, who immediately made himself useful, carrying chairs and heat lamps tirelessly and without complaint. It was the first time since Estes that Erin had been around him for more than a few seconds in passing, and she found she no longer resented him like she had. This whole mess with Lydia had put a lot of things in perspective, and holding on to a twenty-plus-year grudge wouldn't do her any good. That didn't make what he'd done when they were kids right, but she was willing to think he had changed with time. And hell, even if he hadn't, he was good at moving heavy things, which was what they needed more than anything right now.

She, Jen, Lydia, and all the other employees took shifts outside in the beer garden and inside in the overly crowded tasting room. It was bitterly cold out, even with the heat lamps, especially working with cold beer. Hardly anyone could take the chill for long, which meant a constant rotation of employees and customers inside and out all night.

By ten that evening, as the festival wrapped up for the first night, everyone was drooping with fatigue. Erin's shoulders were tight and hot from all the things she'd been carrying. Would she even be able to move her arms tomorrow?

She was sitting backward at the front counter on a stool, resting her back against the bar. A few customers were still in there, but most of the people sitting around the tasting room were staff nursing a celebratory beer. Everyone looked as exhausted as she was. Lottie and Will were next to her at the front. Lottie was sitting, Will standing in front of her, her arms around him. They were whispering and giggling, and Erin couldn't help but grin at them occasionally. Now, seeing them together like she had the last few hours, she could more clearly understand why Lottie liked him. He was obviously devoted to her and very affectionate, and that could go a long way with some people. He would never be good enough for her, but that would probably be the case with anyone. No one was good enough for Lottie because she was basically one of the best people in the world.

Jen was standing by one of the long tables in the center of the room, chatting with Lydia and some of the other employees. They were a little too far away for Erin to hear them clearly, but everyone was laughing at something Lydia had just said. Jen was flushed and happy, and even Lydia seemed to be enjoying herself.

The front door opened, and everyone looked in that direction. While they were technically open for another hour, it was unusual for anyone to show up this late. Further, the two people in the doorway stood out from everyone in the room. Their winter clothes, unlike the Coloradoans', were formal—cashmere overcoats and leather gloves.

It was Charlie and Darcy.

Everyone but the few remaining customers recognized them on sight. All the brewery employees had seen them often enough to know who they were, and everyone who worked here knew what had happened between Jen and Charlie. The room fell completely silent as they stepped in.

Charlie paled visibly, and Darcy's frown was even more grim than usual. She didn't look at Erin. Her eyes, like Charlie's, remained rooted on Jen, whose mouth was open. Erin watched it close with an audible snap a moment later. Her face, like Charlie's, lost all its color.

No one said anything for a long moment, though Charlie opened his mouth a couple of times and closed it, swallowing and licking dry lips. He seemed to make himself take another step or two into the room, and Darcy actually pushed him a little from behind.

Charlie suddenly seemed to realize that everyone in the room was watching him, and he glanced around briefly before gazing at Jen again.

They spoke at the same time.

"Jen, I wanted—"

"What are you doing here?"

They both blushed a little and smiled.

"Go ahead," Jen finally said.

He cleared his throat, his eyes again darting around the room and the audience before settling on her. "Jen, I wanted to see you again. I wanted to talk, to explain..." He shook his head. "No, that's not true—there's nothing to explain. I was an ass, and I was wrong. I hurt you, and I'll never forgive myself."

He took a few steps closer to her. They were still several feet apart, and a few people sat in the stools between them, but their eyes remained locked.

He cleared his throat again. "Jen, I was wondering if you would give me a second chance. You see—I love you. My life these last months has meant nothing to me—nothing at all. And the reason is you. You're why I want to get up in the morning. You're why I want to keep living. I loved you the moment we met, and I've never stopped."

After a tense pause, all eyes in the room turned to Jen. Her face was frozen in shock and surprise. Her lips began to tremble as she held back tears.

Seeming to draw strength from her silence, Charlie took a few more steps toward her. They were now within touching distance, but he kept his hands at his side. His eyes were red too, and he was trembling.

"I'm willing to turn in my resignation at work. Today, on my way here, I drafted my letter to the board of trustees." He pulled out his phone and waved it. "All I have to do is hit Send, and I'm free of them. I can leave Boston behind with no regrets. All I want is here, is you."

Jen burst out sobbing and launched herself at him. His arms were open to catch her, and they were soon whirling together, lips clasped in a kiss. The room erupted in cheers and clapping, whistles, and shouts. Several people rose to clap and cheer, a few of them slapping Charlie on the back. Jen and Charlie pulled apart a moment later, their beaming eyes still locked on each other, smiles wide and happy.

Jen released Charlie a moment later to hug Lydia and Lottie, who had rushed over, and when she stepped away from them, she turned again into Charlie's arms. He paused, held up a hand, and everyone in the room watched as he pulled out his phone. He held it up for the crowd and dramatically hit the Send button for what was presumably his resignation letter. He put his phone away, grabbed Jen, and soon they were kissing again. Friends, coworkers, and strangers began clapping and cheering once more.

Erin was on her feet now, but she remained next to the bar, alone. She'd watched the reunion with a disbelief that gradually changed to joy. Charlie and Jen looked so right together. These last months apart, the problem hadn't simply been that Jen was missing him. Jen had also been missing a part of herself. She seemed whole again there in his arms.

Erin made eye contact with Lydia, who, after hugging Jen, had moved away from the center of the room and closer to her. They shared a wide grin and moved closer together. Lottie joined them a moment later, and all three hugged with simple relief. They'd seen what had just happened. Not only had Charlie returned, but Jen had too.

Jen caught sight of this exchange and released herself from Charlie for a moment, coming over to them. Already her face had regained its usual happy calm. The depression of the last months had slipped away as if it had never been. She and Erin stared at each other for a moment, both smiling, before Erin moved forward to give her a long hug.

"I'm so happy for you," Erin whispered in her ear.

When they pulled apart, tears were falling from Jen's eyes. She was obviously too overcome to say anything, but she nodded. A moment later Jen was turning toward Charlie, and Erin watched her walk toward him and into her future.

The scene between her sister and Charlie had been so absorbing, Erin had forgotten to see how Darcy was taking all this. When she did, a crowd of coworkers and customers stood where she'd been, beaming as happily as she was. But when Erin moved around the edge of the room to see if Darcy was standing behind them, she didn't see her. She looked around wildly, but her growing dread confirmed what she thought she already knew.

Darcy was gone.

CHAPTER NINETEEN

Erin's stomach dropped, and a hot wave of panic swept through her. She searched the tasting room one more time, but Darcy had left—without saying anything to Erin. As far as Erin knew, she hadn't even looked at her. She'd come, she'd done something wonderful, and she'd vanished.

Erin stood outside the ring of well-wishers around Jen, dumbfounded and disappointed. She watched Jen and Charlie again, both of whom had an arm clasped around the other's waist. Charlie was making some kind of speech, but Erin couldn't concentrate on the words. Her ears were ringing, her mind far away.

She might have stood there, rooted to the spot, but Lydia touched her arm. The sensation shocked her into reality, and she jumped, heart once again racing.

Lydia held her hands up. "Yikes. Jumpy much?"

Erin gave her a half-hearted smile, unable to cover her feelings.

"What do you think about them?" Lydia gestured at the reunited couple.

"What do you mean?"

"Is it a good thing? For Jen? After all that mess the last few months?"

Erin nodded. "It's the best thing that could have happened. They're made for each other."

"That's what I think. They just look right together, don't they?"

Erin turned to watch Jen and Charlie, suddenly afraid that if they kept talking, she might start crying. This surprised her. She'd meant what she'd just told Lydia, but the tears in her eyes weren't happy ones. Instead, they came from a deep, sinking loneliness spreading through her as she watched Jen's happy face.

Lydia touched her arm again, and Erin met her eyes. Lydia seemed confused and hurt.

"Why do you look like you're about to cry, Erin?"

Erin opened her mouth and had to snap it shut again. She choked on a sob and turned away, covering her eyes. Any second she would start crying and wouldn't be able to stop.

A moment later, Lydia put her hand on Erin's back and rubbed it. "Is it because she left again?"

Erin, her back still toward her little sister, was still unable to speak. Lydia pulled on one of her shoulders, and Erin turned toward her. A moment later, they were hugging and crying freely. Lydia held her for a long time, and once Erin had calmed down, Lydia's concern moved her. They'd never been very close, and Lydia always seemed so self-centered and cynical. It was a nice surprise to find that she could be caring, too.

Erin finally pulled away, smiling. "Thanks, Lydia. I'm just feeling sorry for myself."

Lottie joined them a moment later, and when she saw Erin's face, she frowned. "What's up? You're upset." She motioned at Charlie and Jen. "Is it about them? Are you unhappy about it?"

Erin shook her head. "No. It's not that."

"She's in love with Darcy, and Darcy left," Lydia said.

Erin and Lottie stared at her in surprise, and then Erin laughed. With Lydia, one thing you could always count on was blunt, no-bullshit truth.

Lottie met Erin's eye, her eyebrows high. "Is she right?"

Erin hesitated and then nodded.

"Well, go find her, then, you ninny!" Lottie said, pushing her toward the door.

"Yeah, you idiot! Go get her! She might be waiting outside!" Lydia added.

Again, Erin hesitated, flicking her gaze back and forth between the door and Jen and Charlie. Jen likely wouldn't even notice if she left right now, and judging from their dreamy expressions they might not notice her again all night.

Again, Lottie playfully pushed her. "Get going, you coward!"

"Run!" Lydia said, laughing loud enough that several people turned their way.

Erin gave them both a wide grin and then dashed for the door, stopping only to fight her way through the throng of people crowding the doorway. A few more people had come in since Charlie had made his announcement, and to Erin, now that she wanted simply to get through them, they seemed to have multiplied tenfold.

Once outside, the cold, like the crowd, seemed to want to drive her back inside. She was dressed warmly, but without a coat, hat, and gloves, she was going to get very chilly very quickly. She paused, almost ready to go back, but she didn't debate her choice for long. She dashed out into the street and looked in each direction, hoping to spot Darcy. While the crowds had basically dispersed at this hour, a lot of people were still out here chatting and milling around before they went home. They'd stopped serving beer outside almost an hour ago, but not everyone here was a customer of the brewery. Some of them were clearly just standing or sitting out in the beer garden under the heat lamps chatting and laughing with friends. BSB was somewhat close to one of the temporary parking lots roped off for the festival, and several people were standing around in the streets saying their good-byes to friends before finding their cars.

Erin took a couple of steps toward the parking lot, thinking that would be the most logical place for Darcy to go, but she stopped a moment later. Some instinct was telling her to turn around and head down the street, toward the festival proper a couple of blocks away. The festival was over for the night, but the city kept the downtown area blocked off all weekend, and even from here, Erin could see some people still standing around in the street admiring the ice sculptures.

She started walking that way, dodging the smaller but still substantial crowds until she stood at the corner of Fourth and

Lincoln, directly in the center of downtown. Here, well away from the parking lots, she was almost alone. A few couples stood around by themselves, heads bent, huddled together near a heat lamp making promises, speaking sweet nothings. Red and pink lights hung from the buildings above, casting everything in a rosy, pale light.

Erin's hopes died as she stood there. While it had been fairly crowded until about half a block back, she would have seen Darcy had she passed her. She'd been so sure she'd find her out here, she didn't know what to do now. She took one more long look up and down the major intersection and turned around, her heart heavy and her eyes burning.

Suddenly, Erin fixed her eyes on a lone figure standing in front of an ice sculpture of a large bird of prey. Despite the cold, the sculpture had apparently melted a little, and the artist was touching up her work with a chainsaw. Ice particles flew into the street, falling like snow onto the lone person standing there watching the artist work.

Even in the dim light, and even with her back facing her way, Erin knew immediately that the lone figure was Darcy. It was almost as if she'd felt rather than seen her standing there. She was still some distance away, maybe half a block, and Erin didn't call out or say anything, but Darcy's shoulders twitched, and then she was turning around, peering into the dim, rosy light. Her eyes found Erin, and both of them stopped moving again, simply staring at each other.

After a pause, Erin began walking toward her again, and Darcy moved to meet her. They stopped a few feet apart. The ice flakes from the artist and the ice sculpture could still reach them, and they fell in little spiraling flakes, resting on their hair and shoulders.

Now that she was in front of her, Erin couldn't think of anything to say. With the ice and the light, Darcy was too beautiful for something as simple as language. Erin's mind whirled, her thoughts spiraling and confused like the ice flakes drifting in the air around them.

Finally, she latched onto one clear thought and took another step closer to Darcy. They were now slightly more than an arm's length apart, a dangerous distance, but Erin needed to be this close to see her face clearly.

"Thank you," Erin said.

Darcy's eyebrows rose, clearly expecting her to say something else. "For what?"

"For what you've done for my family—both of my sisters. First Lydia—"

Darcy actually jumped a little in apparent surprise, and Erin remembered that she wasn't supposed to know what Darcy had done. "Thank you. I don't know how I can ever make it up to you. I realize Lydia wasn't supposed to say anything, but she thought I should know, and her intentions were good.

"As for Jen and Charlie, well, you saw them in there. I'm so glad you helped him see his way back to her."

Darcy took another step closer, and now they were in touching distance. Even here, Erin could feel the warmth radiating off her.

Darcy's expression was serious, almost grim. "I wanted to help your sisters, yes, because I could, and in Jen's case, because I needed to correct my own wrongdoing. But you must know I wouldn't have done anything if it weren't for you."

Erin had suspected as much, and rather than feel angry or disgusted, as she might have if she was being petty, she accepted the simple honesty of Darcy's words.

"Thank you," Erin said again.

Darcy smiled weakly and they stood there, staring at each other, wordless for a long time. Finally, Erin touched Darcy's face, and the cold bleakness died out of Darcy's eyes as Erin brushed her cheek. Darcy clasped Erin's frigid fingers in her own gloved hands and rubbed them briskly.

"What are you doing out here without gloves?" Darcy asked, her tone mock-serious.

"Looking for someone." Erin grinned up at her. "I couldn't wait."

"Did you find her?"

Erin nodded, suddenly emotional, and Darcy smiled widely. She pulled Erin closer, wrapping her arms around her back to warm her. Erin tilted her chin upward to meet Darcy's eyes, and they just stood there, wordless, for a long time. Despite the cold, Erin would have happily stayed there in her arms forever.

Darcy shivered and rubbed Erin's back. "We have to get you inside, somewhere warmer."

"I guess so," Erin said, grinning. "Maybe my place this time?"

Darcy's smiled faded, and then her lips brushed Erin's, gently at first and then with mounting pressure and fire. Erin's knees threatened to buckle, and her head whirled like the drifting ice around them. She soon forgot the cold, once so biting and overwhelming, in the heat and passion of their kiss.

In Darcy's lips, Erin felt her final misgivings die. All the feelings she'd been fighting, all the aching longing she'd been suppressing, rose and presented itself to her one last time as if to say good-bye. She was exactly where she was always supposed to be. Wherever Darcy was, that's where Erin should stay.

They might have stood there kissing all night, but Darcy suddenly pulled away, looking up and behind Erin. Erin turned, not sure what to expect. A few feet away, her sisters, Charlie, Lottie, and Will stood in silence, all of them smiling so widely they looked like an advertisement for a dentist.

Erin laughed and stepped away from Darcy, making the few steps to her sisters and friends. As it had been Lydia who gave her the final push she needed, she hugged her first, but when she turned to Jen, she flushed in embarrassment. Jen had been watching her with something like bafflement, and Erin couldn't help but laugh again.

Jen gestured back and forth between her and Darcy. "So when did this all happen?"

Erin grinned. "It's been going on a long time."

Jen's expression was a little dark and hurt. "Why didn't you tell me?"

Erin shook her head, glancing at Charlie. Jen understood, and her eyes darkened a moment with sorrow and pain. "Right." She touched Erin's shoulder. "You didn't have to do that, you know. I would have understood."

Erin nodded and shrugged, but her omission was already forgiven and forgotten. She and Jen hugged, tight and quick, and then Erin turned around and went back to Darcy. Darcy's arms were open and warm, and when Erin met her lips, she felt as if she was where she was supposed to be for the first time in weeks. Erin was vaguely aware of the others clapping and shouting behind them, but for the most part the world fell away and she was left in Darcy's arms.

By the time they finished kissing, the others had stepped away to give them some privacy. All of them appeared to be watching the ice sculptor finish, but Erin was certain that Jen was watching them surreptitiously. Sure enough, Jen glanced over at them a moment later and winked at Erin before turning her full attention to Charlie. He said something funny, and everyone nearby, including the sculptor, laughed loudly. Erin's spirit soared at the sight. Jen needed someone who could make her laugh.

Darcy was smiling at her, eyes soft and almost sad. Erin rose to her tiptoes and kissed the tip of her nose. "Penny for your thoughts?"

"I'm just a little sorry for you."

"Why?"

Darcy paused, staring at the others. "I'm sorry that you have to leave all your friends and family behind."

Erin froze. "What do you mean?"

Darcy met her eyes, and now Erin could see the little twinkle of mischief in them. "Because you're moving to Boston."

Erin laughed. "Oh I am, am I?"

"Yes. And I'll expect dinner on the table at six every night."

"That I can do. As long as you don't mind TV dinners."

Darcy frowned and shook her head. "No—it won't do. Nine courses or nothing."

She took Darcy's hand and squeezed. "Nothing it is."

Darcy laughed, and for Erin it was a revelation to know that, despite all appearances, Darcy did have a sense of humor. Making her laugh for the rest of their lives would be an absolute pleasure.

Erin pulled on her hand. "Come on. Let's go see what they're laughing at."

Darcy resisted, grinning. "Do we have to?"

"Don't you want to?"

Darcy stepped closer, linking her arms around Erin's back. "All I want is you. It's all I've wanted for months now."

Erin responded to this declaration with a deep kiss. She put the last few months of longing, of dread, of desperation into her kiss—every wakeful, tearful night, every bleak and lonely day. Darcy's eyes were shining when she drew back.

"I'm yours, Darcy. Now come on. I'm going to freeze to death if we don't get inside."

About the Author

Charlotte was born in a tiny mountain town and spent most of her childhood and young adulthood in a small city in Northern Colorado. While she is usually what one might generously call "indoorsy," early exposure to the Rocky Mountains led to a lifelong love of nature, hiking, and camping.

After a lengthy education in Denver, New Orleans, Washington DC, and New York, she earned a doctorate in literature and women and gender studies.

An early career academic, Charlotte has moved several times since her latest graduation. She currently lives and teaches in a small Southern city with her wife and their cat.

Website: http://charlottegreeneauthor.com

Books Available from Bold Strokes Books

A Call Away by KC Richardson. Can a businesswoman from a big city find the answers she's looking for, and possibly love, on a small-town farm? (978-1-63555-025-2)

Berlin Hungers by Justine Saracen. Can the love between an RAF woman and the wife of a Luftwaffe pilot, former enemies, survive in besieged Berlin during the aftermath of World War II? (978-1-63555-116-7)

Blend by Georgia Beers. Lindsay and Piper are like night and day. Working together won't be easy, but not falling in love might prove the hardest job of all. (978-1-63555-189-1)

Hunger for You by Jenny Frame. Principe of an ancient vampire clan Byron Debrek must save her one true love from falling into the hands of her enemies and into the middle of a vampire war. (978-1-63555-168-6)

Mercy by Michelle Larkin. FBI Special Agent Mercy Parker and psychic ex-profiler Piper Vasey learn to love again as they race to stop a man with supernatural gifts who's bent on annihilating humankind. (978-1-63555-202-7)

Pride and Porters by Charlotte Greene. Will pride and prejudice prevent these modern-day lovers from living happily ever after? (978-1-63555-158-7)

Rocks and Stars by Sam Ledel. Kyle's struggle to own who she is and what she really wants may end up landing her on the bench and without the woman of her dreams. (978-1-63555-156-3)

The Boss of Her: Office Romance Novellas by Julie Cannon, Aurora Rey, and M. Ullrich. Going to work never felt so good. Three office romance novellas from talented writers Julie Cannon, Aurora Rey, and M. Ullrich. (978-1-63555-145-7)

The Deep End by Ellie Hart. When family ties become entangled in murder and deception, it's time to find a way out... (978-1-63555-288-1)

A Country Girl's Heart by Dena Blake. When Kat Jackson gets a second chance at love, following her heart will prove the hardest decision of all. (978-1-63555-134-1)

Dangerous Waters by Radclyffe. Life, death, and war on the home front. Two women join forces against a powerful opponent, nature itself. (978-1-63555-233-1)

Fury's Death by Brey Willows. When all we hold sacred fails, who will be there to save us? (978-1-63555-063-4)

It's Not a Date by Heather Blackmore. Kade's desire to keep things with Jen on a professional level is in Jen's best interest. Yet what's in Kade's best interest...is Jen. (978-1-63555-149-5)

Killer Winter by Kay Bigelow. Just when she thought things could get no worse, homicide Lieutenant Leah Samuels learns the woman she loves has betrayed her in devastating ways. (978-1-63555-177-8)

Score by MJ Williamz. Will an addiction to pain pills destroy Ronda's chance with the woman she loves or will she come out on top and score a happily ever after? (978-1-62639-807-8)

Spring's Wake by Aurora Rey. When wanderer Willa Lange falls for Provincetown B&B owner Nora Calhoun, will past hurts and a fifteen-year age gap keep them from finding love? (978-1-63555-035-1)

The Northwoods by Jane Hoppen. When Evelyn Bauer, disguised as her dead husband, George, travels to a Northwoods logging camp to work, she and the camp cook Sarah Bell forge a friendship fraught with both tenderness and turmoil. (978-1-63555-143-3)

Truth or Dare by C. Spencer. For a group of six lesbian friends, life changes course after one long snow-filled weekend. (978-1-63555-148-8)

A Heart to Call Home by Jeannie Levig. When Jessie Weldon returns to her hometown after thirty years, can she and her childhood crush Dakota Scott heal the tragic past that links them? (978-1-63555-059-7)

Children of the Healer by Barbara Ann Wright. Life becomes desperate for ex-soldier Cordelia Ross when the indigenous aliens of her planet are drawn into a civil war and old enemies linger in the shadows. Book Three of the Godfall Series. (978-1-63555-031-3)

Hearts Like Hers by Melissa Brayden. Coffee shop owner Autumn Primm is ready to cut loose and live a little, but is the baggage that comes with out-of-towner Kate Carpenter too heavy for anything long term? (978-1-63555-014-6)

Love at Cooper's Creek by Missouri Vaun. Shaw Daily flees corporate life to find solace in the rural Blue Ridge Mountains, but escapism eludes her when her attentions are captured by small town beauty Kate Elkins. (978-1-62639-960-0)

Somewhere Over Lorain Road by Bud Gundy. Over forty years after murder allegations shattered the Esker family, can Don Esker find the true killer and clear his dying father's name? (978-1-63555-124-2)

Twice in a Lifetime by PJ Trebelhorn. Detective Callie Burke can't deny the growing attraction to her late friend's widow, Taylor Fletcher, who also happens to own the bar where Callie's sister works. (978-1-63555-033-7)

Undiscovered Affinity by Jane Hardee. Will a no strings attached affair be enough to break Olivia's control and convince Cardic that love does exist? (978-1-63555-061-0)

Between Sand and Stardust by Tina Michele. Are the lifelong bonds of love strong enough to conquer time, distance, and heartache when Haven Thorne and Willa Bennette are given another chance at forever? (978-1-62639-940-2)

Charming the Vicar by Jenny Frame. When magician and atheist Finn Kane seeks refuge in an English village after a spiritual crisis, can local vicar Bridget Claremont restore her faith in life and love? (978-1-63555-029-0)

Data Capture by Jesse J. Thoma. Lola Walker is undercover on the hunt for cybercriminals while trying not to notice the woman who might be perfectly wrong for her for all the right reasons. (978-1-62639-985-3)

Epicurean Delights by Renee Roman. Ariana Marks had no idea a leisure swim would lead to being rescued, in more ways than one, by the charismatic Hudson Frost. (978-1-63555-100-6)

Heart of the Devil by Ali Vali. We know most of Cain and Emma Casey's story, but *Heart of the Devil* will take you back to where it began one fateful night with a tray loaded with beer. (978-1-63555-045-0)

Known Threat by Kara A. McLeod. When Special Agent Ryan O'Connor reluctantly questions who protects the Secret Service, she learns courage truly is found in unlikely places. Agent O'Connor Series #3. (978-1-63555-132-7)

Seer and the Shield by D. Jackson Leigh. Time is running out for the Dragon Horse Army while two unlikely heroines struggle to put aside their attraction and find a way to stop a deadly cult. Dragon Horse War, Book 3. (978-1-63555-170-9)

Sinister Justice by Steve Pickens. When a vigilante targets citizens of Jake Finnigan's hometown, Jake and his partner Sam fall under suspicion themselves as they investigate the murders. (978-1-63555-094-8)

The Universe Between Us by Jane C. Esther. Ana Mitchell must make the hardest choice of her life: the promise of new love Jolie Dann on Earth, or a humanity-saving mission to colonize Mars. (978-1-63555-106-8)

Touch by Kris Bryant. Can one touch heal a heart? (978-1-63555-084-9)

Change in Time by Robyn Nyx. Working in the past is hell on your future. The Extractor Series: Book Two. (978-1-62639-880-1)

Love After Hours by Radclyffe. When Gina Antonelli agrees to renovate Carrie Longmire's new house, she doesn't welcome Carrie's overtures at friendship or her own unexpected attraction. A Rivers Community Novel. (978-1-63555-090-0)

Nantucket Rose by CF Frizzell. Maggie Jordan can't wait to convert an historic Nantucket home into a B&B, but doesn't expect to fall for mariner Ellis Chilton, who has more claim to the house than Maggie realizes. (978-1-63555-056-6)

Picture Perfect by Lisa Moreau. Falling in love wasn't supposed to be part of the stakes for Olive and Gabby, rival photographers in the competition of a lifetime. (978-1-62639-975-4)

Set the Stage by Karis Walsh. Actress Emilie Danvers takes the stage again in Ashland, Oregon, little realizing that landscaper Arden Philips is about to offer her a very personal romantic lead role. (978-1-63555-087-0)

Strike a Match by Fiona Riley. When their attempts at matchmaking fizzle out, firefighter Sasha and reluctant millionairess Abby find themselves turning to each other to strike a perfect match. (978-1-62639-999-0)

The Price of Cash by Ashley Bartlett. Cash Braddock is doing her best to keep her business afloat, stay out of jail, and avoid Detective Kallen. It's not working. (978-1-62639-708-8)

Under Her Wing by Ronica Black. At Angel's Wings Rescue, dogs are usually the ones saved, but when quiet Kassandra Haden meets outspoken owner Jayden Beaumont, the two stubborn women just might end up saving each other. (978-1-63555-077-1)

Underwater Vibes by Mickey Brent. When Hélène, a translator in Brussels, Belgium, meets Sylvie, a young Greek photographer and swim coach, unsettling feelings hijack Hélène's mind and body—even her poems. (978-1-63555-002-3)